LOVE AND OTHER HAZARDS

CLAUDIA RIESS

RIVER GROVE
BOOKS

Published by River Grove Books
Austin, TX
www.rivergrovebooks.com

Distributed by River Grove Books

Design and composition by Greenleaf Book Group
Cover design by Greenleaf Book Group

Cover images: Rose: ©iStockphoto.com/JoeLena; within the petals: © Patricia Chumillas, gpointstudio, Artem Furman, MJTH. Used under license from Shutterstock.com

Cataloging-in-Publication data is available.

Paperback ISBN: 978-1-63299-122-5

Hardcover ISBN: 978-1-63299-124-9

eBook ISBN: 978-1-63299-123-2

First Edition

1

Glenda Fieldston's agile little daughter hoisted herself onto the pedestal of the tall bronze statue of the Roman emperor. Only then was she able to reach his genitals. Glenda did nothing to discourage her. The child had never seen a naked man, and Glenda guessed this was as good a time as any to make use of the hands-on theory of learning.

Some twelve yards away, Eugene Lerman was exiting the hall with his daughter Meredith trailing behind him, rhythmically clicking the heels and toes of her patent leather shoes on the marble floor as if she were on a Broadway stage instead of here at the Metropolitan Museum of Art. Raising her eyes to an imaginary audience, she caught sight of the girl on the pedestal.

"Hey, that's Astrid Fieldston! Isn't she gross? She goes to my school!"

Eugene, hanging back, looked in time to witness the last bit of anatomical exploration. He was annoyed with himself for feeling a prudish twinge.

The museum guard, who had been distracted by Meredith's tapping feet, turned. His lanky frame tensed. "Get off there!" he ordered, striding across the hall. He glared at Glenda as Astrid jumped off the pedestal to her side. "Don't you know better than that, lady?"

Glenda concealed her alarm. "Don't get excited, we weren't going to steal him," she assured him.

The guard shook his bony finger at her. "You just observe the rules, ma'am." He marched to the wall, where he positioned himself for a possible showdown, feet apart, arms akimbo. "Fresh!"

"What are *you* looking at?" Astrid challenged, and Glenda noticed Meredith Lerman, one of Astrid's elementary school nemeses—a year her senior, in second grade—crouching across the hall as if preparing to attack. On meeting Glenda's glance, Meredith tossed her braids and scurried after the man Glenda assumed was her father, grabbing his hand and tugging him onward, not without directing a parting tongue-thrust of scorn at Astrid. Meredith's father was a dark-haired figure with a coat slung over his shoulder, and Glenda thought he looked a bit lost and confused. Her own vulnerability bounded out to meet his, but she instantly drew it back, as if it were a flaw he had tricked her into revealing.

Astrid hiked up her jeans. "Can we go now? I'm starving."

Glenda smiled and shook her head. "Already? It's only four-thirty."

"My stomach is making noises."

"That was Meredith Lerman, wasn't it? I met her mother at a parents' meeting last year."

"Mrs. Lerman ran away from home," Astrid said bluntly.

Glenda frowned. "Mrs. *Lerman*? But she was going to law school."

"Meredith said so. Cheryl told me. Can we go home and eat?"

"I think it's a story."

"It's not."

The wind stung for early November, and Glenda and Astrid walked briskly after alighting from the crosstown bus at First Avenue, not even stopping to look inside their favorite gourmet shop or at the antique store with the cuckoo in the window, to Eighty-ninth Street, where they turned east. Their apartment building was in the middle of the block, between First and York. It was an old brick building guarded by Diego, the streetwise doorman, about forty years old and suspicious of all strangers. Sometimes when she had nothing to do, Astrid would sit with Diego in the dimly lit lobby while he told her stories about the good old days, when he used to steal hubcaps and money from his mother. "That was before I got my head straight, man," he always said.

"Hi, Diego," Astrid said outside the doorway, where he was rubbing his gloved hands together.

"Hi, belleza." He tipped his cap to Glenda. "Is freessing cold today, yes?"

"Why don't you go inside?" Glenda asked.

"Freessing days is when people they get stiff fingers. They don't hold on so good. Is when a lot of bad guys, they come around and they think they gonna grab things from my tenants." He thumped his chest. "Not while Diego watches out, man. Nobody gonna bother my people around here!"

"Thanks, Diego," Glenda said. "Have a good evening."

"You too, my ladies."

As they rode the creaky elevator up to the fifth floor, Glenda removed one of her gloves and smoothed back her hair. She wore her thick blond tresses in a neat bun, and a few strands had escaped in the wind. She combed Astrid's hair with her fingers more lovingly, not to smooth the unruly curls but to caress her. Astrid leaned against her.

"Can we have hamburgers?" Astrid asked, looking up into her mother's luminous green eyes.

"Sure. Did you like the new exhibit today—all those sunny paint-ings with the bathers and picnickers?"

"I like the big one with the man and the lady in a boat. Can we go on a boat sometime?"

"Here's our floor. Yes, I'd like that."

For Glenda it was the coziest of Sunday evenings. She had selected a Mozart horn concerto from her iTunes library, and it was playing on her external speaker, sealing up her and her daughter in their warm nest with music and the sound of sizzling meat. Even their unremarkable view of the brownstone roof next door pressed them into each other's company.

Glenda was turning over the hamburgers in the frying pan. She was wearing an apron over her knit dress and had thrown off her shoes. She liked the sound her voice was making as it sang along with a horn solo. At her side, Astrid was breaking up the lettuce for the salad with her cherubic fingers. Her teacher had told Glenda that she had been demonstrating an aptitude for numbers in school. Life was good.

"Mommy?"

"Yes, honey."

Astrid wiped her hands on the dishtowel looped through the refrigerator door handle. "I want a father. All the other kids have fathers."

Glenda's breath caught as she stirred the peas over the burner. This was the first time Astrid had taken a firm initiative on the father issue. "Aren't some of them divorced?"

"Yeah, but they're still fathers. Like Cheryl's. Last week her father came all the way from someplace to take her to see a show. My father is a sperm."

"No, honey, your father is a man we never met. You know. We talked all about it. He has intelligence and a very good health record."

Astrid pouted. "You told me about that official semination stuff. It's just different."

"'Artificial insemination,' honey," Glenda said, cutting into a burger. "They're done. Let's sit and talk about it again. Bring the salad."

Glenda was sure that by being open and honest she was establishing a relationship of enduring trust with Astrid. A matter-of-fact, uncensored explanation of Astrid's conception, she knew, would prevent the air of witchcraft from ever touching the subject.

They walked around the counter into the dining area and set up next to each other at the table. Glenda kept the light natural finish of the wood protected with grass mats, and in the center of the table stood a large vase that contained the crepe paper flowers Astrid had made in school.

Glenda turned to Astrid. "I've always been honest with you, haven't I? I explained how the doctor—"

"Yeah, right. But you showed me in the book, remember? About when two people like each other, and the man's thing gets hard, and he puts it in the lady's thing, and sometimes a baby gets made? You didn't do that—I mean, not with him, anyway. Why?" She cut into her burger. "Why didn't you get married to him?"

"You can call his thing a 'penis,' sweetheart, and hers a 'vagina.' And I told you why. Because I wanted a baby very much, but I didn't want to be tied to a relationship that might be difficult to get out of if it didn't work out." She moved the peas around on her plate. "I know what I want for you and for me. And we get along just great, don't we?"

Astrid chewed her meat. "Cheryl said her father had a beard. He never used to have a beard."

"Don't we?" Glenda repeated.

"'Don't we' what?"

"Get along just great together."

"Oh, Mommy!"

"'Oh, Mommy' what?"

"Sure we get along." Astrid rose from the table. "I need some ketchup."

She went to the kitchen, leaving Glenda alone with her thoughts until she returned.

"Mommy?"

"Yes?"

"What do you think the man was thinking when he was, you know, getting the sperm out?"

"He was probably thinking about the beautiful baby he was help-ing to create." Glenda rose from the table. "Do you want milk or orange juice?"

"Orange juice. Don't lie to me. You said you'd never lie to me."

"What do you mean, lie? Why wouldn't he think about how beauti-ful you would become? Even your name means 'beautiful as a goddess.'" She rounded the counter with two glasses of juice.

"I didn't say I wasn't beautiful," Astrid said. "I mean that the man wasn't thinking about that." She reached for the juice. "In the book you showed me, it says the man is thinking about how much he loves the woman and everything, and that's what makes the sperm come out."

"I remember, yes."

"And you said my father had to make the sperm come out all by himself because you weren't there."

"Yes."

"So what was he thinking about?" Astrid persisted.

Glenda took a drink of the juice while she considered how to respond. "Everyone has different thoughts at those times," she finally said. "Maybe your father really *was* thinking about making a baby just like you. And maybe Cheryl's father was thinking about eating a choc-olate cake with a topping of marshmallows and rats' feet."

Astrid laughed, spraying orange juice from her mouth onto the table. Glenda laughed too, even as a kind of uneasiness rolled in on her like a threatening cloud. She took her napkin and wiped away the residue of orange juice and the growing mist of fear.

Nearby, on Ninety-third Street between First and Second Avenues, Eugene Lerman and his daughter Meredith had just ridden up to the fifteenth floor of their building with Emily Lapwing, an unmarried woman from the same floor who had begun to look at Eugene in a strange, silent way the day his wife had left him. Eugene didn't want to flatter himself that there was much significance in this, but the timing was striking. In one of the friendlier seasons of their marriage, Francine, his soon-to-be ex-wife, had once told him he had the kind of sex appeal that did not spring out at a woman like a beer commercial, but that was there if she wanted it to be. He had a comfortable face, she'd said, with good planes, strong features, and dark, deeply set eyes that could be interpreted as brooding.

As he and Meredith walked to his apartment, Eugene told himself to stop thinking about Francine, and he told himself he was imagining things about Emily Lapwing watching him.

The smell of baking chicken was upon him even before he opened the door, threatening to subdue him, strip him of all he had learned since adolescence. What did his mother do to a chicken that gave it such power?

Just past the living room, the passageway to the two bedrooms, and the dining area was Eugene's modest kitchen, where his mother sat on a bridge chair with her feet planted in a Whirlpool foot massager. Her look of concern was as diffuse and encompassing as the smell of her chicken.

"You look tired, Eugene," she said.

"Well earned—we walked the city," he replied. Sometimes he thought of her as a mirror designed to catch only his bad profile.

The floor was humming with the vibrations of her foot massager.

Meredith strode to the kitchen, and Eugene hung up her quilted jacket and his parka in the hall closet. A flawed prep, he was wearing a white cotton shirt his mother had starched in spite of her arthritis, a navy crew neck sweater, and chinos. "Are you engaged in therapy or hedonism, Mom?" He picked up an apple from the glass-top table en route to her.

"You know the condition of my feet," she said, pulling at her flow-ered hem. "I've been lifting heavy baskets of laundry all day. I overdid."

Eugene wondered if his mother was the only woman in the world who wore a housedress. "Who told you to do the laundry?" he asked brusquely, uncertain what line of sympathy was best to take with a woman of numerous ailments and muscles of steel. "Besides, Mrs. Schmidt came yesterday. Why didn't *she* do the laundry?"

"I told her not to. I told her to reline the kitchen cabinets, which were a disgrace." She sighed. "Can I help it if I forget I'm a senior citizen? Hand me the bowl there and plug in the beater. I'm in the middle of cookies."

"Are you crazy? You'll electrocute yourself. You can't handle an electric beater while you're out wading!"

"So? If I drop dead, it would save you the trouble of calling me a cab for the airport tomorrow." She removed her feet from the appliance, wincing.

"Very funny," he said.

She bent to click off the device. "If you had gone to medical school, you would have been able to help me with my feet."

"And if you weren't a Jewish mother you wouldn't have corns."

"What are you talking about?" She rose to her full height, reaching the center of his chest. "Maureen Macintosh has had problems with her feet all her life! Where did you pick up this—"

"Never mind. I was talking about guilt, not podiatry."

"Again, guilt? I'm trying to help you get through a difficult time! *I* know your game. So you won't have to feel grateful, you want *me* to feel guilt for taking up space here. Well, my friend, you are not going to faze me. I am going to let your abuse go right past me." She made a sweeping gesture with her hand. "Whoosh!"

"Come on, let's not get dramatic." Eugene picked up the foot pool to empty out in the toilet. "I'm not trying to make you feel guilty." He snickered from down the hallway. "Anyway, I forgave you a long time ago for not giving me clarinet lessons like you gave Richie."

"You were tone deaf!"

Meredith handed her grandmother her bedroom slippers. "Let me help you make the cookies," she said.

"No, I wasn't tone deaf, Richie was," Eugene retorted, on the way back. "That's why you gave him lessons. You thought it would improve his condition." Damn, he was getting serious, backwashing onto the old sibling reefs. "Forget it. You want me to be tone deaf? I'm tone deaf. When will the chicken be ready?" He picked up the apple he had left on the counter.

"Twenty minutes. Yes, Meredith darling, you may help me with the cookies. Let me show you how to use the beater."

"I already know," Meredith said.

Eugene flipped through the Sunday *New York Times* on the dining room table, removing the magazine section. He subscribed to the online version of the *Times,* but he still preferred the messier hands-on experience on Sundays. He took the magazine section into the living room area, where he sank into the black velvet couch that only appeared to be comfortable. The furniture in this apartment either offered no resistance to his frame, like the couch and the waterbed, or menaced it, like the sharp corners of the mirrored tables accented in brass.

Ironically, the only item he had bought for the apartment was the clock radio, and his wife had taken that with her to Cincinnati.

He drew a pen from his shirt pocket and turned to the crossword puzzle.

Their meal had all the hilarity of The Last Supper. Rose Lerman was flying back to her condo in Florida the next day after spending two weeks ministering to her son's and granddaughter's needs and reorganizing their drawers, and she was not sure her efforts had been appreciated. The solemnity with which she doled out their food was meant to render her sacrifice immutable in their collective mind. The

occasion was interrupted only by her husband, Abe, calling long distance to tell her that their friend Jake Bernstein had just had a heart
attack and was in the intensive care unit, doing poorly.

"I'm getting back just in time," Mrs. Lerman told Eugene after the
call.

"To see Jake?" he asked.

"To keep an eye on your father. That Hattie Bernstein is a conniv-
ing woman. She'd be plying him with CARE packages in no time. I've
been meaning to unfriend her on Facebook."

"*That'll* show her," Eugene remarked. Amazing: in every aspect of
her being save social media, his mother had not budged an inch from
the weltanschauung of her parents. Ironically, he himself did not have
a Facebook page and resisted advances in communications technology with clenched jaw, bearing them only as much as they provided
convenience. Actual enjoyment of them he regarded as a form of
intellectual capitulation.

That evening, when Eugene tucked Meredith into the waterbed where
she slept with her grandmother during her visit, his daughter sat up and
started to cry.

"Mommy is a bitch. She didn't call me today."

"She called you yesterday, Mer," he soothed, brushing the dark bangs
from her forehead. "And don't use words like that."

"But she calls me every Sunday," she wept. "To remind me to take
my vitamin before I go to school and everything."

"There could be a lot of reasons she didn't call," Eugene said. "Maybe
her cell phone needs to be recharged. Don't worry. You know she misses
you." Sitting on the edge of the waterbed was making him queasy. He
had his wife, Francine, to thank for that. She had bought it to vitalize
their sex, but instead of expanding his imagination, it was all he could

do to maintain purchase on the rolling seas. "We'll try to reach her if you want to," he suggested.

"I want her to call *me*!" Meredith sobbed.

"She will, baby." He felt his chest turning soft as he held her. "You want me to undo your braids? Aren't they uncomfortable when you go to sleep?"

"No, but take them out for me, anyway," she whimpered, her sobs abating.

"It looks pretty," he said, when he had her hair fanned out against her back. "It's all in these neat squiggles. You want me to scratch your back for a little?"

She wiped her eyes on the corner of her pillowcase. "Okay." She lay down on her stomach, and Eugene scratched her back through the light flannel gown. To think, he had once loved his wife almost this much.

"I hope Grandma doesn't snore tonight," Meredith said. "When she goes home tomorrow, do I have to go back to my room?"

"You can stay here if you want to. I don't mind sleeping in your room."

"Oh, it's okay."

"Maybe the hard mattress is better for your back. You know, because you're still growing?"

"Yeah. You can stop now if you're tired, Daddy."

"I'm not, but you should go to sleep."

His mother was leafing through the newspaper when he returned to the living room. He sank into the deceptively plump loveseat and kicked off his shoes. Rose was buried in the sofa. "I want to thank you for your help, Ma," he said. "I'm sorry I never did pick up that container of salt-free cottage cheese you asked for."

"I blame it on Francine," Rose said. "If she hadn't walked out on you, you wouldn't be so forgetful. Do you mind if I ask you something personal?"

"Yes, I do."

"Was it something sexual?"

He shrugged. It was hopeless. "Yes. All Francine could think of was my body. It was distracting her from higher pursuits. She had to save herself."

"Eugene, why did she leave you?"

"She saw an old movie, *Kramer vs. Kramer.*"

"This inspired her to leave you?"

"No, this inspired her to go to law school. The commercial for American Airlines inspired her to leave me."

"Give me a straight answer."

He crossed his legs, trying to find a comfortable position. "We went through this. Francine went to law school. She got a great offer from a firm in Cincinnati. I wasn't about to pull up stakes here, and she didn't want to dislocate Meredith. She wants to take a few more months to get established, and then she'll send for Meredith at the end of the school year. I'd like to have Meredith full time, but I suppose I'll have to settle for shared custody. Also, Francine is involved with one of the partners in this law firm of hers. She'll probably marry him the day after our divorce papers are signed."

"Disgusting."

"Which part?"

"The whole thing. It's sick. I should have known from her background this sort of thing would happen."

"Why? She went to Smith, her father is an accountant, and her mother makes the best beef stew in Scarsdale."

"Her mother is a tramp."

"If you're referring again to the time Pop was coming out of the bathroom with his fly unzipped, I was there. Francine's mother was coming from her bedroom, and they bumped into each other in the hallway."

"You are so innocent," his mother said. "Maybe that's what got you into this trouble. I didn't teach you about street life. I saw by her eyes she was up to no good, that woman, with her black pantyhose. A disgrace."

"Oh, shit, Ma."

"Watch your mouth. And didn't I know Francine was up to no good last year when she turned down a food processor for her birthday? Didn't I?"

"She wanted the latest edition of Mac Word, not Mix Master. That's *word* processing."

"And how does that purée a banana, may I ask?" His mother paused and looked at him for a moment. "Don't worry, Gene, you'll get another woman," she said. "Next to Ben Stiller, you're the best looking Jewish boy in the country."

"I can tell by the way you're eyeing my hairline that you didn't mean that."

"Why, is it receding?"

"No, Ma."

"Richie is seven years older than you—forty-four years old!—and he has a full head of hair."

"I'm his brother, not his clone. You never know how I'll turn out."

"You have a fine head of hair. A nice dark brown with a strand of gray. You won't have a problem."

He could tell by her fixed smile and her eyes, which scanned him like a detective's flashlight at the scene of a crime, that she was not entirely sure.

2

While Astrid polished off her scrambled eggs and the crusts of toast from her mother's plate, Glenda was in their bedroom adding the finishing touches to her Monday attire: the circle pin on the lapel of her gray wool suit, the pearl earrings, the black leather heels. Gathering her luxurious hair into its usual bun, she called into the dining room. "Almost ready, Astrid?"

"Uh huh. The eggs were mushy."

"Sorry, honey. Scrape the dishes and put them in the machine."

"Okay. Are we late?"

"No."

Her hair sleekly confined, Glenda applied a faint smudge of taupe to her lids, highlighting her almond-shaped green eyes, and a touch of neutral gloss to her lips. She tied the bow of her white silk blouse and surveyed the complete picture in the closet door mirror. An office secretary had once told her she looked like a repressed Scarlett Johansson. She loosened the bow.

The daily routine Glenda shared with her daughter felt like the lilt of a familiar rhyme. Every day she locked the door while Astrid ran to press the elevator button, her school bag hugging her back like a turtle shell. At the ride's end, Astrid always trotted ahead of whomever was in the elevator so that she was the first to arrive at the front door, for no other reason, Glenda thought, than that she liked to compete and to win.

"*Buenos dias!*" Astrid chirped to Diego from within the hood of her down jacket.

"Ah, is good pronunciation," Diego said. "Have a good day at *es-cu-e-la*. Yes?"

"Is that 'school'?"

"*Si.*"

"*Escuela!*"

"Good!"

Although the day was cold enough to redden noses there was no bluster to it, and their jaunt to the Houghton School just four short blocks away at Eighty-first and York was invigorating even without the challenge of flying debris. They arrived at the entrance of the modest brick building minutes before 8:30 and the start of the school day. Astrid was just pointing up at a window on the second story, claiming one of the farm landscapes taped to the window as hers, when a snub-nosed bus pulled up alongside the curb to deposit a dozen or so children ranging from about six to ten years old. Among them was Meredith Lerman.

Meredith eyed Astrid and tossed her braids noncommittally as they strode through the gateway in the wrought iron fence that enclosed the school building.

"Have a good day!" Glenda called to the children in general as they filed into the building past the thick oak doors, held open by two staff members.

"I have soccer today," Astrid, hanging back, loudly reminded her.

"I know. Have fun."

"Yo! Astrid!" bellowed a boy of about six who brought up the rear as Glenda headed to the nearby number 31 bus.

At 8:57 Glenda arrived in front of her office building at Rockefeller

Center on Fiftieth, its site graced by the colossal bronze statue of Atlas bearing the world on his shoulders. Directly across the street, Saint Patrick's Cathedral aspired in grand elegance toward the heavens. When she'd first started working here, she'd liked to think that the two buildings showed Man and God vying for the attention of the soul. To Glenda, both images illustrated purpose and initiative, perfect for Monday morning.

The constructive part of her day began here in this smooth terminal of business, now alive with the sound of intent: her heels clicking on the marble floor, the swishing elevator doors, the economy of words. "Up," she called to one of the elevators as its doors were sliding shut; as if by magic, it reconsidered and opened to admit her. "Thanks," she said, stepping aboard. "Floor?" asked a man in a black coat with a token closed-lips arc. "Twenty-two," she replied, returning his smile.

She headed to her cubicle of office space at Business Advisors, LLC, her usual ambition brewing like the coffee at the receptionist's station. The floor was divided into five such areas for consultants like herself, one slightly larger to accommodate two secretaries, and one unequivocally private office for the president of the company, Matthew Crowley.

Glenda sat at her desk and gathered together the material on her most recent client, Richard's Fur Outlets, for whom she had been making systems-streamlining recommendations. That was her job, to ensure that companies were using the most up-to-date computer systems and processes possible, while Matthew, the company president and chief CPA, ensured that their record-keeping was efficient and compliant. She reviewed her notes for her morning meeting with Matthew: *Limited compatibility between departments, need additional cloud storage, tutorial a must!* Printing her notes along with other pertinent documents—Matthew, who had been in the business for twenty-five years, still preferred presentations in hard copy—she got up and went to Crowley's office.

"Hold my coffee for now," she advised the receptionist, Jeff, who was chatting in the pathway with a hyper-active young consultant whose expertise was mailing-list management. "Morning, Danny."

"Morning, babe." Danny's moustache twitched mischievously. "Doing anything for lunch?"

"Why? Has it ever done anything for me?"

"I'm getting through to her," she could hear him confide sotto voce to Jeff as she walked by. "She didn't say no." Her regret for being the cause of his unrequited crush was, as ever, void of self-satisfaction.

Compared to the company's main working area, all commercial carpet and functional furniture, Crowley's office was plush. His carpet was dense; desk and bookcases, sandalwood; chairs, leather; window, draped. A commodious couch and a floor lamp suggested the context of home.

Crowley was not, at the moment, enjoying his comforts. He was jogging in shirt and tie on the moving belt of the treadmill situated alongside his desk, headed for cardiopulmonary efficiency and tireless tennis. "How's it going?" he asked without altering his pace. "Have a good weekend?"

"Yes. You?" She held the printout of her notes to her chest.

"So-so." He frowned, deepening the crease between his dark blue eyes. "Where are you with Richard's specs?" At fifty-two, though twenty-three years Glenda's senior and four years her boss, his tone was that of an equal. He had great respect for her talent.

"I'm about finished with the initial planning," she said. "There are a couple of questions that I'd like to discuss with you before I prepare my final outline."

"Can it wait until tomorrow? I've got a prospective client whom I've promised to get the ball rolling on, and you're the best man for the job." He smiled; the lines bracketing his mouth and etched around his eyes offset the regularity of his features. Time had invested what had been a good-looking but bland face with a past, and thus with character. Along with his graying temples and agreeable diction, he could have been mistaken for an anchorman.

"It can wait, sure," Glenda answered.

There was a lengthy pause while Crowley gradually slackened his pace, taking short breaths with pursed lips, until he came to a halt.

"Whew," he said, patting the modest paunch on an otherwise trim physique. "Okay, let's talk. Sit."

Glenda sat opposite him at his desk as he changed from sneakers to shoes. "Have I ever mentioned my old college buddy Jack Henson? Of Henson and Blackman Publishing?"

Glenda shook her head.

"They publish periodicals in the medical management line. *Perspectives in Neurology* and *Physician's Marketplace*, plus a couple I can't recall. Would you like some coffee?"

"I'll hold off."

"Right. Well, Jack and his partner just acquired *MD Forefront* and *Gynecology Today*, which is a great deal. But it's a lot more volume for them, and they're kind of at loose ends operations-wise. They've got to beef up their system and educate their staff. Blackman is not an enthusiast—he thinks he'll lose touch with the operation if he can't personally wish each of his readers a happy birthday. But that's another matter. What I want you to do is lay the groundwork. Get a general idea of what they're using now to handle billing, mailing, editorial, production, and their online editions, as well as the general stats on distribution, advertising, and pricing. Then, give me a couple of ideas about what you think they'll need, and meanwhile I'll go over their tax returns for the last couple of years to see what compliance issues we may need to address. Excuse me." He buzzed Jeff on the intercom extension. "Has a parcel from Henson and Blackman come in yet? . . . Right. Thanks." He hung up. "They haven't already sent their tax returns over, so you can pick those up when you go. They should include statements from the acquired publishers as well."

"I take it you want me to run over there today," Glenda said, brushing the hem of her jacket.

"Yes. Jack's kind of counting on my being there, but I figure I won't be of much use until I've got a coherent picture of the accounts. I'll come to your next meeting. Besides, I'm up to my ears in that electronics deal Sherm and Danny are working on."

"I'll call Henson and Blackman now, then."

"Appreciate it, Glenda. They're on Madison, in the low thirties. I've got the number here somewhere." He moved the papers on his desk without really searching.

"No problem. I'll find it." She rose.

"Good. Keep me posted." His private line rang as Glenda reached the door. "That'll be the wife. Yes, Sybil," he answered, glancing at her framed photo angled toward him on his desktop. "What? I made him *distraught*? Whose word is that, his or yours? . . . Sure, I'll meet him for lunch." He acknowledged Glenda's departure with a nod. "Yes, Sybil, I realize he's my son too."

Glenda pulled off her knit gloves and thrust them into her coat pockets. "Glenda Fieldston. I have an appointment to see Mr. Henson at ten-thirty?"

A pale young woman made paler by the overhead fluorescent lights tapped a key on her computer. She nodded, agitating a long and otherwise unremarkable ponytail. "Mmm, yes, of course. I just spoke to you. From Business Advisors."

"Yes," said Glenda, just as two men in overalls who carried cartons on their shoulders appeared at the open door of the establishment ten feet behind her. At the same time, a woman in a red coat, who was approaching from down the inner hallway, broke into a run. "Down! Elevator down!" Glenda stepped aside to clear the runway, but the workers and the woman still almost collided in front of the receptionist's desk just as the elevator closed its doors for departure.

"Hell!" the woman exclaimed, and then she looked back to smile at Glenda. "Sorry," she said. "Back at noon, Claire."

"That was Mary Mahoney," offered the receptionist, Claire. "Our creative director."

"Where do you want this stuff from the West Side?" one of the men asked Claire as he adjusted his burden.

"Is it *MD Forefront*, or *Gynecology*?"

"It's heavy," he said.

"Okay, bring it down to the end of the outer hallway. There's an empty room on the right."

"My pleasure."

"We're a little hectic here," Claire confessed to Glenda, holding her ponytail for security. "Moving the files for the new publications and all. We've just acquired additional office space. We've got the floor to ourselves now."

"You must have over two thousand square feet," Glenda estimated, peering down the corridor.

"Mmm, probably," she said. "Oh—if you want to see Mr. Blackman, he's out of the office today. I've already buzzed Mr. Henson. You can go ahead in. Fourth door down, on your left. Just past his secretary's."

The floor of the hallway, although of high quality parquet, could have used a good waxing, Glenda thought. The observation made her feel prissy. She banished it.

Henson's door was half open. There were two men in his office: one sitting behind the desk, and one standing in front of it with his back to Glenda. The man behind the desk rose from his chair.

"Come in. You must be Glenda Fieldston. Jack Henson." He extended his hand as she approached and the second man turned.

Henson, Glenda knew, was about the same age as Crowley, but while the years had sculpted Crowley's face, they had inflated Henson's, obliterating his jawline. "Hi," she said, grasping his hand firmly. The younger man in Henson's office was moderately tall, with a pleasant face: brown eyes, a nose with a prominent bridge, a slightly asymmetric smile. "I hope I'm not interrupting anything," she said, addressing him.

"Not at all," Henson replied for him. "Oh, sorry. This is Eugene Lerman, overworked editor. Take the lady's coat, Gene."

"Glad to meet you, Miss, uh, Mrs—say! Aren't you—"

"Glenda's fine," she said.

"Aren't you the woman—"

"Lerman—you're *Meredith's* father!"

"—from the *museum*?"

"You long lost cousins or something?" Henson interjected.

Eugene grinned, offering Glenda his hand. "We nearly met at an anatomy lesson," he said.

"Our daughters go to the same school," Glenda submitted, shaking Eugene's hand.

"What a delightful coincidence," Henson remarked, with a touch of sarcasm.

Eugene reached out to help Glenda off with her coat, but she beat him to it. She could see him hesitate before placing it on the rack with Henson's old umbrella and spare sweater. "What brings you to our hallowed halls?" he asked.

"Glenda's here to see we're optimally computerized," Henson explained, caressing the place where he might have worn a tie.

"Don't let me hold up the stampede of progress—I was just leaving," Eugene said, taking a pile of galley proofs from the desk.

"You're okay on Dr. Thayer's article, then," Henson said. "You'll have it by the deadline?"

"I'll have the translation ready by tomorrow."

"Oh?" Glenda was impressed. "What language are you translating from?"

"Bad English," Eugene said, backing out of the office. "*Ciao*."

"Have a seat, Glenda," Henson said, pointing to the only one free from papers and mail. "I apologize for the commotion around here. What a time for my doctor to order me to quit smoking—you wouldn't happen to have a cigarette, would you?"

"I don't smoke."

"Damn. You sure?" He rummaged in his bottom desk drawer, unsuccessfully.

"Isn't this a smoke-free environment?" Glenda asked.

"Of course. What a stickler you are. I only wanted a puff." He slammed shut the drawer. "Ah, well, onward to distraction. I'm going to give you a rundown on what we do here, and then we'll call on the office manager, Harriet Vickers, who will tell you *her* side of the story."

"Very good." Glenda removed a notepad from her bag. "I'm all ears."

As Henson progressed with his briefing, Eugene, two doors down, waded through the convoluted prose of Dr. Morton Thayer describing his techniques of pre-surgical consultation. The article had been accepted by a physician on the editorial board with the understanding that all participles would be undangled before publication. Midway through a sentence that grammatically placed a neovascular growth on a patient's bill rather than on his retina, Eugene was interrupted by an office assistant, Connie Falls.

"Excuse me, Eugene, but I'm going to lunch now. Will you be going out, or do you want me to bring you back a sandwich?"

"A roast beef on rye would be great, Connie. Thanks." He started to reach for his wallet.

"Never mind, I trust you," Connie said, her little heart-shaped mouth curling into a grin.

Eugene liked Connie. She was an easy person to co-exist with. There was something vulnerable and nothing arresting about her. She was 5' 2", heavy-chested and hippy, with a round face and an upturned nose like an editor's caret. She was twenty-three, and she took pride in her work. She deserved more attention, he thought. Unfortunately, however, about a month ago he had made the mistake of giving it to her, and he had regretted it ever since.

It had begun with a harmless exaggeration: "That's a pretty dress," he'd said, handing her his hard copy revisions to correct on the computer.

"Oh, thanks! It's as old as the hills, actually. You don't think the color is too bright?"

The color was too bright. "No," he'd said. "You look really good, Connie."

"Thanks. You do too, considering. You know, I heard through the grapevine about your wife and everything, and I didn't know how to approach the subject." She looked forlorn. "I just wanted to say how sorry I am."

"We didn't die, Connie. We separated."

"Don't kid me, I know what it's like. I recently broke up with Eddy, my fiancé, and I was crushed. And we didn't even have a history to speak of, unlike you and your wife."

The conversation had sparkled on for another few seconds, and Connie became encouraged to feel something like a friend. During the following weeks, she had asked him to dinner countless times. He had invented as many excuses, always delivering them, he thought, with utmost delicacy. Now, with her in his office, he awaited the next invitation.

"So," she prompted, cocking her head. "Would you care for anything on your roast beef sandwich?"

"A little Russian dressing, thanks."

"A drink?"

"No, I'm good."

"You know," Connie said, resting her weight on one leg (every day it took her less time to warm up to a conversation), "I got a text from Eddy last night. Would you believe it?"

Eugene put a big check mark near the sentence he was working on in Dr. Thayer's article. It would take him five minutes to find his way back into its labyrinthine intention. "Eddy? Oh yes, your boyfriend."

"Former boyfriend. I mean, this is the person who I was under the impression was the most faithful guy in the world and who I discovered was cheating on me with one of my friends, maybe two. Would you believe it?"

"That they're still your friends? No."

"You're kidding with me. I mean, would you believe the unmitigated gall, for him to think that I would enter a dialogue with him about a lost cashmere sweater he left at my place, who knows where or when? Really, I learned a lesson with him. You don't always know someone as well as you *think* you know them. Never again will I make a commitment to somebody I don't really know."

Dr. Thayer's prose was looking better and better. "That's a good idea, Connie," he said, turning back to his pages.

"I read an article online about dream therapy groups," Connie said. "How people get together and discuss their dreams and learn more deeply about each other. Apparently this is only one of the new approaches to shared awareness. When I think of what I might have learned about Eddy, and of all the time I wasted on him!"

"Talking about time," Eugene broached.

She looked at him. "Don't you notice something different about me?" she suddenly asked.

He studied her, perhaps for the first time in the two years she had been working there. She had short, light brown hair, which exposed dainty earlobes. "You cut your hair," he guessed.

"Only four weeks ago," she replied, disappointed.

Wisely, he ruled out the weight loss category. "You're not wearing glasses," he proposed.

"But I *never* wear glasses!"

"I give up."

"What's the color of my eyes?"

This was the most intimate they had ever been. "Blue," he observed. "And?"

"And *what?*" he asked, beginning to tire of the game. "And *green?*"

"My eyes are really brown—I'm wearing new contacts."

She met his eyes, and he realized that he had been wrong in thinking his mother had cornered the market on poignant stares.

"I'm defrosting a beef stew," she said. "Would you care to join me tonight?"

Eugene moved uncomfortably in his chair. "That's sweet of you, Connie, but my mother—she was visiting for a while—just left this morning, and I think I ought to stay home with my daughter tonight."

"How about tomorrow night?" she asked.

"I think I ought to stay home with her tomorrow night, too. She'll probably still be adjusting."

Now she seemed to be studying him.

"I know it must be hard," she finally said, "after being married to one person for ages, to accept the hospitality of a well-meaning co-worker who only wants to give you a nice meal. My only motive is helping you come back out into the world. I'm really hurt that you keep turning down a simple gesture of good will."

She was wearing him out. How long could she keep this up? Big deal, let her feed me, he thought. Was he such an elitist that he couldn't sit down at the table of a human being who never acquired a bachelor's degree?

"I guess maybe tomorrow will be fine, Connie, if I can find some- one to watch my daughter. Thanks."

He had not been out for dinner in a long time. Maybe it would do him good. Maybe Connie had even seen a foreign film once.

By the end of the work day, Glenda had not only gotten to know the lay of the land at Henson and Blackman's, but she had spent two hours listening to Jack Henson and the office manager, Harriet Vickers, sounding off at the local eatery about business trends in America. Jack and his wife, Rhoda, had also recently spent two weeks vacationing in the Far East, so Glenda had also learned about the magnificence of Oriental rugs and raw fish.

After delivering the publishing company's tax returns to Matt Crowley, she spent the rest of the afternoon working on her plan for Henson and Blackman's, as well as on updating her notes about Richard's Fur Outlets. At 5:15, after the office had cleared out, she rose from her desk and strode to Crowley's private office. She tapped once and opened the door without receiving an answer, as if she were performing a routine act, which indeed she was.

Crowley had already laid the beach towel over the pillows of the couch and was seated on it. He was clad only in boxer shorts. The rest of his clothing was neatly folded over the handrails of the treadmill, and a copy of *Time* magazine lay open on his lap. When Glenda closed the door behind her he stood up, dropping the magazine to the floor.

"It seems like forever," he said, approaching her. "But then it always does."

"I've been frustrated myself," she said, smiling as she untied the bow of her blouse.

He helped her off with her suit jacket and hung it on the back of the chair across from his desk. She placed the rest of her outfit, piece by piece, on the same chair, removing her pantyhose and shoes last, leaving him the duty of pulling off her underpants. It was a task he had reserved for himself from the start, during their first sexual encounter a year ago upstate in Rochester at a CPA seminar on advancements in office planning.

Avoiding anything that could be construed as a pose, she waited as he stood stock still, staring at her as if the sight of her were an effluence, so penetrating that he could inhale it: the long limbs tapering gracefully at the knees and ankles, the girlishly slender waist, the round hips, and, quintessentially, the breasts he could never resist praising. "They're enough to give me tachycardia," he said under his breath, his gaze fixating on what he often hailed as her "perfect globes," a cliché he never seemed to tire of, although Glenda had more than once pointed out its inherent flaw.

When they finally embraced, he buried his face in her hair. As always, she could feel him seeking her soul when he sought out lips. She returned his kiss, but only with corporeal desire. His fingers slowly drew down the middle of her back, continuing into her panties, tracking the furrow of her buttocks and sending a shudder throughout her body.

Were it not for maneuvers like this, Glenda knew, she would be content to relieve herself on her own. Moreover, the situation was convenient: she could satisfy her urges and still pick up Astrid at school before what was called the "child minding" services concluded at 6:30.

She told herself to stay in the present. She lay on the couch, and he stripped off his underwear before savoring the experience of peeling off hers. The newly moist panties removed, he bent to kiss her gently on the pubis, advancing his solicitations up along her belly toward her breasts. These he greedily kissed and fondled, regularly dispatching a hand below.

As sensation refined sharply into clitoral focus, she urged him to mount her, squeezing his member with regard as he did so. She guided his organ into her chamber, and he groaned happily and kissed her lavishly on the neck. She took herself off alone, the stimulation increasing past bearing, a series of pulses expressing themselves from her loins. As usual, the experience fell short of joy.

"I wish I could be with you more often," Crowley sighed, as they were repairing themselves afterward. "How about Friday?"

She felt danger, like the presence of an arsonist in the house. "I don't think so."

"Why not?"

"We didn't want this to get serious."

"If Mondays rank as casual to you, what's so special about Fridays? How does adding Fridays change the landscape?"

She pulled up a leg of her pantyhose. "Fridays lead to Saturdays, and Saturdays lead to chaos."

"Sounds like you've been there."

"Only once, and just as a tourist. I am not going to break up your marriage."

"You don't have to not break up my marriage with such a vengeance," he sulked.

"Besides, I don't want to pick up Astrid after six o'clock more than once a week."

"How *is* your daughter?" he asked, sticking with the safer subject. "I'd like to meet her sometime."

"Maybe not. She knows I have a male friend, but if she met you she'd probably want to adopt you. She's been expressing a need, lately, for—"

He dropped his shoe. "She *knows* about you and me? Christ, I thought she was eight years old!"

"She's seven. And of course I don't go into details. But we have a very honest relationship."

"Who? You and me? Or you and your daughter?"

"All of us." She handed him his shoe. "She knows grownups have social needs."

He whistled. "I can't believe it." He shook his head slowly and slipped on the shoe. "Then again, who knows, maybe you've got the right idea. Whatever I did, at least with my youngest, couldn't have been much use. I had lunch with him today. You know, he took a year off from college, and now he's saying he might not go back. It seems he and a guy he met waiting tables in Philadelphia formed a comedy team. He says they're already booked two whole weeks in advance. I was supposed to be thrilled."

"He must have a great sense of humor," Glenda said, comforting.

"He was a lot of laughs as a business major. That's the way I liked it."

"What does his mother think of the idea?"

Crowley straightened his cuff. "She hates the idea, but she's being sweet as hell about it. Doesn't want him to make her the butt of any of his routines, I suppose."

"You should take an interest in his work," Glenda said. "Go see him perform."

"I didn't say I disowned him," Crowley replied, miffed. "Of course I'll see his act. What do you think I am, anyway?"

She had to be careful how she responded, she knew. She didn't want him to mistake what she felt for him as an avowal of love. "I think you're a wonderful person," she finally said. She realized it sounded like praise bestowed on a wounded war veteran.

There was a long pause.

"You know, Glenda, it's easier to love you than understand you," he said at last.

Eugene's mother had prepared a decade's worth of food for him and Meredith, organized in tiers of labeled packets in the freezer. Their first night alone they ate something called "meat loaf temp 400 for 35 mins."

"I'm sorry it was cold in the middle," Eugene apologized afterward, sprawling on—or, more accurately, in—the couch.

"That's okay, Daddy." Meredith was glutted with love, what did she care about meat loaf? Francine had called shortly before dinner, explaining yesterday's trouble with her cell phone, filling Meredith up, Eugene supposed, on the bittersweet agonies of maternal longing.

Eugene, on the other hand, felt absurdly empty. The apartment was so un-noisy without his mother's presence; passive, without his wife's. He felt undirected, with nothing planned for the rest of his life but a dinner with Connie Falls. Even the prospect of moving up at H and B's seemed

meaningless. It was as if the nerve linking fact and purpose had been severed. He was ready for Camus' dog to pee on his leg—or his life. He took
a gulp of the white wine that, like himself, had not improved with age.

"Vinegary," he remarked.

"Do you want me to get you something else?" Meredith asked.

"No, thanks."

Meredith climbed onto the couch, kneeling next to the slumped
figure. "You're not in a good mood, are you?" she asked, arranging her
skirt so that it lay smoothly across her legs.

"I'm a little down in the dumps," he admitted.

"Do you want me to read to you?"

"Not right now," he replied, smiling half-heartedly.

"Do you miss Grandma?" With one hand she began playing with
his hair.

"I guess I'm just tired," he said, bending his head toward her.

She moved closer to him, directing his head onto her shoulder, and
casually began rubbing his scalp. "Don't you think we'll be able to take
care of ourselves?" she asked. "I can work an egg beater."

"I know, sweetheart. You can do a lot of things." Her fingers manip-
ulated with just the right pressure. "We'll be fine," he said. "You make
me feel better already."

"I do?"

"Yes." Her touch, acknowledging him as a sensitive soul, made him
feel like one.

"You have nice hair," she said.

He held up one of her braids. "You know, I'm not too good at this.
This braid—Grandma's—is so nice and neat. Maybe we should leave it
in forever."

She laughed. "That would be funny," she said.

"Yeah. You know? This couch is more comfortable than that waterbed I never liked.

"Then why don't you throw it away and get another kind," Meredith replied, more like an order than a question.

"That's a good idea," he said, resting his head on her shoulder like a child. "I don't know why I didn't think of that myself."

3

Emily Lapwing played cello with the Municipal Orchestra. She was a reedy 6' 2" with long, fine brown hair, which she wore loose and parted in the middle. And yet her eyes, shoulders, and self-esteem seemed to be directed downward. If she had given herself better billing, Eugene thought, she would be standing tall, her large brown eyes focusing into his own, her thin lips smiling generously, exposing two rows of beautifully even teeth. She could be a handsome, proud, intelligent, lithe young woman instead of Eugene's elongated thirty-year-old babysitter from down the hall. It was a shame, he thought.

"Are you taking the bus or the train?" Meredith asked him.

"The train's the best way to get down to the Village," Eugene sighed, slipping on his parka. "Connie lives near NYU."

"And do we have Miss Falls' telephone number?" Meredith asked.

"Next to the kitchen wall phone," Eugene said, wishing he had canceled the date. He predicted an evening of little kindnesses and big boredoms.

"Don't come home late, Dad. You have to get up early tomorrow."

"Yes, honey." He turned to the sitter. "Any questions, Emily?"

Emily shook her head. He suddenly remembered the last time she had sat here. She had come over to ask Francine's advice about an issue she was having with the orchestra. It had been the evening before Francine's graduation from law school, and the hostility between him and his wife, he remembered, had hung in the air like a brewing storm.

"Say, did you ever settle that wage dispute, Emily?" he asked.

"Oh, a long time ago," she whispered, bowing her head as if she had been responsible for the problem. "We got raises."

"Careful of the train tracks, Daddy," Meredith said.

"Have a pleasant evening," Emily added, her voice lacking conviction.

Connie opened the door to her second floor walk-up wearing an apron over her new polyester dress, deep blue to match her new eyes. "Hi!" she exclaimed, flourishing a meat carver.

"I surrender," Eugene replied, giving the wielding arm ample latitude as he eased into the apartment.

"You're a gas," Connie chirped, her round cheeks broadening. "We're having roast beef tonight. How do you like it?"

"Preferably on a plate," he quipped.

"Oh, I love it!" Connie laughed, her bosom heaving.

"Sorry—medium rare," he amended as he closed the door. "You have a nice apartment."

"If it was one big room it would be, you know, more spacious. The way it is, it has a separate living room, a dining room, a kitchen, but they're all cramped."

Eugene nodded. From his vantage point he could see into the tiny kitchen on one side and the tiny living room, decorated in cheerful yellows and blues, on the other.

"At least I got the landlord to paint," she said. "It took me one whole year to get him to do it. Oops." Hurriedly, she clicked into the kitchen in her stiletto heels, put the knife on the counter, and then clicked back. "Let me take your jacket. I'm glad you could come."

Eugene proffered a brown paper bag, having remembered etiquette as he came upon the liquor store on her street corner. "I hope you like white wine," he said.

"Oh, yes, I do. Excuse me." She quickly traced tracks to deliver the bottle to the kitchen and then returned to take his jacket from him. "I love it, but do you mind if we have red tonight? You know, with the meat and all? I got it 'specially.'" She was panting a little from the scurrying.

"Of course not. Here, allow me." He took back his jacket and hung it up himself.

An appreciative murmur escaped her lips. "Why don't you make yourself comfortable in the living room? There's crackers and cheese, and I'll fix you a drink. What'll you have? Dinner will be ready in fifteen minutes—seeing as how you like it medium rare," she added coyly.

Eugene opted for a Bloody Mary and waited in the miniroom, picking at the Swiss cheese and dropping cracker crumbs on the spotless beige rug. He took a hearty swig of his drink and went about capturing his debris in a cocktail napkin. He was escorted, finally, through the kitchen into the dining room, where a sumptuous meal had been laid out on a floral-patterned cloth and illuminated by candles floating in bowls of water. Connie, now apron-less, glowed in the soft light, her new blue eyes glistening with the intensity of her emotions.

As they ate, she began to speak about what had become her main interest in life: relationships.

"I've been reading a lot about communication since I broke up with Eddy," she said, pouring the wine. "I told you about Eddy, didn't I?"

He nodded, and she launched into an evangelical speech about the need for deep understanding, punctuated by exuberant spasms of chewing.

"I mentioned to you about dream therapy," she said. "Well, there's another theory I've been reading about, and it says that the way to a real union of spirits is through what they call 'living through fantasy.'

The article claims that it's only through what they call the 'external-ization of madness' that we're able to attain mental peace." Her round cheeks were flushed with the fever of her sentiment. "We have to express our wildest dreams, our fantasies. It fascinates me that a real, down-to-earth relationship can come about through that. Does it fas-cinate you?" She leaned across the table, her little nose colliding with his uplifted wine glass.

"Yes," he said. "Incidentally, the roast beef was done to perfection."

"Don't you think it's paradoxical?"

"The roast beef?"

"The theory! I hope to find the perfect relationship someday. It's not like I haven't tried. I did a ton of online dating, but it didn't work out."

"Here's to perfection," Eugene toasted, before gulping the remains of his third glass of wine.

Once dinner was irrefutably over, the inevitable moment came, although Eugene had not permitted himself to foresee it.

"Wait here until I call you," Connie suggested, pirouetting from the room.

Eugene sat staring into a bowl of candles, wondering why he had not thought the denouement of the evening through. Could he reject her now and ask her to type a memo for him tomorrow, or ever?

"Blow out the candles, Gene, I'm ready!"

When Eugene thought about leaving, he thought about Connie's eager expression and remembered the last time he had tried to have sex with Francine, the way he'd felt when she'd turned him down, the way he'd felt all of the times before that in the waning days of their relationship.

He blew out the candles.

It was easy to find the door to the bedroom, across the hall and just past the living room. He knocked and waited.

"Don't be so polite! C'mon!"

He hesitated, and then he opened the door.

He froze.

"Well, how do you like it?" Connie sang, a note of youthful doubt in her voice.

A lamp on the night table shed a soft white glow in the small room. Strings of blinking Christmas lights draped the headboard of a double bed and ran along the top of the bureau next to it. On the wall over the bureau a collection of dolls and carved frogs seemed almost alive in the twinkling light. Connie stood at the foot of the bed, posing as if she had learned how through an online course. She was clad only in a black bra and bikini pants, out of both of which she had cut holes. One of her nipples was partially revealed; the other protruded like an exotropic eye. A patch of fur escaped below through the heart-shaped cutout.

She flung open her arms. "Tada!" she hallooed.

He coughed. "Very inventive."

"Do you think so?" she said nervously. "I'm glad, because I'm trying to set a mood here. I'm really into breaking down barriers. They say you need an environment that's, um—"

"Conducive?"

"God. You're such an intellectual. They say strobe lights are good, but I thought they'd be a bit much."

He cleared his throat again. "These are just fine." He could not help staring at her breasts, which seemed especially large, possibly because the room was so small. He felt a quick twinge of compassion for her. How hard she was trying.

"So," she said.

"So," he answered.

"So, what do you like?" she asked.

"Like what? Popcorn? Lady Gaga? April in Paris?" He wore his discomfort with an air of bravado.

She laughed. "You're such a card. I never used to think such an educated man could be such a card. *You* know what I mean."

"It's too general a question. Narrow it down to animal or vegetable."

Connie laughed again. "Take off your clothes," she said. "Don't be so shy. By the way, I'm prepared, in case you're wondering."

If Francine had not damaged his self-esteem, and if Connie's roast had been less tender, her wine less flowing, he might have demurred. As it was, he awkwardly unzipped his pants, the sound of it as manifest as a fart in a library. Connie sauntered over, hips swaying, to help with the unveiling. She undid the buttons of his shirt meticulously, searching his face with her limpid blue-over-brown eyes for signs of preference. He tried to look away and found himself looking at her breasts again instead.

When all that he wore including his wristwatch lay on or about a small tub chair, Eugene was led to the bed by Connie's gentle hand. However, once he was delivered to the striped cotton sheets, her technique changed. She was no longer sultry. He guessed she was trying for something more tempestuous. However, it seemed more like a domesticated dog turned feral.

"Down," he gasped, struggling beneath her.

Connie, taking the command literally, flung herself at his pelvis.

Ever content with the traditional position, Eugene figured that the missionary was finally getting its comeuppance through the rite of cannibalization. Yet in spite of his concern for the safety of his organ, or perhaps in its own defense, it became enlarged—or enraged—and Connie retracted her canines and sat astride, inserting the member through the most practically conceived of her cutouts.

More curious than enamored by the large appurtenances bobbing over him, Eugene reached up to touch them, perhaps even to pinch the delicate buds peering in rakish asymmetry from the black bra. Seeing this, Connie reached behind her back and unsnapped the constraining garment, throwing it from her with calculated abandon. Free now, the breasts bounced with less formal grace, and Eugene stared in fascination at the lively show.

His appreciation was short lived. In one deft movement Connie bent toward him and reached under his head to bring him in closer. She smothered him with her breasts, pressing his face up against them.

Instantly his mind went to his brother Richie. When they were children, Richie had held a pillow over Eugene's head every night, laughing and threatening greater tortures if he told. Later in life, Richie had said this had all been in fun, but Eugene believed that what Richie had really wanted was to deprive his brother's brain of oxygen to lower his SAT scores. Regardless of the reason, he had been left with a terror of suffocation that Connie was now activating. In a state of panic, he struggled with head and hands while Connie, blissfully ignorant of his history, enjoyed all the frenzied manipulations.

In one of the most politically inspired moves of his life, Eugene raised his muffled voice from the center of stifling flesh. "Let me look—oomph—at your face!"

Instantly, Connie sat up, donning the expression of an angel in heat—cupid lips parted, eyes directed heavenward.

"Ah, lovely," Eugene praised, and the rhythm resumed below. Connie's pelvis rose and fell, rose and fell against him. He reached a fullness that seemed destined for expression, but because he was thinking about it so diligently, it stalled. Syncopating the rhythm, Connie grunted accompaniment to her orgasm.

Eugene, trying harder to escape into pure sensation, perversely became more distant from it. Would she keep thrusting like this forever, like an abandoned sump pump left on automatic, beads of perspiration forming on her forehead, running down her face, neck, breasts, dripping onto him, drop by drop like the Chinese water torture? He never had answered her question: what did he like? What did Eugene like, anyway? Whips, crops, lashes between the thighs? Sucking her toes? Sucking her "down there," as Francine used to say before she was accepted to law school—"my cunt, goddammit," *after* she was accepted? And just how was he supposed to have performed the act on Francine with genuine enthusiasm after she'd asked if the cat had gotten his *tongue*? Bitch finally found her match, he thought, energized—her licking, sucking, fucking, fawning, pursuing, suing, slimy lawyer—

"How's it coming?" Connie panted.

"Great," he said. "A minute more."

She kept going, and then she groaned, in a voice more full-throated than Francine in labor. "Aaaugh! Again! Right in my G-spot!"

He hated the term G-spot. It sounded like something for the dry cleaner to get out. But he was glad she was enjoying herself. He, meanwhile, was evading the question. Just what did he like? Just what did assholes like him like?

He suddenly began to laugh, causing a change in the sensations below. A hopeful sign.

Connie, faithfully thrusting above, asked, "What's so funny?"

"It's a long story," he said.

There was a pause while Connie arched in response to another fluttering. "That's number six," she beamed, as if she were going for the record. "Now tell me the joke."

"I was just thinking of Tigger—you know, from A. A. Milne's *Winnie the Pooh*? The chapter where Tigger's trying to discover just what it is that Tiggers like—honey or thistles or whatever. It just popped into my head."

"Oh!" Connie exclaimed, clutching at her breasts, a gesture that further improved the chances of Eugene's reaching orgasm. "I absolutely *adore Winnie the Pooh*. It's my favorite animated film ever!"

He told himself to ignore that, ignore that, just go harder, faster, while he went for his last hope: the Jones Beach scene. *He was eleven, lying in the sand face down. Five yards away there was a couple on a blanket. He watched as the boy's hand crept into the girl's bikini bottom. Now it was a bulge moving around beneath the taut red fabric. I think he knows I'm watching, but he doesn't seem to care. My own hand is doing things to her inside my own bathing suit. The girl moves her legs apart, just inches, but oh god, it means she lusts. I hear my mother calling me. Richie is running toward me. I have to deto-nate before they . . . hurry, yes, yes . . .*

"Yes!" he exclaimed.

"Oh, honey!" Connie cried, riding the tremor. "Good!"

Moments later, she began her attempt to set up lines of deeper com-munication, taking advantage of the situation he had called "conducive." Sitting cross-legged on the bed—revealing her midmost cutout, mer-etriciously frayed—she asked him questions about life, death, and his favorite colors while he lay there resting, his hands covering his spent shaft. He told her he was for climate control and the New England Patriots, and he watched as she probed within her own soul and discov-ered identical views, which he supposed were newly formed.

Finally, he rose to a sitting position, coming face to face with Con-nie. He moved still closer. He gazed into her eyes. A long silence filled the room, twinkling in the Christmas lights. He realized she was waiting for him to kiss her. He hesitated.

"I think you lost one of your lenses," he finally said. "You've only got one blue eye."

She stared at him, and then she began to cry.

He suddenly glimpsed the depth of despair he had caused by with-holding the post-coital kiss. The omission had surely dashed her hopes of his becoming the agent of her future happiness. His guilt scrambled for a place to perch.

"Gee, maybe we can find it," he said. He began to feel around in the sheets. "Isn't it insured?"

"Forget it," she sobbed. "I'm very emotional. It wasn't my color, anyway."

He wondered, on the subway home, where the blue lens might have gone. Perhaps it had been adhering to his inner thigh when he went to wash up in the bathroom, where it had come loose and fallen onto the floor, unnoticed, becoming one of those recoverable objects that is nonetheless lost forever, brushed by a stranger's toe into eternal darkness behind the sink.

"Did you have a pleasant evening?" Emily asked, smiling forlornly.

Eugene thought she had grown taller and paler in his absence. She reminded him of some sad and stark passage out of an Aaron Copland ballet. "Let's put it this way," he said, falling into the black velvet loveseat while still wearing his parka. "Unless I'm arrested, I'm not planning to leave this apartment any evening in the near future." He rubbed his knee where it had just jabbed into the brass corner of the coffee table. "I guess I'm just a homebody by nature. And to think, I've never even once had a fireplace or an Irish Setter."

He might have been imagining it, but he thought he saw Emily's forlorn smile brighten.

—— 4 ——

Next morning, as Glenda and Crowley were approaching the door to the offices of Henson and Blackman, they came upon Eugene interrogating the receptionist.

"Look, Claire," he said, "me and *Webster's*, we have an organic thing going for us. We *smell* alike, for god's sake. Now, who the hell do you think walked off with it?"

Claire tugged at her ponytail as if this would dislodge the clue her brain had been keeping from her. "I really can't think of who it could be. Nobody uses it but you. Everyone else Googles. Maybe you misplaced it."

"Damn thing never fails to open up more than two pages away from the one I'm after," Eugene went on. "The binding's magic. Where *is* it?"

"Lost your Bible?" Glenda inquired as she and her boss walked up behind him.

Eugene turned quickly. "Someone's swiped my dictionary," he said. "Hello, Glenda."

He offered his hand, and she clasped it cordially.

"Why don't you use your computer?" she asked.

"Did you ever see a computer with its corners gently worn and battered like an old friendship? Name's Lerman," he said to Crowley. "Eugene."

"Matt Crowley." They shook hands. "Any particular word you're looking for, Eugene?"

"I'm afraid the culprit absconded with the entire lot."

"You don't happen to know my son, Pete, do you?"

"Why? Is he a kleptomaniac?"

"No, a comedian."

Claire, having taken the liberty of buzzing through, announced, "You can go right to Mr. Henson's office now." She replaced the receiver in its cradle. "Why don't you let me take your coats. I've got a lot of room in my closet here."

"I'll walk you down the hall," Eugene offered, after stowing the coats. Glenda studied him a moment as they walked toward Henson's office. She liked him, she thought, but from a comfortable distance. The disarmingly askew smile, the somewhat disheveled hair, the one upturned collar tab of his cotton knit shirt, the lost book: these all hinted of disorder. Just as she admired the paintings of de Chirico but would find them too unsettling for her living room, she could appreciate Eugene, but not for her personal life.

"Did you finish that translation you were working on?" she asked.

"Translation? Oh, yes, the Thayer article. I did, yes. And have you decided how to *process* us desultory creatures?" he asked, forcing a smile.

Crowley laughed, his features broadening in classic symmetry, unlike Eugene's. "You have a way with words," he said, "with or *without* your precious dictionary. And yes, incidentally, we have decided. You and everyone else here will shortly be transformed into byte-sized morsels—that's b-y-t-e—and eaten up by our hand-selected suite of office management applications."

Eugene shrugged. "Just what I thought. Is there time to catch one more glimpse of the sun?"

"Barely," Glenda said, smiling. "You better hurry."

Eugene shook his head in mock solemnity as he pushed open the door to Henson's office. "Morning, Jack. You wouldn't happen to have run across a stray dictionary, would you? Answers to the name Webster, may be hungry and frightened?"

Jack Henson, standing near his cluttered desk, one thick index finger pressed into a fleshy cheek, could not have been less attentive. "What the hell did I do with those cigarettes?" he said. "I could have sworn I just put them down somewhere."

"Maybe Webster is smoking in the men's room," Eugene mumbled. "Have a challenging day," he added to Glenda, as he walked off.

"Sorry, sorry," Henson said, jumping toward his guests. "Matt! It's been how long—three years—four? How long have we been meaning to get together? Jesus, you look so fucking trim!" He grasped Crowley's arm warmly. "Pardon the French," he added anachronistically for Glenda's benefit, "but I don't get this man—what do you do, keep a painting of yourself in the attic?"

"Cut it out," Crowley protested. "Dorian never had gray hair or crow's feet."

"He would've wanted them if he'd seen you," Henson said, shaking his head in disbelief. "Sit, sit, you two. Matt, I hope you remembered me to Sybil." He pointed to Glenda. "This is a very competent lady you have here. I was impressed."

"As well you should be," Crowley said, chorusing Glenda's "Thank you." He cleared his throat. "Sybil sends you her regards. She'd love to hear about that trip to China you and Rhoda took. We've really got to—"

"—get together, yeah."

Glenda and Crowley were directed to the two old leather chairs opposite the cluttered desk. Glenda first had to remove some unopened mail from her assigned seat. A packet of cigarettes dropped from between the envelopes she was transferring to the desk.

"I remember you saying your doctor told you to quit smoking," she said, as Henson dove for the packet. "I also remember the government making it illegal to smoke in the workplace."

"Oh, what do *they* know. Anybody got a match?" He rummaged in a desk drawer and his pockets. His guests shook their heads. "Don't go away. I'm going to get a light and also collect Bill and Harriet. You haven't met my partner, have you, Glenda?"

"Just Harriet."

"Yes. A very devoted woman. I only wish she'd find herself a husband. Right back." He brushed past them.

When he had gone, Crowley turned to Glenda. "What do you say I take you to dine someplace elegant this afternoon, like Le Périgord?"

"Thanks, but I can't," Glenda replied.

"Would you prefer Italian?"

"I'm meeting a friend, sorry." She touched one of her gold button earrings and looked straight ahead at the stripes of granite through the slats of the blinds.

"A *friend?*"

"Susan Dudley. We were at NYU together." Her eyes wandered to the wall on their left, where a black-and-white photograph of a bridge at night hung alongside one of a thinner Jack Henson receiving a plaque from a stiff man in a dark suit.

"Have you ever mentioned this friend of yours to me?" Crowley studied his left knee as if the meaning of life were woven into the fabric.

Glenda turned from the photographs. "I don't know," she said. "*Should* I have?"

His eyes rose from his knee, meeting hers in a reproachful exchange.

Back at his desk, Eugene was proofreading while thinking about Glenda. As Glenda had arched to remove her coat, the suggestion of her figure beneath the wool dress had stirred his imagination. Though a benign and fleeting hypothesis, next to her cool neatness his presumptuousness had made him feel like an ape. He'd wondered whether she could make out a tuft of hair through his shirt.

Chuckling at the absurd thought, he looked up from the page of *Physician's Marketplace* he was proofreading and unwittingly met Connie's brown-eyed gaze. She was breathing fast.

"I think you were looking for this," she said, her voice a pitch above normal. She dropped Eugene's dictionary on his desk and stepped back quickly.

Eugene had been dreading their first encounter *after,* and here it was, upon him. "Gee, thanks," he said, his smile feeling like somebody else's. To hide his discomfort he tried a grandly casual lean-back in the desk chair, nearly falling. "So where'd the damn thing turn up?"

She flushed. "Well, you see, my computer froze, and I had to look up the spelling for the word 'germane.' Anyway, I took the liberty, and then I must have been in the restroom when you were looking for it."

Cocking his head, he asked, "Is your computer working now?" He felt like there was a hummingbird in his intestines.

"Yes it is. I mean, I think it is." She clasped her hands in front of her waist.

This was impossible. Maybe the situation would ease up if he could at least make reference to last night. "You know, you're one terrific cook, Connie."

"Thanks," she said, taking another step backward. "I try."

He wanted to define the situation, but, unwilling to mislead her, hardly knew where to begin.

She did it for him, resourceful woman. "I don't think we're really suited for each other," she said. "Like you're more introverted, and I'm more the spontaneous type. I think we should stop seeing each other now, before one of us gets hurt."

Somehow, Eugene hadn't counted on being let off the hook quite so easily. He'd thought she would be making a concerted effort to have at least one more go at his irresistible body, leaving him with the onerous task of withholding it from her. He was grateful for having been extricated, yet it was a victory devoid of that virile smack of satisfaction.

"You're a perceptive woman," he said. "Which is, I might add . . . *germane* to the issue."

She uttered a grateful laugh, affording her the advantage of a buoyant exit.

"Jack knows how I feel about computers—don't you, Jack?" Bill Blackman crossed his long legs and draped his arm over the back of Henson's chair. "Sorry—did I kick you, Jack?" He uncrossed his legs by casting the abuser out to the side, where it lay like a felled telephone pole.

"Computers," Henson said. "Bill hates them, but he accepts them as inevitable."

"Like death and taxes," Blackman said.

Harriet Vickers emitted a curt laugh and glanced down at the hands folded in her lap.

Blackman bent forward, leading with his hawk nose. "I don't like acclimating to a new system just to find out if some fly-by-night medical supplier paid for their ad spot."

"Tutorials," Henson said, looking first to Blackman and then to Harriet, seated on either side of him. "Glenda makes learning easy by coming to hold our hands until we know all there is to know."

"I wouldn't need such an excuse to hold this lady's hand," Blackman said.

Crowley shifted his weight.

Harriet coughed. "May I suggest that I'd be the principal systems coordinator as I have always been, so why worry?" There was a touch of bitterness in her voice.

"I don't like feeling helpless if you should be unavailable," Blackman said unctuously, as if parodying humility. "I've just barely managed to learn the basics of our modest computer set-up, and now Henson is pressing me to gut it."

"You won't have any trouble catching on," Glenda said, disregarding the emotional byplay between him and Vickers. "What you'll be doing at core is upgrading the analytic tools you already have. Your optional modules will streamline your e-commerce interchange, your subscriptions, and your rights and digital asset management, collating your existing customer data with the data picked up by your recent purchase. The system will allow for greater capacity than you have at present and, most importantly, the provider company is reliable, so you won't have a problem with online updates or other service. I think your fears will be allayed by the time—"

"Excuse me," Harriet interrupted, "but will we be able to track and report aged accounts receivable? That's always been a problem."

Glenda was taken aback for a moment. How was tracking receivables still a problem in this twenty-first century office? But she remembered Eugene's *Webster's*, smiled, and recovered.

"Of course," she said. "You'll also have full inventory control and audit trails. The system, you'll see, will be a godsend for your accountant."

"Let's hope," Harriet said, smoothing her deep burgundy sleeve.

Even though Harriet wore a tasteful designer dress, minimizing broadness, Glenda couldn't help picturing her in a Macintosh and orthopedic shoes. "Trust me, Harriet, you'll be happy with the system," she said.

Blackman laid an arm on Henson's desk and crossed his large feet straight out in front of him, invading Glenda's space so that she had to move her own feet to one side in order to avoid contact. He seemed too rangy for the furniture, like a basketball player in a kindergarten, and when he was not talking, he studied her distractedly, as if he were sprawling about her *inner* space as well. Perhaps, she mused, by the end of their meeting he would not only know her ideas on software, but also that she picked out the nasty white globules from her eggs before scrambling them.

"And what do we do," Blackman posed, "if some four-year-old from Topeka hacks into us to win a nursery school dare?"

"Your system will be far more secure than your current one," Glenda assured him.

"That's comforting," Blackman replied. He searched her face, as if for a hidden message. "I suppose the most disgruntled of us will be Eugene Lerman, our resident Luddite."

Henson snorted. "Atavist snob, more like." He took a long drag on his cigarette. "Can't help but love the guy, though. Where were we?"

Glenda and her friend Susan Dudley sat at one of the tables-for-two lined up against the walls at BG, Bergdorf Goodman's top-floor restaurant. The walls were painted sky-blue, underscoring its loftiness, and one row of tables faced Fifth Avenue and Central Park—the other, where they snugly nested, a pair of graceful sconces.

Susan pressed a lock of curly red hair behind an ear and poked at a lump of her chicken salad. "Did I ever tell you I hate chicken salad?"

"Then why did you order it?" Glenda asked.

"*Because* I hate it."

"Come on, share mine," Glenda urged, referring to her generous Croque Monsieur of rich black forest ham and melted gruyere.

Susan shook her head. "I have to work my ass off to stay thin. You know what you can do with your Croque!" She laughed. Susan's voice had a husky, sensuous quality, and her laugh was soft and scratchy—intimate.

"You always had a great figure, and you know it," Glenda affectionately chided.

Susan responded with a bemused smile. "I have to watch it obsessively. Long term, CryoCorp will up its fee if it looks like I'll be taking up more space than I contracted for."

"What's *this* all about?" Glenda asked.

"Didn't I tell you? I'm planning to have myself frozen. Don't react like my conservative husband, Malcolm, please." She sipped her unsweetened tea. "As an actuary, the subject of death is brought to my attention rather regularly. I thought cryogenics was a happy sort of alternative. Why don't you try it?"

Glenda grimaced. "I don't think I want to take a chance of renewing life as a defrosted vegetable. I'll wait until the art is perfected."

"By then you may be dead."

Glenda laughed, her outflung hand nearly knocking over her coffee cup.

Susan stroked the arm of her faux raccoon jacket, which she had slung across the chair of the adjacent table. "See how we take advantage of the latest in freezing? You have a baby like the Virgin Mary, and I sign up for eternal life. We're such planners, you and I."

"We always were, Sue," Glenda replied evenly, chafing at the comparison, but chalking it up to her friend's broad humor.

Susan cocked her head. "Except that I fell in love and got married. You never suffered such a lapse. In spite of the efforts of . . . what was the name of that statistics prof? George Hyman?"

"Hayman."

"Poor man got divorced and everything, and you dropped him, as I predicted you would. He wasn't safe anymore."

"I didn't want him to be hurt."

"You didn't want him to *be available*."

"You know my philosophy about marriage."

"Glenda, everybody's got a philosophy. You're the only one who adheres to it. By the way, how's that beautiful little premise of yours?"

Glenda smiled irrepressibly. "Astrid's wonderful. She's—well, she's just great."

Susan took a sip of her tea and shook her head. "What a puzzle you are. Staunchly independent, yet cloyingly maternal. And here I am, married to Malcolm, the sweetest guy on earth, and what do I do? Check my diaphragm every night under a strong lamp to see if he's poked a hole in it."

"I take it you don't want to get pregnant."

"If I had been clearheaded from the start, I would have realized the significance of the way Malcolm always looked down at his feet when he agreed that my career came first. But love is blind, and so was I. Now that the spontaneity has gone out of our sex, Malcolm's perpetuity drive has gotten out of hand. He stares into windows of children's clothing stores. He buys books like *Delivery Room Daddy*, and he's going to be picked up for child molesting, the way he's been hanging around school yards—well, hello!" she interrupted herself, addressing an elderly woman in a knit cap who aimed to plunk herself down in the chair alongside Susan, and who was therefore removing Susan's coat.

The woman could hardly have failed to miss the disdainful note in Susan's greeting, but she chose to ignore it. "Good afternoon," she said with perfect decorum, as she handed Susan her coat. "They do pack us in, don't they?" she added as she settled in beside Susan, who arranged her jacket across the back of her own chair.

"So anyway," Susan went on, turning from her neighbor as if aging were contagious, "I won't have a child, and Malcolm's obsessed with the idea. But there's just no room in my life for diapers and mashed bananas."

"Tsch, tsch," the woman commented to the handbag in her lap. "In my day we had babies, now they have debates."

Susan turned abruptly. "Excuse me?"

The question was meant to discourage further exchange. But Glenda felt they ought to give this woman a chance to express herself to something more responsive than her handbag. She was about to say something provocative about a woman's right to define herself as she chooses, which she thought might encourage the older woman to elaborate on her own views, but Susan quashed the invitation by introducing another topic.

"Meanwhile, I've been jogging every day at the Y. Aside from toning me up, it's been great tension therapy. You should try it, Glenda." She stabbed at a chunk of chicken, brought it as far as her lips, and returned it to the plate.

"Maybe some day," Glenda said. Over Susan's shoulder she saw the woman's hands move tenderly over the bag in her lap.

"Well, if you ever feel like it," Susan said, "it's on Lex and Fifty-third, very convenient, and they have running clinics for novices on up."

All through the rest of their desultory conversation, Glenda was aware of their neighbor's silence. She felt guilty that she hadn't overridden Susan's unilateral decision to wedge the woman into solitude, and as the two of them finally rose to leave, she wondered whether it was too late. *Say something about her pasta, ask if it's as good as it looks, tell her she has a pretty hat. Speak!* In the end, she aimed a friendly nod, but the woman was concentrating on her water glass.

Glenda tagged after Susan, suddenly feeling like she often had as a child—powerless to express her emotions, uncertain whether they would be accepted or whether they were acceptable. How close was she to Susan? How close was she to *any* adult? With a rush of neediness, she wanted desperately to hug her daughter, to be charged again with the only unrestricted love she had ever known.

That evening Eugene waited, as usual, just outside the entrance of his apartment building for Meredith to be dropped off by the Houghton bus. As he stood leaning up against the brick façade, a memory of Francine wheeling a stroller along this street drifted through his mind like an old film, mixing irreverently with a cartoon of Connie's carved frogs glimmering above her headboard. He wondered if any of the atoms of the stroller tires were still here, embedded in the pavement, and if those frogs would taunt him forever.

Meredith's high socks were riding unevenly as she stepped off the

bus. The sight of her one exposed calf filled Eugene with loving respon-
sibility, dispelling all else. He bent toward her, and clutching her books
to her chest, she kissed his cheek.

"Why's your jacket unbuttoned, Daddy? You're going to catch a
cold," she reprimanded, as he rose to his full height.

"Bossy!" he teased, flipping the end of her long scarf over her
shoulder.

"What should we eat tonight?" he asked as they rode the elevator
up. "I thought maybe we'd like Grandma's stew. Should we stick it in
the oven?"

"Okay," Meredith replied, starting to fidget because she had to go to
the bathroom. "Will you test me on my spelling words tonight?"

"Sure. Will you load the dishwasher?"

"I would've *anyway*, Daddy."

"Joke, honey. Joke."

Meredith dropped her books and bolted for the bathroom as soon
as Eugene unlocked and opened the door. As he was closing the door,
he noticed an envelope at his feet. Someone must have slipped it under
the door in his absence.

He picked it up and turned it over. *Eugene Lerman, PERSONAL*
had been printed on the envelope. He broke the seal and withdrew a
sheet of paper containing a typed, anonymous series of lines:

through bridges twined and

mobile homes unbounding

true rings the best and

ever less than certain

the rivers hide though

tender lures surrounding

night ere draws its curtain

"What is it?" Meredith asked, returning from the bathroom as he was rereading it.

"I'm not sure," Eugene answered. "It's either a love poem or an eviction notice."

5

Whenever a Houghton School bus was scheduled to return late in the day from a field trip, parents were expected to pick up their children rather than allow for changes in the home-route schedule, the administration having ruled that a child stranded at school due to parental miscalculation or forgetfulness was safer than a child stranded in front of his or her apartment house.

On Friday, the first and second graders were taken to see a new adaptation of *The Wind in the Willows* and to participate in an improvisation workshop at a theater school upstate in Glen Oaks. Their bus was expected back at Houghton at about 5:30, and by 5:25 a number of car-pooling parents and others on foot were either double-parked at the curb or milling about in the main corridor.

Glenda, who *always* picked up her daughter at school, was standing in the hallway reading the minutes of the last board meeting posted outside the principal's office when the principal herself emerged, in the process of pulling on her coat.

Lillian Mumford was a handsome, middle-aged African-American woman with deep-set eyes and an earnest gaze. "Ah, Glenda!" she hailed. "The bus has been delayed and will be arriving an estimated forty minutes late. The driver—"

"The children are all right?" Glenda interrupted.

"The youngsters are all safe and sound," Mumford said. Raising her voice to reach the rest of the parents in attendance, she elaborated: "The driver reported in with engine trouble, people. Another bus will be picking up our youngsters in Glen Oaks. The estimated arrival back at Houghton is six-twenty. We're very sorry for the inconvenience." Her delivery was firm without being imperious, engendering acceptance among the parents of the way things were. "I'll be right back to answer any questions just as soon as I notify the folks waiting out there in cars. Coffee is brewing." She imparted a reassuring smile and hastened down the corridor.

On her way to the front door, the principal brushed by Eugene Lerman walking in the opposite direction. Glenda spotted him, waved, and approached. She might have been imagining that he quickened his pace when he saw her. They met in front of the door to the supply closet.

"This must be a rare visit for you," she said. "Have you ever been to a PTA meeting?" She remembered having met his wife at one, and she hoped he wouldn't interpret this as a leading question.

"Up to now I never knew what I was missing."

"Consider yourself reproached."

He raised his right hand. "On my honor, I'll go to the next one."

"It's next week."

"What, so soon? Well, if you promise you won't put me on a committee. By the way, what grade's your daughter in?"

"Astrid's in the first grade."

"Meredith, grade two."

"The drop-off is going to be forty minute late," she said. "Did you know?"

"Why? What happened? Are the kids okay?" he asked, suddenly anxious.

"Would I be chatting here if I thought they weren't?"

"True," he admitted.

"The engine broke down and another bus is coming for them."

He thought for a moment. "Are you alone?"

"Yes," she replied. "Incidentally, did your wayward dictionary ever come home?"

"He did. Since we have time to kill, you want to spend it at the corner pub?"

"They're brewing coffee for us right here."

"I said I'd go to the PTA meeting. You're not going to make me start circulating *now*, are you?"

She conceded.

The corner pub was dimly lit and smelled vaguely of furniture polish. A sandy-haired waitress in a black jumpsuit was polishing one of the many vacant tables. She indicated that Glenda and Eugene could sit where they chose, and they agreed on the table furthest from her spray wax. After they were settled in, the waitress ambled over to their table with menus.

"Care for a hamburger or something?" Eugene asked, admiring Glenda's cheekbones.

"I should wait to eat with Astrid."

"What'll you have? I'm having a whiskey sour."

"A ginger ale."

"That's exciting."

"A Perrier, then," she said.

"You don't imbibe, do you," he said thoughtfully, after the waitress had left them. He moved the pitcher of fake roses, which was obstructing his view of her hands.

"No, I don't," she declared, as if he had challenged her virtue.

"Your adamancy speaks louder than words," he observed.

"How predictable. I was *expecting* a gibe."

After they were brought their drinks, he touched her glass with his own. "Forgive me if I have aggrieved."

"I just don't have a taste for it. I think I have a right."

"More than a right. An obligation. Hell, I'm sorry." He poured his drink into the pitcher of fake roses to atone.

She laughed. "You shouldn't have done that."

"You're right," he agreed, and he ordered another whiskey sour.

"You know," he said, as they sipped their drinks, "my wife and I are divorcing. Finalization is imminent."

"Mm hmm," she said, noncommittal.

He fingered the rim of his glass. "I'm trying to avoid asking you the least subtle leading question ever fashioned, which is: 'what does your husband do for a living?'"

"I see."

"You're a big help. I'll try to be creative. Does your husband ever come to PTA meetings?"

She smiled. "I'm not married."

"Divorced?"

"No."

"Gee, I'm sorry," he said, covering the possibility of her having been widowed.

"Why sorry? I've never been married."

"But your daughter . . . I mean, her father . . . I'm so heavy-handed."

"Let me put it to you this way," she said. "I've delivered a legitimate child, but I've never been a wife."

After a beat, he said, "Is this something like my saying I've got a degree from Princeton, but that I'm not what you'd call a Princeton man?"

"Now, *there's* a circuitous way of flashing your credentials."

"*I'm* being circuitous?" he countered. "You've got my head spinning!"

Glenda disclosed the nature of her pregnancy. Eugene was affected more by the manner in which she related her story than by the facts themselves. This was a woman who left nothing to chance.

"You weren't just screwing around," he commented.

"Motherhood," she stated, eliding his pun, "is a basic need. Monogamy is not." She told him she had chosen to fulfill herself while avoiding the constraints of a relationship. He thought she sounded like a cross between Gloria Steinem and Pope Francis.

"I suppose it all boils down to a matter of self-management," she concluded.

"I think it boils down to a matter of control," he said. "You even thought to plan the genetic input for your offspring. I hope you don't mind my saying so, but although I'm impressed by your courage, I'm kind of put off by your rigidity."

"No, I don't mind your saying so." She sipped the last of her Perrier. "You're entitled to your views. As I am entitled to mine."

There was something about the way she held herself so very straight, the way she stared so intentionally into his eyes, as if she were countermanding the inclination to avert them, that he could not help but feel the source of her credo went deeper than the *seds* and *ergos* of reasoning, that it went way back to the illogic of experience.

"You know," he said, "there's a random side to every atom. No matter how hard you try, some electron or other is going to give you a kick in the ass. What I think is, maybe you're more afraid of losing control than you are happy about possessing it."

"And what I think," she retorted, her eyes fiery emeralds, "is that maybe you missed your calling. You should have been a quack."

"You don't think your views about sex are just a bit—cold, huh?" There was an ache between his legs. This was not a response to her ideology.

"I don't, no," she said. "I separate sex from societal imposition, is all."

He gave a whistle of disbelief. "You don't separate, you alienate."

"You seem to be doing just fine in that area yourself!" She emitted a scornful laugh. "Does it sound like we're married?"

"Not likely. I associate sex with commitment." He frowned: where did his night with Connie fit into this admirable doctrine? He was a hypocrite. He grew silent.

"*Now* what's on your mind?" Glenda finally asked.

"Random atoms. Some of my own."

"I have a feeling I shouldn't pursue this one," she said. "We've been getting along so well for the last millisecond."

"I have one hell of a nerve," he pronounced, "getting on my high horse. Here you are, minding your own business, conducting your life as you see fit and not hurting a fly."

"Don't overdo it."

"I'm sorry." He reached for his wallet to pay for the drinks. "I've had an odd couple of days."

She grinned. "It's okay. We've both been a bit . . . hard sell, or something."

"So I guess I'll be bumping into you at H and B next week," he reflected as they walked back to the school. The wind was suddenly bitter. He raised his collar and widened the distance between them, though his instinct was to draw nearer.

"Yes, I'll be back," she said, pulling out the gloves from her pockets.

They stood together in the warm school corridor for some time and then separated when the first and second graders began trooping in. As children paired off with adults and narrations of the day's events were launched, he stole a glance at her, and he smiled inwardly when he saw her kiss Astrid's cheek.

6

Saturday mornings Eugene often played racquetball midtown at the elegant Le Parker Meridien Hotel at the invitation of his friend, Larry Bloom, a member of its health club. Unlike the set-up at most clubs, the courts and exercise rooms were located in the bowels of the hotel, whereas the pool was on the penthouse level, a facility unto itself. Thus Larry was able to purchase a membership that excluded pool privileges, saving a couple of hundred dollars.

The morning after the Houghton bus breakdown, Eugene was scheduled to play racquetball with Larry at 8:30. He was preparing to leave the apartment when Mrs. Schmidt, the housekeeper, arrived for her weekly four-hour stint. Mrs. Schmidt had been coming for three years, and Eugene felt ill at ease with her, especially now that she was making it clear that she preferred Francine to him. Francine had given her lists, numbered lists, against which Mrs. Schmidt could check her performance. Eugene was uncomfortable assuming the role of feudal lord, which meant that there were no lists for Mrs. Schmidt, and consequently no respect for him.

Before Eugene left for his match, Mrs. Schmidt complained that she had been telling him for weeks to restock the oven cleaner and indicated that his wife would never have been so negligent. She also raised her peppered brow at the sight of his clothes strewn on the chair in his bedroom and grimaced at the dirty socks scattered at the foot of his bed. Eugene was miffed. How had she interpreted Francine's departure, anyway? Did she think Eugene had driven her away with an attack of dishevelment? He was about to object to her attitude toward him, but he recalled Francine's words of wisdom: "It's hard to find good help these days—knock wood that we have Mrs. Schmidt." He held his tongue.

To add insult to injury, Larry, who was the slightly better racquetball player, beat him soundly that morning, wounding him at that tender juncture of athletic fallibility and masculine deficiency. Sitting afterward in the club's subterranean health bar at a little white veranda table furnished with an inapposite umbrella and with only a glass of tepid juice and a bunch of carrot sticks to offset the agony of defeat, Eugene had to contend with a battery of questions put to him by his bulked-up friend. Larry asked about the status of his social life, which led to a confession of the unfortunate encounter with Connie, which Larry irksomely treated as an example of Eugene's touching innocence.

When the anonymous verse that had been slipped under Eugene's door made its way into the interrogation, Larry saw this, too, as proof of his friend's magnetic guilelessness. "Have you researched the possibilities of authorship?" he asked.

"I'm curious but not on tenterhooks," Eugene answered. "I figure the poet will reveal herself, or himself, sooner or later. For all I know, this was an unusual way of submitting an ad spot for *Physician's Marketplace*."

Convinced of the poverty of Eugene's love life, Larry pursued the idea of fixing him up with his recently divorced sister. The spirit with which he approached the mission matched the aggression he had demonstrated on the racquetball court. From their earliest association at *Time* magazine, where Larry still worked, the two had been at odds when it came to matters of socio-sexual protocol. Larry, a devoted husband and ardent womanizer, had always teased Eugene about his old-fashioned notions of monogamy and constancy. However, now that Larry's cherished sister was single, what he had once called Eugene's "hang-ups" he now considered his assets.

As a result, when Larry talked to Eugene about his most recent conquest, a student from Intermediate Aerobics, he didn't try to prose-lytize his own creed on marriage and amour (a "division of church and state," as he had once described it), nor did he play up the three fabu-lous positions of intercourse he and the student had discovered. Instead, his account was sober and modulated, and he made reference only in passing to his prior lover, the blackjack dealer from Atlantic City, whom he used to visit once every two months on what his wife thought was a stag junket.

"She was so upset," he recounted sadly, "and rightly so, to find out I had been unfaithful to her."

"Your wife?" Eugene asked, brushing back his hair, still wet from the shower taken after the match.

"No, the card dealer. She was very hurt when I confessed my attach-ment to Judy. It seemed like the gentlemanly thing to do."

"Aha. The aerobics person."

"Yes." Larry gave his shoulders the smallest shrug, a sign of help-lessness, or possibly even remorse. It was obvious he was trying not to insult the standards Eugene upheld, the very same ones he wanted to be applied to his sister's next marriage. "Now, don't try and evade the issue, Gene. You've never met my sister, Phyllis, have you? No, you wouldn't have, being that she was held hostage in Duluth for the past eight years by a deranged orthodontist. You'll love her."

"I'm sure I would."

"Will. You're coming to dinner with her and me next Sunday. Don't say no. Really, you're kindred spirits—except I believe she plays a better game of racquetball."

"You bastard."

"Listen, my sister would kill me if she thought I was trying to fix her up." Larry rubbed the crick in his muscular neck. "She doesn't need that kind of assistance. I just thought you two would hit it off."

"It's kind of you, Larry, but I'm laying low for a while."

Larry picked up a wilted carrot stick and looked suggestively at Eugene. "Not laying at all is more what you had in mind, eh, buddy?"

"Something like that," Eugene said, grinning openly, as if he were in good humor.

Segueing, with tender ego, to the next item on his agenda, Eugene brought his daughter, at her fervent request, to the neighborhood Cutaway salon, where he waited as she had her locks clipped to shoulder—"grown-up!"—length. He sat on a tufted leather bench against a wall of the busy salon, watching Francine's old hairdresser going to work on Meredith. Though pained by every lock lost, he was unable to leave the scene. He could see the image of Meredith's face in the mirror. Now admiring herself, now timorous in the presence of her womanly potential, she squinted and sighed and cocked her head, forcing a gentle remonstrance from the hairdresser. Eugene reacted with a pressure in his chest.

Meredith looked at her father through the mirror and beamed him a questioning smile. He nodded his approval and mouthed, "Looks great," at the same time feeling an overwhelming grief at having bequeathed to her the inevitability of suffering and death. At that moment, looking at her sweet image in the glass, he was so close to being part of the stream of her perceptions that he could almost feel the tug on her scalp as the hairdresser grasped a section of his handiwork, could almost share that blink of her eyes, the question simmering . . . *Am I pretty?*

The absolute nature of separate awareness—his own from Meredith's—the loneliness of the act of dying . . .

Such thoughts receded when Meredith started complaining about the shorn little hairs itching under her clothes as they walked home, although throughout the rest of the day they periodically interrupted the flow of events, bothering him like existential gnats.

That evening, as Eugene watched Meredith carry out another of her initiation rites—the removal of what she now deemed the "babyish" clip-on bows on her school shoes—Glenda was engaged in a difficult long distance call from her cousin Janet.

"You know how I feel about him," Glenda was saying, "so I can't understand why you go on like this."

"But he's really sick, Glenda, and he's been pleading for me to get you to come see him. He's your stepfather. Can't you forget the past?"

"That's what I'm trying to do. That's why I won't come."

"Your judgment is so harsh, Glenda."

"My judgment is so accurate." Glenda was sitting on the edge of her bed in a terrycloth robe, twisting and untwisting the ends of the tie that went around her waist.

"It's not, I don't know, admirable, your bearing such a grudge all these years."

"You can think what you want, Janet, but don't sermonize." Glenda spoke in a subdued voice. Astrid was in the kitchen area emptying the dishwasher, and Glenda did not want her overhearing. This was the one part of her life that was too painful to share. Even Janet, with whom she had spent so much of her growing-up time, knew only the tenacity, not the depth, of her feelings.

"What should I tell him, Glenda?"

"Tell him the truth. Tell him we have nothing to say to each other."

"I love you, cousin, but you are one stubborn lady."

"Thanks for the affection, anyway. I love you, too, Janet."

The conversation ended and Glenda replaced the landline phone in its cradle on the night table. She sat there pulling at a loose thread in the white quilted comforter until it tore off. She rolled the thread between her fingers and was about to flick the ball to the carpet when she changed her mind and pushed it into the pocket of her robe. She looked up, caught her reflection in the dresser mirror, and although she was not planning on going anywhere but into the shower, she smoothed her hair back from her forehead and straightened the collar of her robe. She felt unkempt, disordered.

Disparate thoughts converged toward her mother. She closed her eyes and tried to elicit an image of her from out of the good years, before the time of changes that ultimately led to her death. She tore at the shades of perception, trying to evoke a living picture of her mother unencumbered by the ravages of those terrible last years—to see, to hear, to touch her completely and intact. With her eyes closed, she focused on the straight nose, narrow at the bridge, like her own, until she could see the textured details of the skin. From the close-up she made the image expand into a holograph of a kneeling woman, a strand of warm blond hair falling across her brow as she looked up from her pruning activity, there in her garden patch, haloed by the scent of earth. She was smiling up at Glenda. There was a small chip in her front tooth in the outline of a crescent moon. Was that its true configuration?

Glenda struggled to get the edges clean, as if her self-image would flatten into conjecture if the image of her mother did. She tried to catch the luster of those deep blue eyes, to inhale the pungent smell of dirt on those fingers as her mother's hand was raised to shield the eyes from the sun. But she could not approximate sensation. She remembered *that* her mother's eyes were blue, *that* her fingers smelled of damp earth, but the concept lacked vitality.

If only she had a photograph of her, not to replace the elusive life-image but to caress memory, objectify it. There were no photographs. Long ago, her stepfather, in one of his drunken outbursts, had seized the precious photograph album from her mother and destroyed it.

Glenda tried again to capture the woman in the garden, turned the face up toward her, lifted the hand to shield the eyes, again and again. She imagined voices added to the gestures. *Hi, honey!* Pause. *Hi, honey!* No. Again. *Hi, honey!* No, she could not hear it.

"Mommy?"

Glenda opened her eyes and turned. Astrid, bestowing an instant improvement in Glenda's judgment of herself, was standing at the door, her hand on the knob.

"I thought you were going to take a shower," Astrid said.

"I was just going to."

"I'm all finished with the dishes. There's this big soccer game on TV starting in a few minutes. You want to watch it with me? I'll explain about the rules and everything."

"I'll take my shower first."

"*Then* you'll watch? You promise?"

"Yes, honey." Glenda's breath caught. The term of endearment had seemed directed as much to herself as Astrid. She rose from the bed. "I won't be long."

7

Her cousin Janet was not the only one to disturb Glenda via the telephone that weekend. On Sunday she was surprised by a call from George Hayman, her erstwhile statistics professor and lover, to whom Sue had made reference over lunch. She had not heard from George since the dissolution of their relationship eight and a half years ago.

George was calling from Berkeley, California, where he was teaching at the university. He spoke with a rapid urgency that bordered on mania, a style that Glenda might have attributed to time constraints had George not seemed determined to go on forever. His call was an expulsion of autobiographical data, passionately annotated. As far as Glenda could tell, she was to blame for all that had gone wrong with George's personal life, yet was at the same time the only one who could set it right. He failed to ask her to bring him up to date about herself, and from references to her in his diatribe, it was evident to Glenda that he thought of her as unchanged, like a mathematical given in what was otherwise an empirical science: the study of his life.

His troubles, he said, had begun when he had divorced his wife so that he and Glenda might attain their amorous potential, and Glenda had rewarded him by ditching him with a flowery excuse regarding her independence. Beside himself with grief, he had applied for an opening in the math department at Berkeley and had let his hair grow. For two years he lived with an unstable economics instructor only because she had a nose like Glenda's, and after the woman moved back with her husband, he grew a beard and took up with a nineteen-year-old cheerleader. This association terminated when a covetous linebacker threatened to report him to his department head if it continued. Since then, he had gone from one unstable relationship to another, including a marriage, presently on the rocks, to a fellow mathematician.

Glenda remembered the reedy, articulate Dr. Hayman, perched on the edge of his desk with a pipe between his teeth and fire behind his tortoiseshells. The voice swathed in petulance at the other end of the line negated the image. He must have nurtured the idea of Glenda being the Prime Mover in his life for so long, she realized, that it had ripened into a full-blown fixation. Now, she learned, he was registered for a math symposium at NYU scheduled for next weekend, and he was arriving Friday afternoon. He wanted to meet her to resume the relationship, which, he reasoned, would resolve his problems.

"I think it's a bad idea for us to meet," she managed to interject.

"Wrong. It's the *only* idea," he amended.

She tried to tell him he was oversimplifying his situation, but there was not a long enough break in his soliloquy to get her point across. Finally, she heard a door slam at his end. Happily, it was George's wife, and he was forced to end the conversation.

Glenda's concern over George Hayman's impending visit was tabled Monday morning when, as de rigueur, her professional responsibilities regained their supremacy.

She was working in Harriet Vickers' office, trying to devise a good process for importing H and B's ancient records to the new accounting system she was building, when she noticed an imbalance. The entry was camouflaged by supportive notations, and under ordinary circumstances she supposed it would probably have gone unnoticed. But given that it might pose a problem for the data import, she became determined to track down the source of the disorder.

She pulled the physical ledgers and files to check them against the computer records, and she pored over entries of income and disbursements with unflagging purpose. In doing so, she discovered more and more similar disparities, along with sometimes mysterious signatures and record-keeping methods. In the end, she called upon Harriet Vickers to help explain some of the records. Harriet seemed not to mind the interruption.

"We should definitely iron out all the minor bookkeeping errors before we debut the new system," she heartily acknowledged. "I would be the last person to say I haven't made one or two errors myself, although I'm confident they're not what we'd call flagrant." She swiveled her desk chair to face Glenda directly. "Will you be going out for lunch?"

"I'd hate to lose my train of thought," Glenda replied.

"I'll order in sandwiches for us," Vickers offered. "I don't want to abandon you with all this." She gestured toward the files.

"I don't want to put you to—"

"I have no other plans. It will be a pleasure to dine in with you and get on with our work."

Glenda yielded, and as her analysis progressed over the next few hours, she was grateful for Vickers' cooperation, especially in the face of the new strata of bookkeeping that had arisen out of the recent merger.

Over the course of the day, after much digging and retracing, the scent narrowed to a single source: Bill Blackman. In each instance, an unremarkable allocation of funds—from $200 to $700—had moved from unrestricted cash to accounts payable. Each of the transactions referenced an invoice vouchered by Blackman. However, the voucher could not be found in the general ledger, and the actual amount transferred was less than the amount withdrawn.

Although there was no hard evidence, and although Glenda was careful not to communicate her suspicions to Vickers, she found it hard to escape the possibility that Blackman had been involved in foul play. The aggregate sum, she figured, was no more than about $11,000, but she did not know if the duplicity had been going on for a year or ten, or if it had been accomplished with Henson's knowledge—or, for that matter, their accountant's. The exact figure didn't concern Glenda as much as the fact that the connivance had occurred at all.

When Glenda returned to her office late in the afternoon, she immediately went to see Crowley about the matter. Crowley listened attentively as she reported her findings and appeared to be sympathetic with her decision to proceed no further with the systems upgrade until the books were reconciled.

"I hate to accuse someone of being unscrupulous, but the facts are pretty convincing," Glenda said. "I didn't think it my place to confront either Blackman or Henson on my own, and I guess I'm counting on your political savvy to help at the showdown."

Clearly delighting in her flattery, Crowley repositioned the pencils on his desk to divert from the displayed emotion. "Let me think about what you've said. Leave your notes with me, and I'll consider how best to approach this thing."

"You'll prepare the field for us?"

"I'll call Henson tomorrow and broach the subject."

"You don't know how relieved I am," Glenda said.

"It's Monday," he said, as if she needed reminding.

Crowley stopped Glenda from rising by exerting pressure on her leg and slipping his hand between her thighs. She could feel the outer edge of his pinky. "Don't get up," he said in a hushed voice.

She closed her legs on his hand, and she gave his knee a squeeze.

"I'd love to loll around here with you," she said, "but I've got to pick up Astrid. You know that."

Crowley looked at her as if he'd plummeted from Eden and landed with a thud somewhere between Fifty-seventh Street and his sixtieth birthday. "You don't have a clue about how I feel," he complained.

"Oh, Matt, don't ruin it." She rose from the couch, trying not to appear languid. "You were never moody."

"Sorry if I'm starting to object to being compartmentalized." He smoothed back his hair and rose. "So be it," he sighed, reaching for his shorts.

"What do you want me to do?" Glenda asked, slipping into her underpants.

"I want you to see how I handle a wine list. I want you to kiss me in the back seat of a cab."

"Don't," she said.

"Does it offend you that I want to break out of this"—he made a sweeping hand flourish—"this *prison*?"

Glenda adjusted her bra. "Please, Matt."

"This is not typical of me," he said. "I don't like myself at this moment."

"Yes, I can see that."

"What makes it worse is that I'm perfectly aware that *you* don't like me at this moment either!" He buckled his belt, noticing that it had become looser over the last week, an observation that helped lighten his mood. "What a jerk."

"Me?" she asked.

"No, me."

She grinned. "I thought so."

They finished dressing in silence.

To avoid the cleaning brigade's suspicions, Crowley always left at least ten minutes after she had gone. As they parted at the door, Glenda frowned. "You *will* call Henson and Blackman tomorrow, won't you?" she asked. "I feel unsettled about the situation."

"Don't mix business with pleasure," he admonished. "Unless you want to talk about it over dinner tomorrow night."

She smiled without answering, as if she did not know his statement was a plea.

"Understood," he said, his commanding figure slumping. "Yes, I'll make the call. I told you I would."

Yet by Tuesday afternoon Crowley's call had still not been made.

"I've decided how to handle the matter," he said when Glenda pressed him.

"How?"

"By letting *you* handle the matter."

Glenda picked a piece of lint from her gray sweater and remained poised before his desk.

Crowley leaned forward in his chair, resting his elbows on his desktop. "The problem you raise is not actually in our realm of inquiry. Our business is to initiate or enhance a system, not enforce law and order."

"Our clients rely on us to keep them in line with the laws of the land," Glenda reminded him.

"*Tax* laws," he corrected. "We're not a detective agency. We've been contracted to improve the architecture of a company's management system. Nothing more. I suggest you carry on as best as you're able, and—"

"Fudge the figures?"

"Leave them as they are."

"I can't rubber-stamp a lie. I would be abetting a criminal."

"An alleged criminal," Crowley retorted.

"Of course," Glenda agreed. "Still, I can't pretend I haven't come to a tentative conclusion. Maybe you should take me off the assignment."

Crowley shook his head. "You're the most familiar with the systems we're using. I have complete confidence you're up to it."

"Aren't you concerned your friend Jack Henson's partner may be bilking him?"

"For all I know, Jack may be fully cognizant. Come on, Glenda, this is all very benign stuff. I'm surprised at you."

"Is that a compliment?"

"Yes and no."

Later in the day Eugene sat down in the vacant seat next to Glenda in Houghton's cozy auditorium, where the PTA meeting was already under way. The president, Vera Held, was on stage suggesting ways of raising funds to purchase a set of uneven bars for the gym.

"You're a man of your word," Glenda whispered to Eugene. "I didn't think you'd come."

"Neither did I."

Vera discussed the benefits of a pancake breakfast, and Glenda crossed her legs. She was wearing brown leather boots and jeans, and were it not for the long strand of pearls she wore over her red turtleneck polo, she might have passed for sporty, Eugene thought. Her hair was in its usual constraining bun, and he thought about pulling out the pins and seeing it fall free, if only out of curiosity. He himself had not bothered to take off his parka, which he now unbuttoned.

"I saw something flash by my office today," he whispered. "Somebody told me it was you."

"I was in only a short time," she said. "I was double-checking something I want to be sure about."

"Do we have any volunteers for the sausages?" Vera put to the assemblage.

"Why the haste?" Eugene asked Glenda.

"Not now," Glenda whispered, turning her attention to the podium.

Eugene raised a hand to his head.

"Great—thank you!" Vera responded, smiling greedily at Eugene. "I don't believe I know you, Mister . . ."

"Who, me?" Eugene replied, nonplussed, to the amusement of the gathering.

"You *did* volunteer, didn't you?" Vera lilted.

"I'm Eugene Lerman, and I was just going to scratch my head."

"You also just volunteered to cook the sausages for the pancake breakfast," Vera informed him.

"Good thing we weren't bidding on a Rembrandt."

"Go for it!" Glenda quietly urged. Then, addressing the group, she announced, "This is the first time he's been to a meeting. Draft him."

Applause.

"Sold!" Vera belted, and Eugene could do nothing but submit.

"You won't get away with this," he told Glenda after the meeting, as they waited their turn at the coffee urn in the rear of the auditorium. "I'm holding you responsible for half the sausages."

"It's a deal. You're a good sport."

"Yes, I am."

With her coat draped over her arm, her bag dangling from her shoulder, Glenda approached the coffee urn.

"Here, let me," Eugene said. He poured two cups. "Cream?" She shook her head no, and he added cream to one cup. "Sugar?"

"No, thanks."

They stepped aside.

"So what were you so interested in double-checking at the office this afternoon?" he asked, after they had found a patch of space in which to talk.

"I can't really discuss it," Glenda said, raising her cup to her lips.

"How mysterious."

"I don't mean to be," she began, just as someone passing behind Glenda bumped her shoulder. The movement jolted her cup, splattering coffee down the front of Eugene's parka. Oblivious to the deed, the perpetrator continued on her way, while Glenda profusely apologized.

"No problem," Eugene insisted.

"Here, hold this," she said, handing him her cup. She drew a bunch of tissues from her bag and began wiping the front of his coat. "I'm so sorry."

"It's okay. But don't stop, I'm beginning to enjoy it."

Glenda laughed, her face becoming warmer than it had been. He wondered why. She took back her cup and tossed it and the tissues into the nearby trash bin. "I'll have it dry cleaned," she said.

"Are you kidding? Say, you want another cup of coffee?"

"Are *you* kidding?"

They shared a laugh.

"What was that mystery you were in the middle of not telling me about?" he prompted. "Your flight from H and B's?"

She hesitated. "It's unethical of me to discuss it with you," she said. "Especially since you work there."

"Which might enable me to advise you about whatever's bothering you."

"I thought of that."

"I've got the ability to keep my mouth shut, you know."

Silence.

"It's unfair of me to make an accusation without allowing him to speak in his own defense," she began. "Or without evidence much firmer than what I have."

"But—?" Eugene encouraged.

"But it looks to me like Blackman may have . . . pocketed some funds from the unrestricted cash account. I've gone over and over the records, and although it's circumstantial, the evidence just doesn't seem to point anywhere else."

"Really?" he replied. "Well, how do you like that."

"You seem less than flabbergasted," she said.

"We live in dangerous times. My threshold of terror has risen." He was joking, but then he began to consider the implications of career instability for Bill Blackman. "Who's hurt by the impropriety, anyway?" he asked.

"Henson, I imagine. Whoever. I'd rather not carry over imbalances to the upgraded system."

"Is that because you're a mathematical purist, or because you're just honest to a fault?"

The warmth she'd shown before quickly cooled. "I should have kept my mouth shut."

"Look, I don't mean to be a spoilsport," he returned, "but with the firm's recent acquisitions, there'll be some personnel shuffling, and the guy pulling for my promotion to editorial director is none other than, yes, Bill Blackman. Don't make trouble for him. Why don't you just call him and ask him to have Harriet look into it? If he's innocent, he'll clear everything up, and if he isn't, you'll probably know it anyway."

He realized Glenda had provoked him into a stance that was out of character. He had always been put off by those heading-up-the-ladder types, and here he was, coming across as one of them.

"I'm not one of those heading-up-the-ladder types," he said aloud. "Seriously, what would be so wrong with just talking to Bill about it? Is exposing guilt more important to you than resolving a problem?"

"Honesty is important to me," Glenda finally said. "I guess I'll figure it out on my own." After a moment, she added: "We should have stuck with the sausages."

"Don't remind me."

She held her bag close to her body as if it were a pacemaker.

"I hope the matter will be resolved without causing you a problem of any kind," she finally offered.

"Save the lofty good will," he muttered. "Meeting's adjourned."

That night in bed, as she berated herself for her schoolmarmishness—
and berated Eugene for having caricatured her as such—Glenda laid
out a plan. The next morning, Wednesday, she would call Blackman, tell
him that she had run across a couple of discrepancies in the transference
of funds from unrestricted cash to accounts payable, and ask whether he
would mind looking into them. She would indicate when the transactions in question had occurred and suggest that if Bill preferred, Glenda
might have Harriet check the records to save him the bother.

She would continue to monitor the accounts. If they had been corrected by the following Monday—Eugene was right at least in that, that
Glenda would be able to tell if cash had been replaced or the numbers
skewed—she would go ahead with her assignment. If not, she would
bring the matter to Henson's attention, again making no overt reference to misconduct. In either case, next Wednesday she would proceed
with the record transcriptions, including a memo with her signed doc-
umentation of the transcription stating that she was not responsible for
discrepancies of prior genesis.

The call to Bill Blackman went more smoothly than she expected.

"It's just a precaution," she said. "No one's accused of anything. But
I do think it would be good for Harriet to look into the issue."

He surprised her, however. "I don't think so," he said. "Bookkeeping
is hardly my bailiwick. But I'm more than capable of looking into this
matter on my own." His tone was friendly but firm, and he got off the
phone as soon as possible.

Two days later, Glenda still hadn't heard from him. She made herself
put aside her worries about the situation. She would wait until Monday before advancing to step two. In the meantime, she had been busy
enough putting the finishing touches on other proposals. She had
been so successful at keeping her focus on her day-to-day that she
was surprised when, that evening, just as she and Astrid were about

to bread their flounder filets, the phone rang and George Hayman's voice greeted her.

"Hello, I'm here!" he announced.

A pause while the realization came fully into consciousness.

"Oh, no!" she cried.

"Glenda! Darling! I told you I was coming!"

"I didn't take you seriously. I thought you got whatever it was off your chest. I never thought I would hear from you again!"

Astrid's eyes opened wide. "Is that my father?" she asked in wondrous anticipation.

Glenda shook her head as a wrenching pain pierced her belly. She drew Astrid in tight against her body, and Astrid wrapped her arms around her mother's waist, clutching her in return with equal force.

"Did you think I was kidding around?" George was saying. "I'm beside myself with expectation!"

Glenda took a few deep breaths and stroked Astrid's shoulder. "And did you think *I* was kidding around when I told you I didn't think we should see each other, George?"

"Nonsense," George countered. "You're only afraid of all those feelings you decided to bottle up eight years ago. Well, fate has given you another chance. I'm at the downtown Marriott. I found your address through phone reverse. Shall I come to you, or do you want to come to me?"

"I'm not going anywhere," Glenda clipped.

"Then I'll come up to your place. Of course it'll take a little while to—"

"No, George, you're not coming here. You've got an idée fixe. Work it out."

"Glenda, you're not denying us this second chance," George declared.

"I am hanging up," Glenda enunciated. "You do not know me. You are thinking of a woman you would like me to be. Good-bye." She reached up to replace the receiver back in its wall cradle. "That was weird," she said to Astrid. She kissed the top of her head.

"Was that a crazy person?" Astrid asked, separating from Glenda and looking up at her. "It sounded like he was crazy."

"Maybe not crazy," Glenda said. "Obstinate. Definitely obstinate. Sweetpea, I didn't mean to frighten you . . ."

"It's okay, Mom. Can we make supper now?"

She was about to say *yes* when the phone rang.

"Don't hang up on me again!" George bellowed, as soon as Glenda picked it up.

Glenda spoke slowly, guardedly. "I had to do that to make you understand," she said. "If you must talk, I'll call you later at your hotel. If we decide a meeting is still necessary, we can get together where you're giving your lecture."

"You're lying!"

"I don't lie."

"I want to see you tonight," George insisted.

"Then I'll have to hang up again. My god, George, you're a brilliant man, why are you making me sound like a condescending bitch?" She hung up.

Seconds later the phone rang again. Glenda turned the phone off and placed the receiver on the table. "I don't like doing this," she told Astrid.

"Who *is* that guy, Mommy?"

They went back to breading the fish as Glenda explained that George was an old boyfriend who wanted to see her again, and that Glenda didn't want to see him. Astrid asked her a few when-and-where questions as they finished and she wiped her hand on Glenda's apron.

"What if he comes here?" Astrid asked. "Will you let him in?"

"No—and thanks for reminding me!" Glenda hurried over to the intercom panel on the wall next to the door to the apartment and pressed the asterisk button. Diego's voice rose from the speaker: "Hello, Miss Glenda."

"Please, Diego, don't let anybody up!" Glenda squawked. "A man I don't want to see may try to get past you!"

"Lady, lady, I never hear you so jumpy. I don't ask you why you are so jumpy, but I say you must not worry. I protect my people."

"Yes, I know, Diego, and I'm grateful. The name's George Hayman, but he may use a fake name. Don't let any man up!"

"This man, does he maybe have a gun?"

She gasped. "Oh, no, Diego. He's excitable, but I'm sure he's not *armed!*"

"I would not want to see my brains all over the lobby floor, so I just ask, okay? Don't you worry."

"I'll try not to." Glenda's legs felt unfamiliar, like recent grafts. "Thank you, Diego."

Friday at H and B was eventful, to say the least, and Eugene couldn't wait to tell Glenda all about it. Doing so, however, was more of a problem. He tried Glenda's landline and cell phone numbers three times each before trying to find her address online. She only lived about five blocks away.

He explained to Meredith that he had something important to tell a business acquaintance of his and that he had to walk over to talk to her directly. "You know her daughter, as a matter of fact. The girl you almost had a fist fight with—Astrid Fieldston?"

Meredith gave a disdainful toss to her newly cropped hair. "Oh, terrific, Dad. This is really terrific."

"One thing has nothing to do with the other, Mer. I'm going to call Emily Lapwing to see if she can babysit for a while, all right?"

"I don't need a babysitter. I'm not a baby."

"Well, you're *my* baby." *Shit, that sounded like Fran.* "I mean, you're

not a baby, but I would feel more comfortable leaving you with somebody who's older. So do me that favor, okay?"

She sighed. "Okay."

He dialed Emily's number. "Hello, Emily. Meredith and I would like
to know—"

"I think I'm gonna puke," Meredith mumbled.

"Hold on a sec, Emily." Eugene held the mouthpiece against his
thigh. "What's wrong?"

"It sounds like *we're* inviting her over," Meredith said. "Instead of
just *you*."

Eugene raised the receiver. "Sorry, Emily."

He explained the situation. Emily sounded flustered.

"I'm happy to sit," she said. "But maybe—would Meredith like to
come over to my apartment instead? She could listen to me practice
the cello?"

Eugene relayed the message. "I don't care," Meredith replied.

"She'd be delighted," Eugene told Emily.

"Does she have a TV?" Meredith whispered.

Eugene lowered the mouthpiece to his thigh again. "What?"

Meredith groaned. "Stop doing that! She's going to think I'm crying
or something! I'll go there. C'mon!"

Eugene unzipped his windbreaker and scanned the dimly lit lobby.
There was a doorman there, and he watched Eugene carefully while
securing his cap.

"Can I help you?" he asked.

"I'm looking for Glenda Fieldston," Eugene said. "I didn't see a list
of residents at the door."

"Aha!" the doorman said incongruously, with a self-congratulatory
yank at the jacket of his uniform. "I thought so."

"Huh?"

"Don't make trouble, mister. You just turn yourself around and go away nice and quiet, yes?"

"What's going on here?" Eugene started to make his way across the somber maroon and brown carpet toward the front desk, where he was hoping to find a list of tenants.

"Hey, hey!" the doorman warned, coming between Eugene and his goal. He was easily a head shorter than Eugene, but his cap gave him a couple of inches, and he seemed eerily confident. Eugene stopped dead in his tracks.

"Tell me why you're being so goddamn rude," he said.

"When my tenant tells me she wants to see nobody, nobody is who she sees. You get it, mister?"

"Jesus, is she in trouble?"

"The name's Diego, mister, and it's you who's in trouble if you take one more step."

"Get out of my way!"

"Don't take another step!"

This was not normal doorman behavior. Was this an imposter? Eugene wondered. He felt a growing alarm for Glenda's safety. It was essential he find that list of tenants. After that he could run up the stairs to her apartment if this doorman—or whoever this was—prevented him from using the elevator. He tried to push Diego out of the way.

Diego uttered his battle cry—"That's it!"—and went for him. Eugene, ill prepared for combat, and certainly not for Diego's brand of killer karate, found himself quickly sprawled on the floor of the lobby, with not enough hands to clutch all his hurt parts.

"Had enough?" Diego asked, as if the pummeling had lasted more than five seconds.

Eugene moaned. His left cheek stung, and the vision of his left eye was blurred.

"What the hell!" came a voice several yards away.

From what Eugene could make out with his good eye, a tall man with a scruffy beard and strands of brown hair combed over his baldness had just entered the building. He appeared caught between seasons, wearing corduroy pants and a linen jacket.

The man approached. "Is someone calling the police? What happened?"

"He tripped," Diego replied. "He's okay."

"Is this true?" the newcomer asked Eugene, his tone skeptic.

"Yes," Eugene said, appeasing Diego while he planned his next move.

"Is there anything I can do to help?" the man offered.

"What do you want here, anyway?" Diego snapped.

"I'm looking for Glenda Fieldston."

Diego flinched. "*What* you say?"

"I'm looking for—"

"Never mind! Don't move, either of you!" Diego scurried to the intercom behind the reception desk and signaled to Glenda.

Eugene heard her answer almost instantly: "Yes, Diego?"

"Listen, when you talk to me I think you worry about one guy. So far I got two down here. Maybe I don't hear you so good. Just how many you say you expecting?"

Silence.

"Two?" Glenda's voice was almost inaudible. "What are their names, Diego?"

Eugene was rising to his knees.

"Stay on the floor!" Diego ordered. "You want me to hit you again, mister?"

"I *thought* that's what happened!" the newcomer said.

"You *hit* someone, Diego? Whom did you hit?" Glenda's transmitted voice was shrill now. "Who's *there*, Diego?"

"What's your name?" Diego asked Eugene.

"Eugene Lerman."

"I got a Eugene Lerman here," Diego announced into the speaker.

"Eugene Lerman's down there?" Glenda shouted.

Diego turned to the other man. "You! What's your name?"

"George Hayman."

"I got a George Hayman here," Diego said into the device.

"I'll be right down, Diego!"

"Tell her to bring a couple of ice cubes," Eugene said.

"Who the fuck are you, anyway?" George asked.

"An angry bastard like yourself," Eugene retorted.

"The man says to bring him a couple of ice cubes," Diego added into the speaker.

"Lock the door and don't let anyone in," Glenda told Astrid. "If you don't hear from me in five minutes—look at the clock, it's when the big hand gets to the three—"

"I know how to tell time, Ma."

"Okay. Call the police—that's nine—"

"I know how to call the police, Ma."

"Right. I'll call up to you within five minutes." She ran back to the refrigerator, added another couple of ice cubes to the plastic bag, and re-zipped it.

"I want to come with you," Astrid enjoined. "You're not as strong as me. Mrs. Nielson says I'm the strongest girl in junior soccer."

"I'll be just fine. There's not going to be any more fighting."

Before going downstairs, she threw off her apron. It didn't occur to her to ask herself why she'd done that until she was in the elevator.

The three men were arguing when Glenda stepped out into the lobby. They fell silent when she appeared. Glenda rushed to Eugene, where he was sitting on the floor, ignoring George altogether; time to deal with him later. She dropped to her knees. "I'm calling an ambulance!"

"No, I'll be fine. I can stand. The Gestapo just wouldn't allow it."

"This is awful!" She was close to tears.

"Thanks for the ice," Eugene said, taking the bag from her and pressing it to his bruised cheek. "You must be wondering why I dropped by."

"Glenda!" cried George. "Aren't you happy to see *me*, for chrissake?"

Diego was attentive, on guard.

Glenda was suddenly aware that her hair was falling apart, she was in stockinged feet, and George bore only a remote resemblance to someone she was once infatuated with. "I told you not to come," she reminded him. "But of course, it's good to see you," she added. From her position on the floor she extended her hand up to him, and he gave it a mechanical pump.

"So, how have you been, George?" Eugene asked with mock solicitude, rising from the floor. He winced, and with Glenda's support he hobbled over to the couch and fell into it.

"I'm going to use the intercom, Diego," Glenda said.

"Yes," Diego acknowledged, his tone seeming to say that he no longer expected explanations.

"Everything is under control, Astrid," Glenda transmitted, after the connection had been made. "I'll be up soon."

"Sure. I'm watching the New York Rangers. They just got a goal."

"Who's Astrid?" George asked.

"That'll be Glenda's daughter," Eugene said.

"Her *daughter*?" George was finally being forced to accept Glenda as integral to the space-time continuum. "Then she's married!"

"I take it you mean the mother," Eugene said. "No, she's single."

After a beat, George exclaimed, "God, am I the *father*?"

"No!" Glenda shot back as she padded to the couch.

"Is *he*?" George scowled, pointing at Eugene.

"No!" she replied.

"Yes!" Eugene replied simultaneously, infuriating her.

"*What*?" George sank into the couch, put his head in his hands and began to weep uncontrollably. Glenda sat down on the couch between

George and Eugene while Diego watched the men closely, as if either of them might become rabid at any moment.

Residents Mr. and Mrs. Wendell Fisk stepped into the lobby from the elevator. More than good Samaritans, the Fisks were known for keeping abreast of the standards of behavior maintained in the lobby of their building. "What in heaven's name!" uttered Mrs. Fisk.

"They tripped," Diego ad libbed.

"Actually," Eugene said, removing the bag of ice and exposing his injured cheek, "*I* tripped. George, here, is empathizing."

"Well, really!" Mr. Fisk admonished.

"They're okay," Glenda said. "Just a bit disoriented."

Mrs. Fisk eyed Glenda's stockinged feet and Glenda flushed. "Perhaps I should fetch a doctor," Mrs. Fisk said, surveying the group. "Of *one* kind or another."

"I was going to call a doctor myself," Glenda said, peering at Eugene's bruised cheek.

"That won't be necessary," Eugene said. "As a professional boxer I'm accustomed to facial injury."

Mrs. Fisk snorted and took off for the exit with her husband. "You never know what'll turn up these days." She flashed Diego one of her severest looks—eyes squinted, thin lips pressed together—as if he were responsible for this and all other problems that had ever existed in the building, and perhaps beyond. As soon as the Fisks had gone, Diego crossed himself.

"Eugene, I think you really ought to see a doctor," Glenda implored. "Your cheek is black and blue."

"I don't want to."

"Then why don't you both come up for a . . . for some kind of beverage?" She gave George's knee a maternal pat. George was still sobbing, though less noisily. He waved off the suggestion.

Eugene also declined. "I don't think I'm up for another go-round with you, Glenda. Nothing personal, but they all seem to end in disaster. I'm still not quite sure why *this* one turned out so poorly."

"I told Diego not to let anyone up," Glenda explained. "I knew George might try to see me"—another pat on George's knee—"and I didn't want to get together with him."

"Next time try to be more specific," Eugene advised. "That way you don't put all males in harm's way."

"What time is it?" George sniffed from within his cupped hands. "Never mind, I've got the time." He emerged to look at his watch. His eyes were red and his tears had plastered his beard to his jawline. "Maybe Richardson will be at the party, and I can get some information out of him there, at least." He began to weep again.

"Who's Richardson? What party?" Glenda asked, trying to draw him out.

"A math and science book club is giving a cocktail party for us tonight," George replied faintly. "Richardson gave a lecture that I missed today, being so distracted and all, and I promised my wife I'd take notes on it."

"What lecture?" Eugene asked, curious.

"It was on the heuristic method of teaching math. My wife wrote her doctorate on the subject. I can't do anything right. She said she wanted to register for this conference. I said no, I wanted to be alone to straighten out my life—ha. I could have at least taken notes on the—"

"If you scoot off real fast," Eugene interrupted, "you can still catch Richardson at the cocktail party."

George rose from the couch. Although he appeared lost, Glenda supposed that this meant he was entering the first phase of adulthood. "I'm giving a lecture myself, you know," he informed Glenda's feet. "On Saturday at—"

"That's tomorrow," Eugene prodded. "You better hurry."

"Yes, Saturday. It's on the three fallacies engendered by statistical astronomy. My wife typed it." He paused before bending forward to grasp Glenda's hand. "It's been truly—"

"Enlightening," Glenda finished.

"Yes," George agreed.

"You okay?" she asked him.

"Yeah. I'll catch a cab. Do you think I'll have trouble at this hour? Never mind, I'm good." He started to move away and then turned back, as if he had forgotten something. He shrugged his shoulders. "Well, good-bye."

"Good-bye," Glenda and Eugene returned in unison.

Diego ran ahead to hold the door open to guarantee the departure.

"Oh, yes," George remembered, just as he reached the door. He looked back. "My talk's at one-thirty, if anyone's interested."

Glenda waved. "Good luck."

"Knock 'em dead," Eugene called after him.

Glenda took a moment to absorb George's final exit from her life. Then she leaned away from Eugene, as if she was seeing him for the first time.

"Eugene!" she pronounced.

"Yes?"

"Why are you here?"

"I thought you'd never ask."

"I'm asking," she said.

"I said our encounters end disastrously. I come with glad tidings, and I leave with bodily damage. Although at this point the whole thing seems to belong on another planet." He rubbed his calf. "Okay, it's about the business with Blackman."

Glenda shot forward.

"Whatever your strategy was, it worked," he said. "It all happened this afternoon. I tried reaching you—in the spirit of unrequited good will, I might add."

"Don't say that!"

"Why? You gonna get Diego to work me over if I do?"

"Eugene!"

"Yeah, I know. I have some nerve, haven't I? Let me explain. First, it wasn't Blackman who was doing the skimming. It was set up to *look* as if it was Blackman. The culprit was Harriet Vickers, killing two birds with one stone."

"Harriet Vickers?"

"The one and only. Whatever you said to Blackman must have stirred him up, because he went digging in the records. He turned up the irregularities you pointed him toward—withdrawals and entries he hadn't made, invoices he hadn't vouchered, checks he hadn't written. All faked and forged. He suspected Harriet right off the bat because she has access to all our records. And, as it turns out, there's a personal issue as well."

"I thought I detected some rancor between them," Glenda submitted.

"Observant. I hadn't noticed. Well, Blackman didn't have any real proof of her wrongdoing, but he put pressure on her, and she spilled the beans without putting up much of a defense. She's essentially an honest person. I suspect the burden of guilt outweighed the pleasure of revenge."

"I guess there was an affair—or the semblance of one—in the picture," Glenda suggested.

"Yes." Eugene touched his bruised cheek, shamelessly garnering sympathy. "Ouch. It all came out today. Bill and Harriet had at one time been having what Harriet interpreted as a serious affair. According to Harriet, Bill had treated her badly, refusing to divorce his wife and, on top of that, ditching her for yet another woman. 'He toyed with me'—those were her actual words at the site of her catharsis, the coffee station."

"I think you should reapply the ice," Glenda said. "So Harriet committed a reactive crime. He deceived her, and she went and deceived him back. If the improprieties were ever disclosed, Blackman would find himself in trouble with Henson. Sweet revenge. Am I close?"

"You're hotter than hot," Eugene said, staring at her.

His remark could not have been more obvious. Eliding it, she said, "The other of your 'two birds with one stone' would be the cash she acquired—remuneration, from her point of view."

Eugene nodded. "I think she did it more for the mischief than for the money—although, come to think of it, she does have a penchant for expensive tweed suits. At any rate, Blackman's not filing charges and is chalking up Harriet's ill-gotten gains as separation pay." He dropped the plastic bag, now filled mostly with water, into Glenda's lap. "And so they all lived remorsefully ever after." He rose and saluted Diego, who had returned to a post within protective range: two feet away. "I'm going now."

Glenda jumped to her feet. "Can't I do something for you?"

Eugene shrugged. "Distract Diego while I head for the exit." He started to walk in its direction. "And Glenda?"

"What?"

"When you come to complete your work over at H and B's, let's try not to get too close. I like admiring you from afar."

In the void created by Eugene's departure, Glenda realized that despite his barbs, more jaunty than pointed, he had been a real sport about being caught in a melee not at all of his making. She thought of his parting shot and wondered if, on the contrary, she herself might enjoy reviewing his positive qualities nearer than "from afar."

The music coming from Emily's apartment began its healing effect as Eugene stood outside it, leaning up against the door. Before ringing the bell, he savored a few moments of music unbroken by conversation, listening to the orchestra from which was emerging the voice of a cello riding the swells of a dulcet melody. The walk home had loosened his bruised and stiffening muscles, but the music began restoring his parts to harmonic unity. As he listened—eyes closed, thoughts guileless as the cello's line—he remembered a Princeton sanctuary, an old tape player, a notebook laid aside, bowed head, torso accenting downbeats, guttural sounds coming from his throat reinforcing the Alberti bass. When had he last *lived* a musical performance?

The cello receded as the orchestra became more assertive. He opened his eyes and rang the bell.

Emily clapped her hand to her chest. "Oh, dear Lord!"

"Looks that bad?" He touched his hand to his cheek. "I return in a worse way every time, don't I?"

It was strange, he thought—her posture seemed to improve as she kept looking at his injuries, as if she was gaining strength from the prospect of treating them.

"Your cheek's discolored and there's an abrasion—what *happened* to you?"

Her long fingers were spread against her white T-shirt. He could see where, at the edge of her hand and between the thumb and index finger, the muscles had been developed by what must have been countless hours of her percussing at the strings of her instrument. He could not help but admire her for the devoted persistence the muscles indicated, bulging as they did on what would otherwise have been the hand of Botticelli's Venus. "Let's pretend I ran into a door," he said. "May I come in?"

Emily reddened. "I'm sorry—of course!" She stepped back, allowing an entry without contact.

Two floor speakers were broadcasting what had developed into an animated passage. "Your daughter was watching television in my—my bedroom," Emily said, "and she fell asleep."

Looking in on Meredith, they found her on her back on the Indian print spread, her hands innocently above her head, her feet sweetly toeing in. On low volume, Keanu Reeves was plowing a car through the roof of a barn. "I was afraid it would wake her up if I shut it off," Emily said, tilting her head. "Isn't she adorable?"

"*I* think so," he said.

Emily's lips formed a beatific, if somewhat regretful smile, as if she couldn't quite get past the Platonic Ideal of a young girl to the immediacy of one in particular: Meredith. Her affection had a touchingly legato quality about it. "Shall I take off her shoes?" she asked.

"I should bring her home," Eugene said.

"Why not stay and let me make you a cup of green tea?" she said suddenly. "I can clean your cheek with peroxide."

She seemed ill at ease, somehow, after she'd said it, as if she were worried about having been too aggressive, but after the incident with Diego, Eugene appreciated the modest recommendation. "Why, indeed, not?" he replied.

Emily removed Meredith's shoes and covered her legs with the afghan she said her mother had given her last Christmas. The child stirred and then was still. Madonna-like, Emily touched the girl's forehead, and then she and Eugene left the room, he closing the door halfway.

The one-bedroom apartment had a similar layout to Eugene's own, but on a smaller scale. Layout was where the similarity ended, however. His place had that Francine-is-inspired-one-Tuesday look, whereas Emily's arrangement seemed to have evolved over a period of time. One bookcase held books. Another, which didn't quite match, contained musical scores. One chair, a butterfly, looked like the type carted around after college until it falls apart or its owner gets married. Another, a Chippendale wing, resembled something donated by an elderly aunt. There was also a music stand, a cello, and a bridge chair centered between two speakers against the wall, the speakers playing music that for some reason kept skipping, or going silent for long stretches.

But it was the difference in art selection that made the real impression on Eugene. Unlike Francine's chosen school (she called it Modern, he called it Neo-natal), which included monochromatic washes, stone spheroids, and generic fish, Emily's choices abounded in detail, forming a kind of Italian Renaissance-Eclectic-Zaire School mix. A copy of

Raphael's "The School of Athens" was tacked to a wall. On a lamp table stood a reliquary of wood and copper and a small wooden model of a tribal war god or ancestral figure. Elsewhere hung a formidable mask of wood and fiber and a framed reproduction of Tintoretto's "St. George and the Dragon." Eugene saw the collection as a kind of symposium, "The Search for Beauty and Order, An Overview." Scanning the art, he cocked his head and frowned.

"There it goes again," he said. "It sounded great from the hall, so why is it skipping now? What's wrong with your CD player—or is it digital?"

Emily smiled. "Nothing's wrong. You're listening to Schumann's Concerto in A minor with the solo cello left out. This is a Music Minus One CD." With both hands she swept her long hair back behind her shoulders, exposing her delicate gold hoop earrings.

"You mean that was *you*?" Eugene asked. "Gee, I thought it was Yo-Yo Ma or—"

"Or somebody really *good*, you mean!" Her thin lips curled into a strangely seductive grin.

"No, I didn't mean that," Eugene objected, attending to her words rather than the configuration of her mouth. "It's just that I've never been in such close proximately to a real artist. Did I ever tell you about my brother?"

She uttered an uncharacteristic demure giggle. "No."

"He plays the clarinet like a dead cat—no, I'll give my mother the benefit of the doubt. He plays the clarinet like *Benny Goodman's* dead cat. You see my point?"

"Yes." She was laughing now, brazenly exposing her gum line. It was the first time he had ever seen Emily laugh.

"Would you mind playing for me?" he asked suddenly. "I mean, I hate to sound like a visiting grandparent, but would you?"

"Of course. Just let me fix you that—"

"Forget the tea and sympathy. Just sit down and play."

"If you insist," she said.

"I do." He removed his windbreaker and threw it over the butterfly chair, waving off her intention to hang it up.

"Would you like me to play something else? Some Haydn, maybe?"

"I was enjoying the nostalgic flavor of the Schumann," Eugene said. "Let's save Haydn for another day." He planted himself in the couch of nubby fabric, propped an embroidered pillow behind his back, and sighed, contented.

Emily took up her cello at the bridge chair. She set her thonged feet firmly apart, adjusted the instrument between her jean-clad legs, and reached behind her to reset the CD player. After three introductory chords of the orchestra, Emily came in with a curving melody in the middle register, and Eugene was struck first by the wonderful clarity of her tone and second by the idea that prior to seeing her with a cello between her legs, he hadn't thought of her as having a crotch.

A deliberative half step in the cello's bass register thrust its musical line into a flurry toward the treble, and with this dramatic phrase, Emily gave up the world and became immersed. Eugene saw it happen. Her right foot shifted and her shoulders curved, as if to allow space for the instrument to expand.

The music itself, through its passionate sweeps, its imploring turns, its progressive drive through the heart of memory, was enough to take Eugene back to the days of unencumbered love and the pursuit of truth, both discovered in the remote corners of Princeton's library. But it was not just the music that affected him in this way. Emily displayed the kind of intense concentration and dedicated effort he associated with his college days. Now that she was absorbed, her face had begun exhibiting reflexive grimaces and tics that Eugene saw as an escape valve for what he imagined to be the total mind-body coordination required in this deceptively effortless production of sound. He marveled at the phenomenon and at the musician herself.

Fifteen minutes into the concerto, during a fervent dialogue between the solo cello and the violin section, Eugene felt a series of sharp raps beneath his feet. Having already been the victim of violence once today, he responded with a jump of considerable force. Recalled to reality in another register, Emily completed the phrase and lifted the bow. The orchestra continued without her.

"I shouldn't be playing so late," she said. "I have an agreement with the people downstairs." She turned to shut off the music. "I'm sorry."

"How can they complain? You're great," Eugene commented.

Emily colored. "Maybe they prefer country music."

Eugene brushed the sole of his shoe over the gold-toned carpet. "You'd think this would absorb most of the sound."

"It's thick, I know," Emily said. "I got it to appease them, really." She rose, propping the instrument against the chair and placed the bow on the seat.

"What happens if you want to play until two in the morning?"

"There's a comfortable area off the storeroom in the basement that the building manager lets me use. It doesn't happen often." She adjusted the bottom of her T-shirt. "I'm going to fix you some green tea now."

"No, no, Emily. Thanks. I'd like to take a rain check, though. Any time you need an audience. Do you know how affecting your playing is?"

"Thank you," Emily fairly cooed. "Shall we get Meredith?"

"Yes." Eugene stood up and, performing the only vestige of his mother's influence that had remained intact, smoothed the spot where he had been sitting and replaced the embroidered pillow against the back cushion.

Meredith was still lying on her back. Eugene scooped her up in his arms and carried her to the apartment door. Emily grabbed Meredith's shoes, clicked off the TV, and followed him.

"Oh, my jacket. Could you reach inside the right pocket and get my keys?" Eugene asked.

Emily fetched his windbreaker from the butterfly chair and dug into his pocket for his keys.

"Now, would you just throw the jacket over my arm?" He tried to rearrange Meredith.

Emily held on to it. "I'll open your door for you," she said.

"Sure, if you wouldn't mind."

When Emily turned the key in his lock and looked back at him, Eugene could not help but notice her eyes. At 6' 2" she was two inches taller than he, and her eyes were about level with his, and definitely glazed.

A possibility arose in his mind. "Emily?"

"Yes, Eugene?"

"Do you—oh, never mind." He was about to ask if she ever wrote poetry, and whether that poetry ever happened to slip under doors. But with Meredith in his arms, and especially with her elbow digging into one of his sore spots, the ensuing conversation would be awkward. He'd ask her some other time.

But curiosity notwithstanding, Emily had been working on a question of her own. "Would you like to come to a rehearsal some time—tomorrow, even? Meredith is welcome, of course. We're preparing for a tour."

"Sure, I'd love to."

"Tomorrow we'll be playing Mozart and Smetana." She handed him—parted with—his jacket.

"Sounds great. Oh, and I owe you for babysitting."

"No, you don't," Emily objected, her spirits visibly deteriorating.

Eugene understood. "That's so sweet—thank you, Emily."

As soon as the Lerman door clicked shut, Meredith opened her eyes. "Gross," she said.

"Hey, were you awake?" Eugene let her down.

Meredith noticed his bruise. "Daddy! What happened to you?"

"I ran into a door. What's gross?"

"You and her."

"'You and she.' Why?"

"I don't know. Why did you carry me like a baby?"

"You were asleep."

"You should have waked me up."

"Why?"

"Because I told you. I'm not a baby. I woke up in the hall, but I had to keep my eyes scrunched because I was embarrassed to say I was awake. Your cheek looks awful. I'm going to put some medicine on it for you. You get ready for bed, and I'll get the iodine and cotton balls."

"Look, Florence Nightingale, *you* get ready for bed and *I'll* get the cotton balls." Her face fell, and he regretted his insensitivity. "Actually, it would be nice if you'd help me. I'd like that."

He watched her as she stood on the bathroom stool to get the iodine from the medicine cabinet. There was a small bottle of Francine's perfume on the shelf above. He watched as she noticed it, hesitated, and then reached for the bottle of iodine instead.

Late that night Eugene was awakened by the phone ringing. In his haste to answer it, he knocked it off the night table, sending it crashing to the floor.

"I hope I didn't wake you," Glenda said.

"That's okay; I had to pick up the phone from the floor, anyway. What can I do for you?"

"I just called to see if you were okay and to apologize."

"Oh, good. I thought maybe you were calling to warn me your doorman was on his way over."

"Sometimes injuries don't bother you until hours later. You're feeling okay, though?"

"Yes."

"Do you know there are thirteen E. Lermans and three Eugene Lermans in the neighborhood?" she asked.

"Did you wake them all?"

"Only two. You sure you're all right?"

"Positive," he reassured her. After the noncombative interlude at Emily's and the doting care from Meredith, Eugene was feeling smug, definitely not amenable to exposing himself to an attraction that endangered life and limb.

"Nothing hurts?" Glenda persisted.

"Well, maybe the spleen, but they say it's expendable. No, really, I'll be fine. Just *fine!*"

It was strange. When she said goodnight, following this firm prognosis, she sounded as if she was perturbed, and he wondered at whom.

8

Emily's Music Minus One performance so impressed Eugene that he decided to take her up on her invitation to attend a rehearsal of the Municipal Orchestra the following morning. He asked Meredith to go with him, but she refused.

"Mrs. Schmidt's here today. She's going to help me with my sewing. I'm taking sewing after school hours."

"I thought you were taking dancing."

"I decided it was dumb. I changed to sewing. Mrs. Schmidt's going to help me with my backstitch."

Eugene, as a result, went alone with Emily, carrying her cello to the bus that took them to the Sixth Avenue rehearsal space where the Municipal Orchestra met four times a week. He carried her cello in and then retired to the corner, where he spent the morning becoming an intimate in a world he had never entered and listening, with fascination, as the orchestra fine-tuned pieces by Mozart and Smetana through subtle tweaks to approach and delivery.

On Monday he spent an hour and a half of his workday at the rehearsal space, to where he brought sandwiches for himself and Emily to eat during the rehearsal break. The next day he did the same, Elgar and Bartok comprising his listening pleasure. On Wednesday he sat in on Emily's cello lesson at the Manhattan School of Music and stayed to observe at least the beginning of one of the string ensemble classes Emily herself conducted several days a week. On Thursday night he got Mrs. Schmidt's niece to sit for Meredith so that he could take Emily to a revival of the movie *La Traviata* at the Angelika Film Center in Soho. At 10:30 that night, when he brought Emily to the door of her apartment, he kissed her on the mouth because he had grown to admire her so deeply as a musician, and also because he was curious to find out what it was like to kiss somebody that tall.

On Friday he again dropped in on the orchestra rehearsal. During her half hour break, as they were eating the ham sandwiches he had brought, she told him that she had just been informed that as of the first of the year, following Moe Gimplemeyer's retirement, she was to occupy the second chair in the cello section, which meant she was moving up not one but three chairs. Eugene planted a congratulatory kiss on her cheek.

"So are you as dedicated a poet as you are a cellist?" he finally asked.

"You guessed, didn't you?" she said. "I was going to tell you some time."

They were sitting next to each other and could speak freely, the nearest person being a trumpeter connected to an iPod three seats behind. Balancing his sandwich on his lap, Eugene reached inside the vest pocket of his blazer and drew forth a folded sheet. "This seems as good a time as any to ask. Would you interpret it for me? Blank verse has always been a weakness of mine." He started to hand her the paper.

"I know it by heart," she said, waving him off. "Where are you having a problem?"

"Kind of all over, I guess." He unfolded the sheet. "Starting with 'bridges twined and mobile homes unbounding' right on along to 'rivers hide through tender lures surrounding.' I mean, don't misunderstand.

I really appreciate the timbre and all, it's just that my mind seems to function on a more concrete level." He folded the paper and put it back in his pocket before taking a hefty bite of his sandwich.

Emily looked at him, then looked down at her own sandwich, hardly touched, and explained. "The first few lines refer to the confusing landscape of our lives. 'True rings the best and ever less than certain' refers to those loyalties we feel instinctively, but are reluctant to accept as valid because they are grounded in faith rather than in reason."

"Aha!"

"'The rivers hide'—the rivers, that is the flow of consciousness, hide our secrets, those pure truths that exist amid all the confusion mentioned earlier. 'Though tender lures surrounding'—though we are tempted to divulge our secrets."

"I see, yes."

"'They ope their gates to night ere draw its curtain'—we finally reveal to each other . . . before . . . night . . . I mean . . . oh!" Emily choked back her emotion.

"I understand, Emily. I see now." Eugene patted her arm. "It loses its provocative force in the translation, but for thick heads like mine, well, we have to make the sacrifice for understanding, right?" He tried to keep her from losing control and embarrassing herself. "You better eat, Emily, or I won't be able to distinguish you from your cello bow."

That was Friday. On Saturday, after almost beating Larry at racquetball and again finding excuses not to attend a dinner for the purpose of meeting Larry's sister, Eugene picked up Meredith and walked her to the home of a classmate who was having an all-day birthday party complete with sleepover. He bussed over to the office to work a few hours on the upcoming issue of *MD Forefront*. Afterward he returned to join Emily in her apartment.

Emily awaited him there with high trepidation and eagerness, even as she cut the crusts from the dainty paté sandwiches that she was preparing for their mid-afternoon snack.

Emily's admixture of emotion was due to the fact that she was a virgin anticipating a change in status. There was nothing terribly anomalous in her background to account for her virginity. It was just that she had been a shy teenager with protective parents who had allowed her to leave Bozeman, Montana only because Juilliard had such a great reputation. Since her growing-up years had largely been occupied with practicing the cello, it had not been difficult to transpose her pubescent energy into musical expression with, here and there, a flight of fancy she'd make manifest through a poem and heavy masturbation. She had merely continued this lifestyle when she had settled in New York.

Time had passed. The shedding of her virginity had been delayed and delayed, looked upon more and more as a singular event, separate from the natural flow and almost impossible to ease into. That is, until the confluence of factors leading to this Saturday afternoon, when she cut the crusts from the paté sandwiches and awaited Eugene's arrival.

None of the men she had ever had occasion to fantasize about had ever been as accessible and pleasant as Eugene. She had never fantasized about any of the men in the orchestra. They were too close to her, like children brought up together in the same kibbutz. Eugene was far enough from her calling to instill an air of mystery, yet close enough to be considered an ally in the arts. In addition, he lived just the right distance down the hall for her to be exquisitely tormented over the nearness of his physical being, especially between the hours of 10:00 p.m. and midnight. To top it off, they had the same initials. This was something that, like a Debussy arabesque, moved her deeply without the need for reason's compliance. Added to all of this, her recent career boost had charged her with enough confidence to keep her from flinching. She had been moved up three chairs in the orchestra, and this morning before rehearsal a member of the percussion section, pianist-composer

Paul Scheinberg, had asked her to join a small chamber group he was putting together, though admittedly for the purpose of getting his own avant-garde works performed.

Emily was as ready as she would ever be.

Which is why, a short time later, after serving Eugene and herself the delicate sandwiches and Formosa oolong tea, she was able to serenade him with a piece that seemed custom-made for cello and transcendental virgin: a melody she had found in a Dvorak cello concerto, which the composer had taken from one of his own piano songs.

"Dvorak composed the melody to the original German," she told him as she tuned her instrument. "He structured the adagio movement of the concerto as a three-part song. I guess you could say I relate to the lyric—'Let me wander alone with my dreams.'"

She played the cello part through, and then she played transpositions of the clarinet and flute parts. Eugene was touched by the honesty of expression as she sounded the strings of her heart.

"That was really beautiful," he said, when she at last laid the cello aside and joined him on the couch.

"Thank you," she said. "I think you must find me overly sentimental."

He reached across the seat cushion that separated them and took her hand. "No. I find you sincere, something which you can never be 'overly.'"

"We have the same initials, you know," she said.

"Yes, we do," he said.

"I know it means nothing, but it feels significant to me," she confessed.

"That's sweet." Having the same initials did nothing for him, but she had lowered her head as she spoke the words, her hair falling over her shoulders and partly concealing her face. This, he found charming. He squeezed her hand.

"I've always been a private person," she said.

"I kind of thought so."

"A *very* private person."

"Oh."

"I mean I never . . ."

"Oh?"

She nodded. "That's right."

"Oh."

"I mean there's nothing *wrong* with me."

"Of *course* not."

"It's just that—"

"I know. The opportunity—"

"The opportunity," she fugued.

"Never arose," he completed.

Her head was bowed as if in prayer.

Eugene stroked her hand. Why should he be surprised? After all, who knew where *he* would be today without the timely aid of Tillie "the Hun" Bernstein, a Princeton classmate whose appetite for knowledge was at once ravenous and diverse and who had led him, their freshman year, into a secluded aisle of the library stacks where, between Whitehead and Wittgenstein, he was divested both of his virginity and of all that he knew about the Punic Wars? Wasn't it only after Tillie had broken his barrier of shyness and he saw that he could not only penetrate a vagina but do it standing up and proximate to the text of Alfred North Whitehead, that he became relatively confident in his prowess? Emily, here, had just never been pushed to overcome her timidity.

"The first time is always the hardest," he said. *Big shot! You're suddenly an expert?*

She raised her head and looked at him, her large round eyes filled with tears. "It *is* difficult."

He slid closer to embrace her.

Compared to the women Eugene had been with, Emily was so unfamiliarly tall that for a second he panicked, believing he had forgotten everything he knew. This lapse in confidence passing, he led her to the bedroom and closed the door to promote intimacy.

Emily had already drawn the shades, allowing only a small amount of daylight to filter through. Perfect visibility for a deflowering, she thought: dim enough to allow for modesty, light enough to permit adequate observation.

Eugene kissed her long and hard then stepped back, smiling in a way he realized was patronizing. However, at a time when Emily wanted nothing better than to be directed, the smile was a comfort to her. It indicated that he assumed authority and that he thought kindly of her.

"Are you on the pill?" he asked. "How stupid. Of course, you wouldn't be."

"I was just fitted for . . . I mean, I was hoping we would be . . . I mean, it's okay."

The mood was deteriorating. He kissed her again, this time while undoing the back button of her prairie skirt, hoping to encourage her to disrobe.

In order to get through the difficult transition to intercourse, Emily pulled back her perspective to third person. This had saved her from mortification on other occasions: when she had been singled out for criticism by her math teacher in high school, when her junior prom date had publicly poked fun of her height, and two days ago, when the gynecologist had fitted her with a diaphragm.

She is unzipping her skirt and stepping out of it now, she said to herself as she performed the deed. *She is calmly pulling off her T-shirt just as easily as if she was going to take a shower,* she continued, as she pulled off her T-shirt. *She is regarding Mr. Lerman as he drops his jeans. He is now stepping out of his shorts. She is following his example and is removing the last of her garments. She is now unclad and ambling over to the bed. She is now supine.*

Eugene sat on the edge of the bed, unable to speak.

At the precise instant Mr. Lerman touches her, she will switch to the sub-jective mode and participate with pleasure in all that follows, Emily advised herself.

Eugene was dumbfounded. Not because of the silent, mechanical manner in which Emily had undressed and lain down on the bed. He was curious about that, but not stunned. It was her body itself that held him speechless.

He had never seen anything like it—such a long, flat expanse. There was something mystical about Emily's body—its homogeneity, its con-tinuity. It fascinated him like the Great Wall of China and the Sahara Desert. His arousal came from the sexual content present in all things mystical and from the awareness that there was something profoundly enigmatic within reach.

And then to discover, when he touched the monolith, gingerly at first, that it was sensate at every point on its surface! And further, get-ting past his initial generalization, to find there were indeed fine rises and slopes, ridges, concavities here. He became acutely aware of every deviation, so titillated was he by the very notion that such deviations even existed on what he had at first perceived as a grandly uniform sur-face. The nipples, miles apart, were precious jewels, alive to the touch, emerging with the contact of a finger or its approach. From there, tra-versing a great plain, gently curved like a heavenly arc, he attained the distant navel, its delicate convolutions inspiring questions akin to "Is there life on Titan?" Then, exploring further, through a clean-waxed clearing, rounding the bend he at last came upon . . . Emerald City? Sparkling wonderland of Disney dreams? No! Instead, he found a dark and secret place of unknown depth and design, from which oozed a slimy exudate! All the lascivious dreams he had ever had that in any way pertained to subjects prepuberal, from choir boys to the maidens of Uganda, were filed in this Pandora's box.

Before he knew it, he was rising and falling on her. By the time he was fully aware that he was in the throes of raping a ten-foot Venusian girl, it was too late to turn to a more civilized image. He was already coming, and coming.

As for Emily, it was as if she had been preparing all her life for this tee off, only to take a swing and miss the ball. Of course her failure was partly the fault of Speedy Gonzales, but the fact remained that for years she had been playing miniature golf in pleasuring herself. Over time, she had gotten her strokes down to a science.

Immediately after his paroxysm, Eugene realized how negligent he had been. "Oh my dear," he said, burying his face in her neck. "I know I didn't give you time to . . . I'm so sorry."

"That's all right," she said, basking in the ardor of his contrition.

"And I was going to make sure the first time would be good for you." He ran his hand down along her side. "I got carried away . . . just, carried away!"

This sentiment also delighted her. He had been swept away with passion. This was certainly worth more than an orgasm. She caressed his back.

Determined to bring her to climax, he began a solicitous round of stroking, pinching, probing, running through the full range of pressures and guided only by the subtle variations of her chirrups and purrs, until finally, with a bleated series of James Joyceian yes-yes-yesses, she indicated she was experiencing orgasm. Eugene was overjoyed, both for her sake and because the muscles of his hand were starting to cramp up.

It took a few weeks for them to remedy the timing difficulties, at least in part. As Eugene became more accustomed to Emily's terrain, he was able to slow down his orgasmic rpms and give some attention to fore-play. As for Emily, being a creative individual used to long hours of dedicated practice, she came up with a corrective exercise to which she applied herself with determination and love: she forced herself to masturbate with her left hand. By using the "wrong" hand, she struggled to break herself of those clitoral habits to which she had for so long been inured and, in so doing, to train herself to seek orgasm through new patterns of arousal from a different instrument entirely.

9

Eugene stood at the kitchen counter spreading peanut butter on a slice of rye bread. He hadn't bothered to sit down to a real meal since Meredith had left at dawn to visit Francine for the Christmas vacation. He folded the bread in half and bit into his lunch, or whatever, and thought again about seeing her off at the airport that morning.

Meredith had looked so brave and small, and it had broken Eugene's heart to open his arms and let her walk out of their last hug. Although the charming flight attendant had acted like she was leading Meredith to a ride on a merry-go-round, Eugene had felt as if he was sending her off on a perilous mission into outer space. He hated himself for having delivered her to the indifferent arms of technology, not to mention the fellowship of the son-of-a-bitch lawyer who was fucking Francine and who probably wanted Meredith to call him Uncle Bob.

That evening Emily hadn't been able to cheer him up, not with all the ebullient music and earnest sex she could muster. That was especially sad because she herself was leaving the next day on her orchestra tour. He wished she was departing with her confidence riding high.

Eugene was just beginning to feel sorry for having been morose with Emily, and for not properly attending to the area behind her knees where she so dearly loved being fondled, when the phone rang.

"How're you doing?" Glenda asked.

After the evening of Diego's misguided assault, Glenda and Eugene had been relating with one another during the duration of her assignment at Henson and Blackman in a way that was at once casual and remote. Communication was confined to banalities, to office business, and to a minimum. Therefore, her call tonight came as something of a surprise.

"Okay, I guess. You?"

"Me, too, I guess," she replied. "I saw you at the Christmas—or, I mean, seasonal—party at school."

"Yeah, Meredith wanted me to go."

"The cheese dip was good."

"I wouldn't know."

"The pancake breakfast is in a couple of weeks. Do you want me to pick up the sausages, or do you want to?"

"Makes no difference. You get them, I'll reimburse you."

"I was at your office the other day to check out the new system we installed. I didn't see you, Eugene."

"I must have been out to lunch."

"I met Harriet Vickers' replacement. Sara. She seems to be a bright woman. Very competent."

"We were lucky."

There was a pause. "Eugene, I'm really calling to ask you to dinner tonight. It's short notice, I know, but I said to myself, oh, why not just go ahead and do it."

Odd. He thought she had been quite sanguine about their rather detached mode of communication. Had he misread her? "Spontaneous. I didn't think you were the type."

"I'm not the type. It's just that I'm getting uncomfortable with this cold shoulder business. After all, we may be bumping into each other for years—at the school, I mean—and I'd rather we—"

"Meredith will be going to school in Cincinnati starting next September."

"Oh, I'm sorry. Well, I . . . actually, I'm also trying to make up for what you went through last month in my lobby. And to be honest, I think I'm getting complacent. I miss the hostile way you attack my ideas on just about everything. To solidify my theories, I need to be challenged."

"Try reading Kierkegaard."

She laughed. "But I'm in the middle of a John Grisham. Oh, and of course we'd want you to bring Meredith."

"Meredith's with her mother for the holidays."

"Then bring yourself."

"Glenda, I don't know what you have in mind, but I've been seeing someone."

"I'm not inviting you to *see* me, just to eat my food."

"Not that it would matter to you, I suppose—being unfaithful, that is."

"As a matter of fact," she clipped, "I'm *seeing* someone myself!"

"Is he married?"

"He is."

"Figures."

"It so happens, Eugene, I do more to stabilize his marriage than anything else. His wife will never go through the upheaval of divorce as long as I'm in the picture. If not for me, he'd be looking for another woman, and quite possibly he'd find one with a more acquisitive nature."

"Altruistic of you."

She laughed. "You see? That's what I miss—your piercing objectivity."

Astrid ushered Eugene in. "Hi, I'm Astrid. It was my idea to invite you over."

"Do you mean everything your mother told me was a lie?" he asked.

"No," Glenda answered from the kitchen, where she was cutting up tomatoes for the salad. "Everything I said was true. Take off your coat."

"It was my idea *first*," Astrid qualified.

"Astrid thought we should have you over weeks ago."

"I didn't even know you then," Astrid said. "I only knew that you got a black eye because of my mother."

"Astrid is more courteous than I am," Glenda said.

Astrid adjusted a shoulder strap of her painter's jeans. "I'll take your coat, Mr. Lerman."

"Don't be so formal. Call me Eugene—only don't call me Uncle. I think that's silly."

"It is. I don't even have an uncle." Astrid held out her arms. "Your coat."

"It's heavy." Maneuvering the package he was holding, he took it off.

"But I'm strong," Astrid said. She took his parka. It was a little on the heavy side, but she managed not to show it. She carted it to a side chair and dropped it there.

"Have a seat," Glenda said. "Or grab a knife and a celery stalk. May I offer you a drink?"

"A *real* drink?"

"No. Just something that quenches your thirst."

"Have any club soda? Maybe I'll make myself a wine spritzer."

"We do. I'll get it, Eugene," Astrid said.

"Thanks." He took a box of dried fruit and a bottle of white wine out of the foil bag he was holding and brought them to the kitchen counter. "I hope you don't mind about the wine, Glenda. I'll be discreet."

Glenda laughed. "Thanks. I might not have a corkscrew."

"I thought as much. I came prepared." He drew one from his pants pocket, worked off the cork, and poured some wine into the juice glass Astrid delivered to him. Then Astrid poured the soda until he said "when." He let the drink sit on the counter and began to cut up a celery stalk on the butcher block as Glenda dumped her cut-up tomatoes into the salad bowl.

Eugene was wearing a red long-sleeved cotton knit shirt and jeans, and Glenda had on her red turtleneck sweater and navy fitted pants. "You guys match," Astrid observed.

"Yeah?" Eugene returned. "I thought only *one* of us was tall, dark and handsome."

Astrid giggled.

Eugene added the celery to the salad. "Now what?"

Glenda bent to get a pot from the cabinet, but his legs were in the way. "You and Astrid go sit in the living room while I finish here," she said. "It's too crowded."

"I was hoping you'd say that." He picked up his drink.

"We're having lasagna and garlic bread," Astrid told him as they settled in on the couch.

"Fantastic. I love it."

"Do you want me to slice you a piece of cheese?" Astrid asked, referring to the wedge of Jarlsberg and crackers on the coffee table.

After what he'd been living on for the last couple of days, he realized he was starving. "That would be nice. Thanks."

"I play soccer," Astrid informed him, leaning over to slice the cheese.

"I used to be on a soccer team myself in high school. What position do you play?"

"All of them. We take turns. We mostly practice and play against each other. The older kids get to play matches against other schools. My coach—Mrs. Nielson—she says the junior team has to learn the techniques of every position. I like being goalkeeper the best because you're allowed to use your hands, and I've got very good hands. What position did *you* play?"

"Center halfback most of the time. I was on the defensive team."

She handed him a cracker topped with a big chunk of cheese. "My coach says I'm the strongest girl in junior soccer." She flexed the muscle of her upper arm. "Go ahead. Feel."

He felt the undefined muscle. "Wow. I'm signing you on for a five-year contract."

Astrid grinned.

Eugene sipped his drink. "We should teach Meredith how to play."

"I don't think so."

"You wouldn't want to teach her?"

"She wouldn't want me to. She tap dances!"

"Actually, she switched to sewing, but does that matter? I mean, I can't see her dancing or sewing and playing soccer at the same *time*, but I think she'd enjoy learning how to—"

"She called me a boy because I play soccer with the boys," Astrid cut in.

"That was silly of her, wasn't it? I'll talk to her about that."

"There are mostly boys on the team," Astrid explained. "That's why Meredith said that. I take soccer once a week after the regular school day. Two other days I take Computer."

"Well, we know what parent you got *that* talent from," Eugene said.

Immediately he realized his gaffe. He glanced at Glenda in the kitchen area for help. She was at the oven monitoring the lasagna she'd prepared earlier in the day. Hearing Eugene's comment, she looked over at them and smiled.

"Astrid's father was classified as a nuclear physicist, so I wouldn't be too sure of where to award the credit."

No taboos, then, Eugene thought, relieved.

"Were you good at heading the ball?" Astrid asked. "That's the thing I'm not so good at. I don't get the power I should."

"Let me see how you jump when you're heading the ball," Eugene suggested.

Astrid moved to the open space and jumped up, making a butting motion with her head.

"Hold it," Eugene said. "It looks like you're attacking with the top of your head, not the center of your forehead. When you jump, you should kick your legs behind you so that your back arches and you hit the ball strongly with the forehead. Like this." He jumped a few times to demonstrate. "See?"

"I think so. I wish you could show me with a ball."

"Maybe outside sometime. Do you have a soccer ball?"

"No," she said. "But I have shoes with regulation cleats. Do you want to see them?"

"Sure."

"I don't get to use them much. We usually play in the gym."

The two of them kept returning to the subject of soccer and its strategies and rules throughout dinner, Glenda noted, and they ended with a heated argument over the matter of committing fouls and awarding direct and indirect free kicks. Eugene and Astrid's differences were finally ascribed to the fact that the rules of indoor soccer, unlike outdoor soccer, were partly derived from those of ice hockey, and Eugene had never properly learned those rules. Glenda was unable to contribute to the debate except to act as a mitigating ump. But she enjoyed seeing her meal devoured and Astrid having such a good time. It was Astrid's first time in the paternal aura, and she was basking in it. What Glenda tried not to focus on was that she herself was, too.

Following the meal they cleared the dishes, and then Eugene performed a passing maneuver by taking off one of his shoes and kicking it along the floor to Astrid. Astrid, kicking it just right with the inside of her feet, returned it to him nicely and won his praise. After that, Eugene put his shoe back on and sat down on the couch. Astrid, prefacing her statement with an exaggerated yawn, announced that she was going to bed early and encouraged her mother to make herself comfortable on the couch.

When Astrid was washed and ready for bed, she returned to the living room and kissed them each goodnight. Then she slammed the door of her bedroom, and Glenda heard her TV turn on, loud. When Glenda came into the bedroom to turn down the volume, Astrid whispered authoritatively, "I like him, Mommy!"

"What a kid," Eugene said, after Glenda returned to sit beside him on the couch.

"I hope she didn't force you into the soccer exchange," Glenda said. "I'm afraid she senses my lack of zeal when it comes to team sports. I guess I can't blame her for holding you hostage."

"You kidding? I had a better time than she did. You know, with that face and that mop of curls, your tough athlete looks like a cherub. I thought of Emily's bas-relief."

"Emily," Glenda said. "Must be the woman you're *seeing*."

"Yes. She lives on my floor. A fantastic cellist—plays with the Municipal Orchestra. They're on tour now in the Midwest."

"She sounds terrific."

"She is. A very sensitive and caring person." He was using Emily's image to arm himself against his instincts. Glenda's lip gloss had worn off during dinner, which made her seem more accessible. "How about you?"

"You're asking me if I'm a sensitive and caring person?"

"No, I'm asking about the man or men in your life."

"Only one, and he doesn't play a musical instrument."

"That's it?"

"Well, he's married, and you must know that doesn't disturb me, and you know my ideas about sex, so you must also know he's a good lay. Suffice?"

"That could be anybody. Does he have any hobbies?"

"Why do you want to know?"

"I want to know how the other half lives."

"By the other half, do you mean me or Matt?"

"So it's Matt, is it? Who's Matt?"

"I didn't mean to—"

"Of course! Your boss, Matt Crowley, the Clint Eastwood lookalike."

"I don't understand why I do this," Glenda chided herself. "I have to watch myself with you. You make me talk."

"That's all I'll make you do, too," he volunteered. "Don't worry. I'm not about to tweet *The National Enquirer* with your confession."

"I know. I think that's why I keep shooting my mouth off."

"Not that the publicity would bother you."

"Don't be abusive. You just ate my lasagna."

"Has Matt eaten your lasagna?"

"No, why?"

"I don't think he deserves to enjoy *all* of your talents."

She crossed her legs and put her arm over the back of the couch, unintentionally drawing attention to her breasts. "I think you had too much of your wine," she said.

"On the contrary, I haven't had too much of *anything* lately. Sorry. This conversation needs to be rerouted." He laughed at his own discomfort. "What have you and Astrid been doing with yourselves this vacation?"

Realizing her postural oversight, Glenda dropped her arm to her side. "She's had more time off than I, and she's spent most of it at a friend's. During the last couple of days we've managed to see an awful spy movie, and we've gone ice skating at Rockefeller Center. Nothing unusual. And yes, the Metropolitan Museum."

"Ah, the Met," he said, thinking back on his first sight of her.

"Speaking of which," she said, "have you ever taken Meredith for any of what they call their 'family weekend' programs?"

"At the Uris Center? No, are they any good?"

"The one on parks and gardens in art was. I've been meaning to register us for another. The one on medieval celebration sounds good."

"Why don't we join you?"

"Sure," she agreed. "I'll let you know about dates and the other programs offered in the series."

"Great."

"So, what have *you* been doing lately?" she asked.

"Nothing much. I've got a couple of days off, and I'm going to visit my parents down in Florida."

She winced.

"You have something against my parents?"

"Of course not. I just couldn't help thinking . . . never mind."

"No. What is it? Tell me."

"I don't want to," she said.

"You wouldn't have started to if you didn't want to."

Silence.

"Tell me," he urged.

She looked down at her lap. "It always seems worse this time of year," she said, almost inaudibly. "And now that my cousin Janet's been after me to see him, I find it's even harder to keep him out of my head."

She was harboring either love or hate, he couldn't tell which. "Whom don't you want to see, Glenda?"

She looked up, and it was clear what emotion she had been holding back. "My stepfather," she said.

"I can tell you're not particularly fond of the man. Why?"

"I can't talk about it." A red blotch appeared on each of her cheeks. "You wouldn't understand. It's the past."

"So you think you have the monopoly on familial rage, do you?"

"If you mean between yours and mine, yes, I do."

He leaned toward her, his head thrust forward. "Oh, yeah?" he challenged, poised in the posture of the tango. "And how do you think I felt when my mother always gave my brother the biggest, least scarred boiled potatoes? And how do you think a five-year-old boy feels when his mother is washing his 'privates,' as she called them, with the same expression on her face as when she's scouring a pot? If they're my privates, why are you putting them to public shame? Am I so dirty? Are Richie's balls better than mine? Today, I know she was as much a helpless victim of her favoritism as I was. But to the five-year-old boy, the questions rage in his little brain, and he squelches them, not realizing why the next time she serves him two inferior boiled potatoes with little brown spots, he chokes on them and vomits."

"How do you make it sound funny?" she asked, as they were laughing.

"Because it *is* funny."

"I wish I could laugh like that," she said.

"You just did."

"About what bothers *me,* I mean. Actually, if it was about me, maybe I could. I'm not angry at what happened to me."

"You sure?" Eugene interrupted.

"I'm angry about what happened to my mother. What he did to her!"

"Nothing about you, huh?"

"He robbed me of her, if that's what you're driving at."

"I don't know what I'm driving at. What did he do?"

"He killed her!" she shot back, as if in reply to a challenge.

Eugene got quiet.

"No, he didn't actually push her down the stairs," she said. "At least that's what she told me before she died and the ambulance took her away—do you know what it sounds like, the sirens, coming too late? And he was the cause, he was the cause!" She punched her thighs and stared at Eugene, fury having disabled all other emotions. "So what do you think I should send him for Christmas?" she seethed.

He touched her hand. "Some Florida oranges, maybe?"

This, with such stunning tenderness, it seemed to bring her to her senses as effectively as a slap in the face.

"What happened, Glenda?"

The words came disjointedly, gathering momentum like a lame animal given chase. "My mother—she was a sensitive woman—artistic, smart. She was a school teacher—the kids adored her, they used to send her notes, give her presents. But he made her quit, said what he earned as a carpenter was enough for us. He was just jealous of her capabilities—of her style. He let her have a small garden in the backyard to grow her flowers. That was her world—a patch of earth. He used to come home at night drunk and abusive, and she would do nothing, *nothing* to stand up to him. She would take it all. And then she began drinking too, out of hopelessness. Out of his rotten example. He had wild bouts, but she slid downhill quietly, every day retreating more and more into herself. I could do nothing to stop it." She paused to catch her breath.

"Your stepfather," Eugene began. "Did he . . . care?"

"Care? He pretended to. Empty hysteria."

It was too simple a story to be complete. "What about your birth father?" Eugene asked. "Where does he fit into the picture?"

"He doesn't. He died in a car accident before I was a year old. I like to think he was a good man. My mother said he was."

"It must have been hard for you, not having a memory to comfort you."

She nodded, almost child-like. "When I was little, my mother and I used to sit on the porch, and she showed me things in this catalogue of paintings she had from the Buffalo art museum. She'd pick out a painting, and first she'd ask me what I thought of it and what story the picture made me think of. Then she'd tell me about the artist and about technical things like perspective and brush strokes. This is the woman I want to remember. Not the one killed from a fall down a staircase because she was drunk. Destroyed. By *him*!"

"How old were you, when . . ."

"I was thirteen years old when my mother died," she said.

"Just becoming a woman," Eugene said. He touched her hand then just as quickly withdrew it.

"I moved in with my aunt and uncle."

"And Janet."

"My cousin Janet. Yes."

"And your stepfather wants to see you now."

"Supposedly. He's very sick, Janet says."

"He must want to . . . he must love you."

She cracked a wry smile. "Oh, of course. He took me to the zoo once. Please don't. What he wants from me is absolution. Nothing more."

"Are you sure?"

"Yes. I just wish I were better at managing my antagonism. It's like a demon in me. I try to keep it at bay by disregarding it. I cover it up with work, and organizing, and tons of . . . *matter*. But when I give it a chance to breathe, it—it impairs me."

"Tell it it's a goddamn incongruous demon and call its bluff," he said hotly. "It's probably counting on your never taking a good look at it. You can't just acknowledge its existence. You've got to pick the damn thing over. Doesn't mean you'll render it harmless, but the act of scrutiny is in itself an act of disassociation. You're handling it, it's not handling you. Take me, for instance. Sure, my stomach turns when I see a brace of boiled potatoes, but do I spit up at the sight anymore?"

She gave a half-hearted smile. "That was a rhetorical question, but no."

"Correct!"

"So?" she asked.

"So *look* at things."

"Like what, for instance?"

"Like, say, your attitude about drinking. I think your mother died when you were just beginning to identify with her as a woman. Are you sure you're not angry with her for not taking better care of herself for *your* sake? Are you sure you don't identify with her weakness for

alcohol? Is that why you don't drink? Because you're afraid you're sus-
ceptible like she was?"

"I don't drink because I don't like the taste of—"

"Just the taste?"

"Maybe I don't like the taste of alcohol because I've seen what lik-
ing it can do to you," she said.

"Or *you.*"

"To *anyone.* You make me dizzy."

Eugene hesitated. "You ever think maybe you . . . never mind."

"No. What were you going to say?"

"I better not," he demurred.

"This is going to sound familiar: you started to tell me, so you must
want to."

"I'll be the judge of that."

"No, I will," she insisted.

"A priori?"

"No, a posteriori, you bastard."

"I forgot what I was going to say," he equivocated.

"Like hell."

He smiled. "I just remembered. I was going to say—to suggest—that
maybe you use men out of fear and revenge. You're afraid you're prone
to ruination like your mother, so you protect yourself by maintaining
the upper hand. At the same time, you punish your admirers, make
them suffer—as you'd like to make your stepfather suffer—by making
them play the subservient role, and by dumping them in the end, like
I would guess you dumped poor George Hayman. All this with the
added bonus of indirectly hurting their wives, and thereby getting back
at your mother for depriving you of her companionship when you
needed it most. Why are you pointing that gun at me?"

"Contrived garbage," she said.

"You mean there was nothing of value in all that shit?"

"Talk, it's so easy to talk."

"Not always," he countered.

"How did you manage to get me into this phony analysis, anyway?" she asked. "My problem is not so damn multidimensional, Eugene. Pure and simple, I witnessed a crime. That never loses its immediacy. My problem is in living color. I'm thirteen years old, coming home from school that day. There's an essay on American history tucked in my backpack. On the bottom of page three there's a note in red ink praising my work and a big fat A+ to prove it. All the way home I'm picturing the scene when I show my mother the note on page three and make her eyes shine, make her better—make her *want* to get better. The illusion that I could do so was particularly keen that day. I ran the last part of the way—expecting, expecting—and then, to find her lying there, sprawled crazily . . . him, howling and stupid . . . and the blood running down the side of her face . . . and the eyes . . . "

Glenda burst into tears. Eugene took her hands in his, but she pulled them away. "Don't touch me!" she cried.

He wanted to comfort her. He tried again, but she reacted more fiercely. He realized that she must not be touched when she was helpless. He withdrew.

Then, like a summer squall, the outburst was over. Her nose was running, and she went to get a napkin from the dining room table. "I'm disgusting," she said, returning to the couch.

"For *crying*?"

"Yes."

He rose to get her a drink of water. "I don't know what the hell you expect from yourself or who the hell you think you are or should be," he said, reaching for a glass in the cabinet over the stove, "but it sure isn't something that grows hair or takes a crap."

He handed her the glass of water, and he was surprised to see a look of gratitude on her face.

Eugene heard his phone ringing as he approached the door to his apartment, but by the time he got to it, it had stopped.

He took the plastic container of lasagna out of the Macy's bag and put it in the refrigerator. He had tried to refuse Glenda's gift of leftovers, but he was too worn out following their marathon conversation to present an airtight case against accepting it. At any rate, he was going to enjoy it cold for breakfast.

He had just hung up his parka when the phone rang again.

"Where *were* you, Daddy?"

"Hi, sweetheart! What do you mean, Meredith? Is anything wrong?"

"I've been trying to get you all night, Daddy. It's eleven o'clock!"

Immediately he felt guilty about having had a good time with another little girl. "I'm sorry, Mer. I didn't think you'd be worried. I just talked to you last night. Are you okay?"

"Yes. I tried your cell phone."

"Oops, I left it home. You know how I hate the little beast."

"Where were you?"

"I was having dinner at Glenda Fieldston's."

"*Oh?*"

He heard muttering at the other end. "Mommy wants to talk to you now, Daddy. Don't hang up after you're done."

"Hello. Eugene?"

"Yo, Fran. How's tricks?"

"Just a minute. Meredith, why don't you go talk to Uncle Bob for a minute. He's going home in a little while, and he wanted to chat with you."

Meredith said something that Eugene couldn't make out.

"Go to the bathroom, honey," Francine responded. "You're wriggling. I promise I won't hang up." There was a pause. "She's gone. Sorry, Eugene."

"*Uncle Bob?* Jesus."

"Listen, Meredith will be back in a minute. Bob has been marvelous this vacation. He sacrificed a business trip to the Virgin Islands just so he could get to know Meredith. He hasn't had to deal with kids in quite a while. His own are all in top graduate schools. He has been trying to be warm and giving with Meredith, but she can't seem to relax and enjoy herself. She's worried about you constantly. What ideas did you put into her head? Have you made yourself out to be some kind of invalid? What's going on?"

"I don't know, Francine. I didn't expect her to react like this."

"Well, she seems very insecure."

"Maybe Uncle Bozo's trying too hard."

"I'll let that pass. She's coming back. You talk to her, Eugene. Assure her you're okay. Please!" There was a note of desperation in her voice. She almost sounded like the vulnerable woman he had once loved.

"I'll try, Fran. Really."

"Here she is. Here you go, Mer. Good-bye, Gene."

"Take care of yourself, Fran."

"Daddy?"

"Yes, sweetie. I miss you very much. I can't wait to see you."

"Me too."

"But while you're there, don't worry about me. I'm going to be flying down to see Grandma Rose and Grandpa Abe in two days. I'll call you from home tomorrow night, and I'll call you from Florida the night after."

"Okay."

"In the meantime, try to like Mommy's friend. He wants you to like him, so why not, right? Mommy loves you so much, and she'd be very happy if you did."

"I'll try. But he has bad breath."

"Did Mommy hear that?"

"No."

"You'll try, then?"

"Yes."

"I love you, Mer."

"Me, too."

After trading loud kisses, they hung up.

Eugene tried Emily's cell phone. Her message center was full. Rather than text, he looked over the itinerary stuck on the refrigerator door with a banana magnet and learned that she was booked in a room at a Holiday Inn in Denver. He dialed the number and asked for her.

"I'm sorry, but we don't have a Miss Hapling registered with us, sir."

"Lapwing, Lapwing, with an L," he fretted, feeling deflated and alone.

"Ah, yes, here we are. Ringing, sir."

"Hello?"

"Hi, Emily. Did I wake you?"

"Eugene! Oh no, darling. I just got in. I went for a bite to eat after the concert."

"How's it going?"

"The Smetana was inspired. The Mozart was adequate."

"I mean you, Emily. How are you?"

"I'm fine. I miss you."

"Same here."

"I tried you earlier, but you must have been busy," Emily said.

"Yes."

She didn't ask doing what. "I was invited to dinner at the Field-stons'," he told her anyway. "They insisted I take some lasagna home with me. It's waiting in the freezer for us," he said, switching the container of lasagna to the freezer compartment.

"That's nice," Emily said.

Two boxes of frozen peas fell to the floor as he was rearranging the contents of the freezer.

"What was that?"

"A book fell."

Hailstones of guilt were falling everywhere.

10

Eugene had challenged the moorings of Glenda's lifestyle, and for her own protection she needed to keep her distance. On the other hand, he seemed not to be throttling her psyche but arousing it, and she was drawn to the marauder in spite of the potential risk.

For his part, Eugene found Glenda's dichotomous creed of sex and self-preservation untenable. Yet at the same time, he was haunted by the idea that beneath the surface her feelings contradicted her creed, and for this reason he was drawn to her.

The stopgap solution to their problem of ambivalence was simple enough: the children provided an excuse to get together, as well as a buffer between the two of them. Thus Eugene carried on his affair with Emily with a clear conscience, and Glenda continued her liaison with Matt, her convictions secure.

As a result, Astrid and Meredith found themselves thrown together in a cultural siege of Manhattan. The family weekend program at the Uris Center called "The Medieval Celebration" led to an extended tour of the Cloisters, which in turn led to a compensatory lecture on Grandma Moses at the American Folk Art Museum. A film shown at the public library depicting the history of the South Street Seaport from the nineteenth century to the present was subsequently illuminated by a tour of the area itself, and a performance of Balanchine's *Bugaku* by the New York City Ballet led to a visit to the Asia Society Museum to see their survey of Japanese calligraphy.

Emily, not to be outdone by her platonic counterpart (whom she'd met at Houghton's pancake breakfast), rallied with ideas of her own. She took Meredith and Eugene to one of the Philharmonic's Young People's Concerts at Lincoln Center, to the Cooper Hewitt Smithsonian Design Museum, and to the United Nations. On these occasions, Glenda countered by taking Astrid to a folksingers' fest, an evening of mime, and the Empire State Building, respectively.

One particular weekend, schedules converged on the ice-skating rink at Rockefeller Center. That Saturday afternoon, Eugene supported Meredith as she struggled around the rink while Emily alternately clung to the rail and to his arm, pretending she was having the time of her life in her improperly fitted rental skates. On Sunday, the Fieldstons and the Lermans attended the morning session. Meredith, expecting to be a star after her previous day's practice, was horrified to find that it still took countless flailing cartoon steps to traverse a foot of ice, while Astrid appeared to be a born Olympian. To make matters worse, Glenda looked beautiful in her white turtleneck sweater, and even though she stood against the railing most of the time, a picture of graceful incompetence, Eugene went ahead and gave her his gloves to wear because she had forgotten her own.

"She can keep her hands in her pockets, can't she?" Meredith complained.

"Maybe next time you could help me teach my mother how to skate better," Astrid suggested to Eugene as the foursome sat down at a table in the Rock Center Cafe after the session was over. "It's hard for me to balance her on my own."

"You did all you could, Astrid," Glenda said, hanging her down vest on the back of her chair. "I enjoyed myself, even though I'm hopeless at it."

"A terrible attitude," Eugene said. "Anyway, you're not bad. You just lack confidence. Astrid's right. We should be more attentive."

Meredith rolled her eyes. "Can't she just take a lesson or something?"

"Why don't *you* take a lesson?" Astrid rebutted. "You need it more than my mother."

"Don't be rude," Glenda chided as a waiter in a black suit laid their menus in front of them.

"Ditto!" Eugene seconded, staring hard at Meredith.

Astrid looked out the glass partition at the ice skaters happily streaming by.

"Emily Lapwing writes dumb poetry," Meredith sulked. "Do you write dumb poetry too, Glenda?"

"Meredith!" Eugene warned.

"My nose is numb. It makes me glum," Glenda offered, looking up from her menu.

"Yup, that's bad," Meredith responded, sustaining her ill humor.

"Meredith," Eugene repeated, not knowing what to expect.

"I fell on the ice. Twice," Glenda said. "Not nice."

"Dumb," Meredith said, fighting off a smile.

Glenda shrugged. "Who's complaining? It could have been raining."

The waiter approached. Addressing Glenda, he asked, "Something to drink, ma'am?"

"Do you have sparkling spam?" she replied.

"*Ma'am?*"

"Ham? Or jam?"

"What?"

"Kumquat?"

The waiter emitted a polite laugh. "I see. You're playing a game."

"And I'll have the same," Eugene added, getting in on the act.

"This is stupid," Meredith said, resenting Glenda for engaging her father's imagination.

"You ruined it," Astrid grumbled at Meredith.

"I'll give you guys some more time," the waiter decided, backing off.

"Meredith didn't ruin anything," Glenda reprimanded her daughter. "How long do you think we could have kept the rhyming scheme up?" She glanced down at her menu. "The soup of the day is lentil. Who's interested?"

The children's bickering continued throughout the meal, although Glenda and Eugene were able to carry on an unruffled discussion of world events over it.

The comfortable polyphony at the Rock Center Cafe came to Eugene's mind the following Friday night as he was lifting a *ponchiki*, a kind of sweet doughnut, to his lips in the Russian Tea Room. Beside him on the continuous leather bench that ran along the wall, Meredith was eyeing his pastry as she scooped out her cantaloupe. Emily sat opposite, delicately spooning up the *morozhenoe*, which Eugene knew Meredith hadn't ordered for spite just because Emily had been so eager to teach her the correct pronunciation of the Russian word for *ice cream*.

The sedate gathering followed a recital of Emily's chamber ensemble in an auditorium at Carnegie Hall, to which Emily had invited Eugene earlier in the week. "There'll be some Webern and Bartok," she had told him over the phone.

"That sounds interesting," he had said.

"And some Scheinberg."

"Schönberg?"

"Scheinberg. Paul Scheinberg. The director of the group."

"Oh, yes. I'd forgotten the name."

"I hope your daughter will come."

"Sure. It'll be good for her."

"Like medicine?" Emily asked.

"Sorry. Of course not."

The benefits of music appreciation had been lost on Meredith. After the Bartok, Eugene had asked her if she had been able to catch Emily's solo parts, and Meredith had replied that Emily was wearing a dumb-looking dress. "You have a keen musical perception, like your Uncle Richie," Eugene had remarked, looking heavenward, although later in the program, listening to Scheinberg's atonal avant-garde opus, *Hypothesis for Piano and String Quartet,* he had found himself similarly unmoved. In spite of Emily's lengthy explanation of serial music preceding the recital, he had been ill prepared for what the program notes called the composer's "argument for reductive materialism."

And now Eugene was uncomfortable at the dinner table, too. As he raised his *ponchiki* to his lips he wondered why this meal had been so awkward compared to the one with the Fieldstons. Why, for instance, had Emily even noticed that he was spooning up his borscht in the wrong direction?

Meredith was looking at the doughnut in his hand. "Want the rest of it, Mer?" he asked. "It's good."

"Just a taste, Dad."

He broke off a piece and gave it to her. "I hope you liked the *shashlik.* You didn't eat much of it, hon."

"It was okay. I like hamburgers better."

What made him uncomfortable, he thought, could not be attributed to the difference in the group's composition, or to the fact that Meredith had enjoyed the Rock Café's hamburger more than the *shashlik* he had talked her into. What made him uneasy was the manner in which Emily dealt with Meredith's negativity. When Meredith had shown resentment toward Glenda, Glenda had rhymed with their waiter to deflect her hostility. For all her rigid ideas about how to conduct her personal life, Glenda could happily wing it with the children. Emily, however, approached the child's hostility head on, drawing attention to it as if it were an instrument playing out of tune. Moreover, unlike the voice of her cello, which seemed effortlessly produced, Emily's own voice reflected the strain of conflict. When Meredith had accusingly stated, "I don't know how anybody can eat cold beet soup," Emily had replied, "I think we should be tolerant of other people's tastes and try to understand them, don't you?" Eugene pictured Glenda telling the waiter to "scorch the borscht."

Poor Emily, Eugene thought as he sipped the remains of his coffee. With what must be an intense desire to enrich and be enriched, she sometimes tried too damn hard. He smiled at her with a conscious show of affection.

Emily returned with a tentative smile. "Meredith," she said, "would you like a taste of my *morozhenoe*? It's excellent."

"I thought you said it was ice cream," Meredith retorted. "Why do you have to use the foreign word?"

"You're very rude," Eugene said.

"Why? What did I do?" Meredith asked, agitated.

"You know very well," Eugene said.

"I used the long word because I thought it was pretty," Emily explained, a Joan of Arc smile frozen on her face. "Don't you think it's pretty, Meredith?"

"No."

Meredith's aggravated resentment demanded further intervention. "I'm surprised at you," Eugene admonished. "If you can't be courteous, don't say anything at all."

"That's all right," Emily said, her pharynx constricted. "Meredith, *would* you like some of my dessert?"

Meredith, capitalizing on her father's injunction, shook her head.

"No thank you," Eugene translated, glaring at his daughter.

The meal ended as it had begun, in awkward silence.

"Why weren't you nice to Emily?" Eugene asked Meredith as he tucked her into bed. "Don't you like her?"

"I was tired. I didn't like the music."

"That's not an excuse for being discourteous."

"Daddy?"

"Yeah."

"What does 'screwing' mean?"

She felt him shift his weight at the edge of her bed.

"It's an unattractive word for making love. Where did you hear it?"

"Astrid. She said you and her mother were screwing."

"Why would she say that?"

"Because I called her a boy."

"Again? Didn't I tell you not to say that?"

"No."

"It must have slipped my mind. Astrid told me you called her that."

Meredith rose to a sitting position. "When? When did she tell you?" Her flannel gown was off one shoulder, drawing attention to her innocence.

"When we were talking about soccer at her house—over Christmas. She mentioned it then."

"You were playing *soccer* with her?"

"We were talking about it, not playing it. You were away. At Mommy's."

Meredith folded her arms. "Well, *I* didn't have any fun!"

He brushed the hair away from her forehead. "I thought you said you had a good time."

"I *didn't.*"

"You said you went to the park and things, with Mommy and Mr.—"

"Uncle. Uncle Bob."

"Yes. Didn't you enjoy that?"

"I only pretended. I heard them fighting one night. They didn't think I heard." She took a few quick breaths to hold back the tears. "He wanted to go someplace alone with her for Christmas."

"That doesn't mean he doesn't like you. Try to understand," he said, scratching the back of her neck.

"He said Mommy spoils me. I heard him."

"Listen, honey, Uncle Bob"—he cleared his throat of the name—"and Mommy, they, well, they love each other. This vacation might have been the first time for him to have gone off with her alone. You know, like new friends and stuff. So they had a fight. So they got mad. But I happen to know he likes you a lot. In fact, I happen to know he feels sad because he thinks you don't like *him*!"

"I don't."

"If you stop thinking about whether you do or you don't, maybe it will just happen naturally."

"What will?"

"You'll get used to him, and like him."

"I don't want to."

"Then you don't have to. Nobody's making you. Just like nobody's making you like Emily. Just be nice to them, that's all. Just let them be nice to you. It can't hurt, can it? C'mon, kid," he said, feigning gruffness, "give 'em a break!"

She bowed her head. "You're silly."

Late that night, he woke up to the sound of her cry: "Ouch!"

"Huh?" he yelped.

"I bumped my toe on the bottom of your dresser!"

"Are you okay?"

"Yes."

"It's the middle of the night, Mer."

"I couldn't sleep, Daddy." She climbed onto his bed and sat

cross-legged on top of the covers. "I thought you were getting rid of this waterbed."

"I keep meaning to."

"You shouldn't put things off."

He rolled onto his back. "Hey, listen, the stores are closed at this hour."

"Daddy?"

"What's wrong, sweetheart?" Eugene asked.

"You didn't tell me."

"About what?"

"Screwing." She looked away from him.

"I thought I said it wasn't a nice word for making love."

"But how does it work?"

"Well, two people hug and kiss—didn't Mommy tell you about this?"

"I didn't ask her."

He took a deep breath and sat up, the covers falling from his chest. He wasn't wearing pajama tops, and he could see her looking at the hair on his chest, the tufts of it under his arms.

"Okay," he said. "The man and the woman who love each other are hugging and kissing and want to get as close to each other as they possibly can." (The words "penis" and "vagina" were sitting on his brain like canons ready to be fired.)

"It's all right, Dad," she said quickly. "I don't want to hear about it now."

He was grateful and hurt. "Why? I was just telling you. The man and the woman—"

"Stop." She put her hands over her ears. "La la la la." It appeared she was suddenly uncomfortable hearing such a secret from him now. "Mommy will tell me next time I see her." She took her hands away from her ears.

He felt as if he had failed her in some way. "Whatever you say."

"Just tell me if you did it with Astrid's mother."

"No."

"Why won't you tell me?"

"I mean no, I didn't do it with Astrid's mother."

"Then why do we see them so much?"

"Because . . . because they're pleasant people to be with, and because Glenda has some good ideas about where to go with you girls. We're friends."

"You do it with Emily, don't you?"

He hesitated a moment. "Yes."

"She's not going to live here with us, is she?"

"I don't know. Maybe some day . . . but you know, don't you, that you're going to be living most of the time with Mommy soon."

"That's what Mommy said, but I'm sure she doesn't want me to. She has Uncle Bob."

"Gee, I never saw the guy, but I can't believe if he puts on a dress he could pretend he's you."

"Oh, Dad!"

"Nobody can sit in for you, honey. Uncle Bob has nothing to do with Mommy's love for you, or needing you."

"Well, I saw them, and I know."

"Well, I'm older than you, so I know better. So there!"

She was quiet for a moment. "Will you need Emily to live here when I stay with you?"

"Emily has nothing to do with my love for you, either. That's the thing about love between parents and children. It's as big as the whole world. As big and slobbery"—he kissed her arm noisily, as if he were going to eat it like a corn on the cob—"as it can possibly be. Even with all that, there can be love of another kind, for another grown-up. It doesn't cut into my love for you, or Mommy's love for you. Love isn't like a pie you divide up between this one and that one. It doesn't have boundaries. Let me ask you a question. Do you love chocolate chip ice cream?"

"You know I do."

"If you *didn't* love chocolate chip ice cream, would you have more love to spend on *me*?"

"Oh, Daddy!"

"Silly, right? Well, just think of Uncle Bob and Emily as ice cream flavors. Only don't make Emily cherry vanilla. If there's one flavor I don't like, it's cherry vanilla."

Meredith smiled. "Mommy said you would only get me for visits. Don't you want to keep me?"

"Of course I do. But it wouldn't be good for you if Mommy and I had fights about which one of us you should live with most of the year. You'll always belong to both of us, no matter where you are. You know that." He tugged at the hem of her gown. "C'mere, you."

She crept over to him and he hugged her. He turned the cover up around her, being careful not to leave any part of her feet exposed. She stroked the fur on his chest as she curled up inside her nest and was soon sedated.

He sat there with her for a long time. Feeling her folded up against him like this, he found himself wondering what it would be like to have this unity internalized, to feel the mystery of creation concretized within his own body, like a mother. Would it change the way he perceived the world? Would his connection to the Milky Way be more intimate?

At last he carried Meredith back to her own bed and arranged the covers over her. He waited, stroking her cheek as she resettled into sound sleep. Then he left the room, closing the door behind him.

Halfway to his bedroom, he returned to set her door ajar. Tonight the closed door seemed designed to cut her off from him. As he slipped back between the sheets, which had grown cold so quickly, he realized how fiercely he regretted having signed that damned chivalrous custody agreement.

11

There was a break in the Fieldston-Lerman culture tour of Manhattan the last weekend in January: Glenda and her co-worker Danny were accompanying their boss to his annual CPA convention in Chicago, while Eugene, having offered to babysit Astrid, was back home refereeing the diverse power plays between Astrid, Meredith, and Emily.

Glenda and her colleagues were staying at the Hyatt Regency overlooking the Chicago River, a convenient shuttle bus hop to the convention center. The bustling complex was about the largest Glenda had ever visited, with accommodations and amenities arranged in tiers visible to the entering guest, the composite looking like a luxurious yet somewhat antiquated spaceship.

Glenda and Crowley were sequestered in the pod of his room, just off the public spaceway. They had spent the day with Danny, attending a seminar on advances in management technology, touring the endless booths of product vendors, and finally dining with Danny at an Italian restaurant. It was there where he openly revealed his affection for Glenda. So intent was Danny on making progress with her that he never for a moment considered the possibility of competition from Crowley.

Even after the group had returned to the hotel and Glenda and Crow-ley had claimed a sudden onset of fatigue, Danny's fervency protected him from the truth.

"It's heaven knowing we have *time*," Crowley said, leisurely folding his shirt. "I can't help feeling sorry for Danny. I didn't know he had it so bad for you."

"He'll be fine," Glenda said, draping her skirt and blouse over the back of the lounge chair. "I saw him eyeing a pretty brunette by the escalator as I was coming up to your room."

"I doubt it. I think he's fixated on you like I am." Crowley sat half naked on the edge of the bed, admiring the natural grace with which Glenda performed the simplest of acts: unhooking the front of her bra. He rose, pulled back the bedspread, and removed the remainder of his clothing, all the time watching her undress.

"You're not leaving that for me?" he asked, as she stepped out of her bikini briefs.

"I forgot," she smiled. "Shall I put them back on?"

"Oh, darling, just come here." He sat back down.

"Let me undo my hair."

"No, let me."

She knelt at the side of the bed, and he removed the pins that held her hair in place. As he stretched to lay them on the night table, his organ brushed her cheek. He slipped his hands beneath the fallen tresses and exerted the gentlest pressure to the nape of her neck. "Take me," he urged.

She did so not out of passion, but as quid pro quo for the pleasure he would shortly deliver to her. As his excitement intensified, he grasped her hands and drew them away from his hips.

"Let me finish inside you," he whispered, and he lay back, pulling her toward him.

She joined him, sliding upward along his body until her breasts met his face. She swayed over him, allowing him to make successful passes at her breasts with his mouth and tongue, and then slowly she slipped downward until his member was caught against her thigh. She lifted her pelvis, guided him to her entry, and fell, engulfing him.

His fingers pressed down along her back, circled at the base of her spine, and finally delved between her buttocks to abrade the hotline to her vagina. It was an exercise that never failed to heighten her arousal, but as she rose and fell against him, it seemed not to be having the usual effect. They rolled over, and within a moment he ejaculated, unable to hold himself back any longer. She was still laboring against her impassivity, disturbed by her failure.

Freed from the ballast keeping him earthbound, he seemed to drift aloft, euphoric and solicitous. "Darling, you didn't climax," he said, running a finger along the line of her frown. "Did you?"

"I didn't," she said, still straining toward the event by constricting her muscles against his diminishing organ.

He dove from the clouds, and with lips and tongue he attempted to save her from the grip of inertia, while she contrived to undulate in response. But like a piano piece memorized without understanding so that it could only be played straight through, her orgasmic composition, interrupted by fretful appraisal, could not be successfully resumed.

"Stop," she said. "It's not working. *I'm* not working."

He helped her to a sitting position and pressed her head to his shoulder. She was damp from perspiration, and he lifted her hair from her back and blew on her neck. "You talk like you're a machine."

She moved away from him. "It *is* some kind of dysfunction." She had never failed to climax with him. Her distress seemed justified. At the same time, she sensed that she was overreacting, which only increased her anxiety. "I was looking forward to this weekend," she said, her voice rising.

"You sound skeptical."

"I don't know why I should."

"Neither do I, but don't get maudlin. It'll be better later. Let's sleep on it."

"I don't feel like sleeping." She rose to her feet. "I'm going to wash up and go down for a while." She scooped up her things, grabbed her bag, and started for the bathroom.

"You want to be alone," he said.

"I hope you don't mind."

"Of course I do. Will you be back?"

"I think I'll go to my room. Don't be angry."

"You look like Ophelia," he said. "How can I be angry at someone so lovely and so distraught?"

After departing, Glenda descended by glass elevator and short escalator glide to the mezzanine-level lounge, where she shimmied into a high seat at the bar and ordered a ginger ale from the on-the-spot bartender. She was feeling out of sync with herself, as if her body was rebelling against its set curriculum. She thought of Eugene's meddling with her memories and fixed beliefs and was wondering if she should assign blame to him, when a man arose from a nearby cocktail table and approached, drink in hand. "Brian Cook," he announced in affable baritone.

Of medium stature, medium coloring, sporting a gray suit and talk-show smile, Brian appeared to Glenda to have been generated as an adult, given life by the aptly named organization printed on his lapel tag: *A. I. Corp.*

"Remember me?" Brian asked. "You threw me all those smart questions on robotic subjectivity earlier today?"

She recollected having participated in an exchange at A. I.'s display booth, but not with whom. This man could murder someone and slip into the crowd unnoticed. "Sure. I'm Glenda Fieldston." She shook his hand.

"Coming from an accountant, your questions were especially astute," he remarked. "Mind if I join you?"

She nodded toward the vacant seat beside her. "You may want to reconsider," she said. "I'm not an accountant. I work for one. My area is modernizing computer systems, so my informed questions were no indication of a diversified intelligence."

Brian pulled the vacant chair closer to Glenda's and planted himself in it. "Who cares? It provided me with an opening line." He smiled and took a slug of his drink.

The bartender served Glenda her ginger ale and exchanged the nut dish for a full one.

"You're very lovely," Brian said, as Glenda's finely tapered fingers plucked a cashew from the dish. "You made an immediate impression on me."

"You flatter me."

"No, I'm honest. I know class when I see it." Before popping a peanut into his mouth, he suggestively rolled it between his fingers as if to demonstrate how attentive he could be to anatomical nubbins. "Where'd you get your degree?"

"New York University—math. You?"

"Illinois State. Business major."

It occurred to Glenda that her lack of sexual diversity might have been the root of her malfunction earlier in the evening. If so, she decided, she ought to rectify the problem.

"How long have you been with A. I., Brian?" she plied.

"Eight years, some good, some bad." He smiled, revealing as much inner disturbance as a paper towel. He emptied his glass and motioned the bartender to return. He ordered a refill of scotch. "Anything for you, Glen? Hors d'oeuvres, maybe?"

"I'm fine," Glenda replied. Even as she considered having intercourse with him, she could feel the disparate elements of her mood uniting to promote action.

Over Brian's second drink, their conversation settled on those products of A. I.'s that had drawn her to the display that morning. "I have all the literature on our philosophy up in my room. Why don't we run through it properly?"

She was compelled to say yes, to defy some weakness gnawing at her resolve. This was a test of her mettle, her mastery over her body, the situation—*him*. With his un-remarkability, he gained significance, representing no man in particular and therefore every man. The thought, though not formulated to syntactical threshold, was capable of investing her with swagger.

"I'd like to take a look at that material," she asserted, as if she had made the suggestion, not he.

Even as Brian escorted her up to his room, she felt that it was she who was leading him to the place. She followed him as a director of a play follows his actors through a rehearsal, with passive omniscience. All through the subsequent ritual, during which they eased themselves with civility from A. I.'s scientific literature to the bed, she felt like she was coordinating the event. And when, finally, she sat astride his naked form in the calculatedly dim light of the room, a Wagnerian sort of triumph visited her loins so that she could not help but thrust down on him with more force than he had anticipated.

"Outrageous!" he sang out, meeting her strength with a forceful movement of his own, in which he grabbed at her buttocks and drove up into her as if his target were her throat. "Give it to me, baby!"

With her hair up in its bun and herself above the replaceable mate, she could not help but receive this proposal as more than a happy cry from the subjugated. Intending to draw her own delectation from his penis, and secondarily to grant a dollop of pleasure to him, she proceeded to move over him in a spirited and varied manner—now bending forward to exert pressure on her clitoris, now backward to change the concentration of pressure and afford him a wide-angle view of her crotch.

The activity continued in this fashion until, without pause, it began to change, not in fact, but significance. Glenda's pleasure line, for all her frictional resourcefulness, was not rising. Just as earlier, with Crowley, it was flattening out like the line on a hospital monitor. Cunt-dead.

Glenda went on moving, shifting, pumping, trying to resuscitate, but with dwindling hope. The exercise soon appeared meaningless. Without the distraction of its immediate appeal, sex was exposed as a set of variations on an overworked theme. Thrusting from above, pushing from below, at right angles or on the parallel. What did it matter? It was all the same clown act from wherever in the heap the asses arced. Even the rooms, she thought, looking around as she hammered at him, were the same, with little modifications to trick you into thinking they were not. A gray lounge chair in Crowley's room. Here, a blue one. The beige commercial carpet was unvaried, she confirmed, deep-bending to her right—"ach, oh, gee," Brian sputtered—her focus coming to rest on the man's shoes lined up next to the bed.

Black shoes with tassels. The image appeared in the impotent generic. Black shoes. With tassels. She could not recall ever having sex with—ever *knowing*—a man who wore black shoes with tassels. The image, no longer blurred by the abstract, alarmed her, directed her back to the objects themselves. Alien things with unpaired creases and bulges, with density and odor and marks from other places.

Her perspective turned inside out. What had just been ludicrous in its generality became fearsome in its specificity. The hotel room was cluttered with foreign matter and hauntings—with echoes, acts, follicle mites, scuffs, gouges, secrets, silences. Her own movements were particular to the instant, never to erupt in the same sequence again. The man beneath her, who called himself Brian Cook, was a stranger, someone who existed apart from the use she would have him serve. Did he have a wife? A criminal record? An allergy to cats? Who was he?

This event was supposed to be an expression of independence. Instead, she controlled nothing—look how he pushed her against his belly, maneuvered her thighs, pinched her ass, as if she were nothing more than a curious slab of flesh. Who—or what—was *she*, anyway?

He clutched at her. "I'm good for—keeping it going—really good—known for it," he panted. "But you—you got me now, baby!"

A barrage of images exploded in her brain as he released. She was being stabbed by him. The warm substance was a rush of him, a hemorrhaging of herself. She was an empty vessel into which he was ejaculating his past, his symptomology, his madness. He was displacing her identity with his own, as a scientific experiment, injecting her with a serum that would make her forget the world.

"You move like an angel," he said, when he was done. It was irrelevant gibberish. "Did you come?" he asked, stroking the place where they connected.

"No, I didn't," she said, welcoming the sound of a familiar voice.

"What can I do for you? Your wish is my command."

"You can lie very still while I get dressed," she said, uncoupling and stepping from the bed as smoothly as possible. "I should not be here."

"Recriminations *already*?"

"May I use your bathroom for a few minutes?"

"Yes, yes. I won't ask any questions—you on a honeymoon or something?"

"Please." She collected her clothes and walked quickly toward the bathroom, already sensing the washcloth scrubbing hard between her legs.

Brian remained in the bed, inwardly humming a happy tune or seething with indignation. Who knew which?

Victimized by her own foolishness and invaded by a foreign body whose cells still clung to her, Glenda thought of her hotel room as another entrapment. She needed air. She did not even want to be confined by an escalator for the ride to street level. Instead, she ran down the staircase intended for emergency escape.

The night cold dealt her a punishing, welcomed blow. She pulled up the collar of her suit jacket and drew the lapels together, but she was far from adequately protected as she walked the several yards to the drawbridge overlooking the Chicago River.

"Brrr!" a woman in a fur coat directed at her, as she and the man on whose arm she was clinging overtook her. "You're brave!"

"No, just stupid," Glenda answered.

Arriving at the bridge, she stopped and leaned against the railing. The harsh wind pressed reality in on her, and she was forced to huddle up and embrace herself, a person for whom, at the moment, she felt no affection.

She looked out across the river. The Wrigley Building stood just on the other side, its baroque lines coldly illuminated by the street lamps directed on its white granite façade. It appeared as a testament to architectural design, impressive but uninhabited, like she herself. It made her shudder. She looked down and saw herself here, too, in the dark water, silty and uninviting. The river must have been unpolluted once. Had *she* ever been?

She leaned over the railing, looking for an answer.

"Lose something, miss?" a man's voice came from behind.

She turned, about to utter something self-derogatory, and realized, upon seeing the look of concern on the elderly man's face, that in view of her posture and foolhardy attire, he must have been worried about her jumping. "No, I haven't lost anything," she said. "I'm at the hotel here—just thought I'd catch a breath of air."

"Catch your death, that's what."

"Don't worry."

The man shook his head and walked off. "Crazy."

He had cut her depression down to size. Next to thoughts of suicide, it was absurd. Laughable. Sex and the appendix, vestiges of a baser age. All they can do is cause trouble. Who needs them? True self-mastery would entail abstention. At the least, a moratorium must be called. She flung her thought into the murky waters below and drew herself up, combatting the cold with willpower.

She realized, on her walk back to the hotel, that her decision was consistent with what had always been her attitude toward sex. Hadn't she always held it in contempt, segregating it from the more advanced passions: music, art, thinking, nurturing?

In her room, she threw off her clothes and showered, scrubbing herself more thoroughly than she had been able to earlier. It was almost 2:00 a.m. when she finally crept into bed.

She had given no thought to the possibility that her affection for Eugene might have obstructed her ability to climax and, conjointly, rattled her instinct for self-preservation. She thought of him now, as she had briefly done at the lounge bar, but only to amuse herself, she told herself, with what she imagined his reaction would be to her newly adopted position on celibacy. He'd probably run her through her development *in utero* to come up with the cause, she guessed.

She pulled the cover up to her ears and harrumphed, scorn being the best way to prevent a more subversive emotion from rising to the surface.

"All I said to Danny was 'What were you and Glenda up to last night?'" Crowley complained. "I don't see why that should make him choke on his bacon."

"We were having breakfast," Glenda said, unsnapping the suitcase she'd placed on her bed. "You took him by surprise."

"I'll bet." Crowley was leaning against the dresser with his hands jammed into his pants pockets. "Why didn't you wait for me before ordering breakfast?"

"We thought you were sleeping late. This is absurd, Matt."

"Danny's always been after you. You didn't meet him after you left my room last night?"

Glenda laid a folded sweater into her suitcase. "No, I didn't."

"Have you ever been with him?"

"Only through innuendo—yours." She folded a blouse and tucked it into the suitcase.

"I tried your number after midnight," he said. "You didn't tell me where you were going."

"I forgot to punch out. Excuse me."

"I don't know if I should. I thought we had an understanding."

"I meant excuse me, I have to get to the drawer."

He moved away from the chest, allowing her to retrieve her lingerie. "Why the hell are you packing now? Our flight's at four o'clock."

"Aren't we going to the wrap-up luncheon?"

"I suppose."

"I won't have to rush later." She pressed the garments into the bag.

He shook his head. "So organized." He took a pair of pantyhose from her bag and tied it loosely around his neck. "Where were you last night, anyway? Fucking a stranger?"

"Yes," she said, without losing a beat.

"Oh, splendid!" he replied, with a grand sweep of his hand.

"I didn't have to tell you," she said in measured tones. "As a matter of fact, it was the first time I've been with anyone else since we were first . . . together."

How sad he looked, she thought, with the pantyhose in rude contrast to his characteristic air of runway perfection. She had demeaned him. "I'm sorry, Matt."

"I suppose I should be grateful for your honesty, but it gives me little comfort," he said.

"I can't help that." She plucked her nightgown from the bedclothes and was about to drop it into the suitcase when he grabbed it from her and flung it back onto the bed. He held her by the shoulders and jolted her once.

"What is it? What are you holding back? Why won't you let me love you a little? What did you think I wanted from you last night? For you to sign your soul over to me? No. All I wanted was to wake up with you next to me. I wanted to be your husband for a night. Was that so terrible? Why wouldn't you allow me one lousy illusion?"

She was silent.

He caught their reflection in the mirror above the dresser. He released her and pulled the pantyhose from around his neck, tossing them to the floor. "The court jester."

"That, you are not," she intoned, as if concluding a prayer.

"What is with you?" He glared at her, waiting for an answer, but she said nothing. "Tell me, why did you go off last night?"

"I didn't really want to. It was a . . . test."

"Of what?" he barked. "To see if you could chase down your orgasm while whistling Dixie?"

"Something like that."

"Did it work?"

"No."

"Who was the guinea pig, anyway?"

"It doesn't matter."

"Wait a minute," he said, struck by a new idea. "Is it possible this is a ploy? Do you think you can tease me into a state of desperation so that I'll drop everything and pursue you like what's-his-name, the fellow in the opera chasing after Carmen—"

"Don José."

"Because if you do think so, don't. I am not a man of drama. I admit, there are times when it depresses me that being content with my mediocre life is an indication that I myself am mediocre. But damn it, when it comes down to brass tacks, I like having my underwear ironed. I like having my low cholesterol dinner waiting for me when I walk in the door. So if you think you're going to drive me crazy, forget it."

"That was never my idea, Matt, and you know it."

"Do I? Hell, maybe I do, and maybe that disappoints me. You don't even care enough to make an effort to destroy me."

They shared a faint laugh.

"You know I'm very fond of you," she said.

"The last time I heard that word used was by my great-aunt," he said, "and she was talking about creamed spinach. You know, Glenda, it's going to take me a long time to get over what you did last night. I suppose I'll have to tolerate your way of thinking and hope at some point you'll come around to mine. I'm hoping it's just a rebellious phase, like what my son may be going through." He started to unzip his pants.

"Please don't do that," she said.

"I'm sorry, that was patronizing, wasn't it?" he reflected, stepping out of his pants.

"I mean don't take off your pants."

"But we have time."

"I've decided not to have sexual relations," she announced.

"All day?"

"Indefinitely."

"You must be joking."

"Why would I joke about a thing like that?"

"You tell me," he said. "I can't make you out."

"It's the natural evolution of how I've been thinking all along."

"I don't understand. Is it something about me?" He was covering the front of his undershorts with his trousers, as if a bellhop had just walked into the room.

"No, not at all. It's a function of me. It's about my feelings about sex in general and about its place and purpose in my life."

"This is making me very tense." He stepped back into his trousers. "This is going to give me an ulcer. If there's one thing I don't need at this point in my life, it's an ulcer."

She picked up her pantyhose from the floor and stuffed them into a side pocket of her suitcase. "It wasn't my intention to upset you."

"This is it, then? Just like that?" He snapped his fingers. The sound wasn't as crisp as he had doubtlessly intended.

She watched him buckle his belt. "I hope our working relationship won't be affected," she said.

"What do you mean? You think I'm going to send you down the river or something?"

"I could see your wanting to fire me."

"You insult me, Glenda. My business acumen does not have a direct line to my cock. Was that too crude for you?"

"I was only concerned you'd be uncomfortable."

"Uncomfortable? Sure, I'll be uncomfortable. But that too will pass." He strode toward the door. "I'll see you at the luncheon."

Reaching for the door handle, he turned suddenly, having just realized, she supposed, that he might never again see her body. "You think you might reverse your decision?" he asked with apparent coolness.

"Probably not, Matt."

He took a few steps toward her. "You told me why, but I didn't really understand. Maybe I'm dense. Tell me again."

"Last night the feelings I must have been harboring for a long time came to a sort of head."

"Yours."

"Pardon?"

"*Your* sort of head."

She smiled. "Yes."

"And?"

"And they formulated themselves into a decision. It's about establishing distance, about needing to be sufficient unto myself."

"Are you talking about masturbation? Never mind. We must be on different wavelengths." He pressed a finger to his temple. "And yours is giving mine a headache. Have you got an aspirin?"

"In the bathroom. I'll get it."

"Never mind. It'll only upset my stomach, which is already under siege."

"I would like you to understand, Matt."

"I don't have to understand. I have to be resigned. Tell me again it doesn't have anything to do with me."

She embraced him. "Nothing at all. You've been wonderful."

He held her tightly, as much to confirm his own shape as to feel hers, she guessed, and she suddenly felt like a black widow spider about to perform an act of mercy. She let him go. He stepped away.

"I haven't ever wanted to hurt you," she said.

There was a streak of delicate malice running through her solicitude, which only she felt the pain of, piercing her through the middle like a collector's pin.

— 12 —

Glenda went directly to Eugene's from JFK Airport. Despite his insistence that she and Astrid stay for dinner (Emily was to join them with a mystery covered dish), Glenda wanted to get home, to be alone with her daughter. She was not up to meeting Emily and making conversation requiring editing of the weekend's events.

Meredith was delighted with the decision. Astrid was not. She cornered Glenda in the bathroom. "How is Eugene going to get you like you better than Emily if you don't stay and be nice?" she protested.

"I am not in a competition," Glenda explained, cupping Astrid's face in her hands. "Let me look at you. I missed you."

"He promised to play soccer with me when the weather gets warm. Don't get him mad, or he won't."

Maybe they should have stayed for dinner, after all, Glenda thought the next morning as she stared blankly at the unopened mail on her office desk. She might have missed her cousin Janet's call and at least have delayed the quandary she had been in ever since.

Janet was again pressuring her to visit, only this time the emphasis was on sustaining the relationship between the two women rather than on Glenda's refusal to see her stepfather. Glenda felt a close kinship with Janet. Her cousin was not only a friend, but the only living reference to her pitiful bank of happy childhood memories. Although she saw her only rarely, their getting together existed as an ever-present possibility. Now Janet had made it clear that Glenda was putting her goodwill at risk.

It was not like Glenda to permit her private life to interfere with work, but this morning her glazed look at her desk proved that the precedent had been broken. The ringing of her cell phone snapped her to attention. The caller was Susan Dudley. Glenda pulled herself together.

"I tried to reach you last week, Sue," she said. "I called your office. They told me you were away. I texted you."

"I was preoccupied," Sue replied. "Sorry. We just got back. I dragged Malcolm off to the Bahamas to see if I couldn't crack the uterine connection with idyllic sex. I got a tan, anyway."

"He still wants you to have a baby," Glenda said, smiling to herself.

"I must have wasted a gallon of massage oil."

"What are you going to do, Sue?"

"Nothing. I haven't got time to think about it now—things are busy as hell in the office. I wouldn't be surprised if Malcolm left me for some unattached egg sac. There's at least one of them giving him the eye—his secretary. How about lunch? I've got a free slot between one and two. Booked solid before and after. Want to meet at Cafe Fiorello? I like their salads."

"You're still dieting?"

"Ever watchful. So?"

"I'm looking forward to seeing you."

As soon as Glenda stowed her cell, her extension lit up and a buzzer sounded. "Mr. Crowley would like to see you," Jeff informed her.

She hastily leafed through her mail and gathered the files of the accounts she was currently working on. Before knocking on his door, she took a deep breath and smoothed the sides of her hairdo.

"Come in," he beckoned.

"Good morning, Mr. Crowley."

"Shut the door."

She did so.

"It's Monday," he said.

"Yes."

"Are we on schedule to . . . I mean, I thought perhaps it was all a misunderstanding."

"It wasn't."

"You haven't changed your mind, then," he declared, maintaining a stiff upper lip.

"No." She held onto her files as if to a life preserver.

He aligned his classic features with her files. "Well, now, what have we got here?"

After talking over her assignments with her, Crowley clapped his hands to his thighs and produced a complacent sigh. "Sybil and I are going to see our boy perform in Philadelphia next weekend. We hear he's quite a hit."

"That's really terrific, Matt."

"Yes. Well . . . I guess that will be all."

"Thanks for the advice on the Regal account."

She was careful to close the door gently so as not to bruise an already delicate situation.

There was a note on her desk from Jeff. Eugene Lerman had called at 9:35 a.m. and had requested that she return the call as soon as possible. She dialed his private line.

"Hello, Glenda," he said, picking up before the first ring was complete.

"How'd you know it was me?"

"I didn't. I took a chance."

"You sound very chipper this morning," she observed.

"I've been informed of my promotion to editorial director of Henson and Blackman."

"Congratulations!"

"I called to ask you to celebrate by joining me for lunch."

"What about Emily?"

"Emily's involved with rehearsals."

"I've already made a date for lunch with my friend, Sue," she said.

"Can you cancel it?"

"Yes, I suppose I can. Yes. Of course."

"How about Chez Charles? It's closer to my office than yours, but I know it's good. Do you like escargot?"

"I do."

"They have the best. Is one o'clock okay for you?"

"Great. See you then."

Sue was more than understanding. "Don't tell me you're about to break the heart of another poor schmuck," she said when Glenda called to postpone their date.

"This is nothing like what you're thinking. Eugene is a friend who got a promotion. Don't read into things."

"Well, I wish the guy luck. He's going to need it. How about tomorrow, same time, same place. Cafe Fiorello."

"I'll be there."

"Maybe we'll have more to talk about by then," Sue chuckled.

"Only if you're the bearer of glad tidings," Glenda rejoined.

Eugene waited outside the restaurant for her. His dark hair had been tousled by the wind and his hands were jammed into the pockets of his parka. He looked more like a lost waif, she thought, than a newly appointed editorial director.

Glenda peremptorily kissed his cheek and brushed a wild lock from his brow. "Congratulations again. Why didn't you wait inside?"

"I don't know." Removing a hand from his pocket, he tucked a stray wisp of her hair behind her ear. "Maybe I thought you'd have second thoughts and pass it by."

"And forgo the escargot? Not a chance."

Chez Charles was a small and unpretentious place. Amateurish oil paintings depicting well-known sites of Paris gave it a cozy touch, as if an artistic relative had contributed to its décor. The smell of garlic suffused the air. They checked their coats and were led to a little table against the wall, just under a Primitive rendition of the Eiffel Tower.

"Your nose is red," Eugene said. "How are you going to warm up without a glass of wine?"

"Don't worry about me," she replied, straightening her suit jacket. "It's nice and warm here. I like your sweater. It looks hand-knit."

He nodded. "My mother. For Hanukkah."

"Beautiful."

"With her arthritic hands," he added, with a loving smirk. He pulled at the crew neck of the navy blue cable-knit. "So now I'm packaged in guilt." He picked up the menu. "I think you'll like the food here."

"I'm not ordering a thing unless you let me treat."

"Don't start. I invited you. I'm paying."

"We're celebrating your promotion, and I'm taking you out."

"Don't argue with me," he protested.

"I'm not arguing. I'm stating."

"No you're not."

"Yes I am," she insisted.

"We sound like our kids."

"That's right," she agreed. "Which reminds me, I never properly thanked you for taking care of Astrid over the weekend. Another point in my favor."

They were interrupted by their waitress, who asked if they wanted drinks. He ordered a glass of merlot; she, a Perrier with lemon. The waitress reeled off the lunch specials and departed.

"Well? Am I going to eat?" Glenda asked him.

"You're serious about the hunger strike?"

"Yes, I am."

"Anyone else, I'd dismiss it as coy. But you're so maddeningly tenacious that I don't know. I guess I'll have to relent."

"Thank you," she answered pertly.

"Wait till you see what I order *now*! Shit, here comes someone from the office." He projected a studied smile at a guest who had just checked her coat.

Glenda, her back to the entrance, leaned toward him. "What's wrong? Shouldn't you be here?"

"Don't be silly, I just didn't want to get involved in a conversa— hello, Connie!" he sang, as she and her date approached their table as they were being ushered to their own. "Connie Falls, Glenda Fieldston."

"Hi!" Connie chirruped. "Of course I know you, Glenda, from your work at H and B's. And this is my boss, Eugene Lerman," she followed up, addressing the musclebound young man with permed hair at her side. "Gary Zaleski," she informed Eugene and Glenda. "Gary's in circulation at *People*. We're celebrating our third."

"Week," Gary amplified. "Third week." He displayed his evenly capped teeth.

"We met on Match.com," Connie piped. She emitted a nervous flutter of giggles while Gary studied the attendant tremor of her angora-sheathed breasts. "Each of us joined as a lark. Does that sound like destiny?"

"Well," Glenda and Eugene replied simultaneously, but fell silent.

"Glenda," Connie said, "do you remember *me*?"

"Yes," Glenda said. "There's something different, though . . . your hair?"

"And eyes," Connie said. "I had blue eyes for a while, but they gave me corneal abrasions." She glanced furtively at Eugene.

"You had tinted contact lenses," Glenda deduced.

"Uh huh. And the hair is"—Connie tugged at a short blond tuft— "is, well, just a whim. Well, have a happy!" she concluded, linking her arm through her escort's as they headed for the table in the rear, where the hostess was waiting to seat them.

Glenda smiled. "There was something between you," she said, tilting her head. "Wasn't there?"

"Why do you say that?"

"I don't know. You looked uncomfortable, and she was fitfully gay."

"Why shouldn't I be honest with you?" he said. "A couple of months ago she coerced me into a one-night stand. It was quite out of character—mine, at least. I think hers, too."

"What a smug son-of-a-bitch you are!" she whispered, repressing a laugh.

"Don't make a production. It happened. That's it."

Glenda was shaking her head as the waitress brought their drinks.

"We better order," Eugene said, glaring at the menu. "We're not ready," he muttered to the waitress.

"Come on," Glenda urged, touching his hand. "I'm ordering the escargot and the veal specialty. How about you?"

"The same," he mumbled, and the waitress withdrew.

Glenda squeezed a wedge of lemon over her Perrier and dropped it into the glass. "Listen, Eugene, I'll tell you about my weekend, and you can have the last laugh on me," she said. She took a sip of her drink. "I wasn't going to, but you would have eventually wheedled it out of me. You always do." She raised her glass. "Before it gets ugly, let's toast your promotion. Cheers."

They clinked glasses. She had already revealed so much of herself to Eugene that recounting her experiences with Matt Crowley and Brian Cook seemed to come easily.

"You always do me one better," he commented, as their appetizers were served.

"Not anymore." She dipped a piece of bread into the garlic butter that surrounded the snails. "The piece de resistance—I've ruled a ban on sex." She took a bite of the saturated bread. "Aah, heaven."

He lay down his cocktail fork. "Are you kidding? You mean you're quitting altogether?" Her lips glistened from the butter, filling him with undefined regret.

She nodded.

"On second thought," he reconsidered, "I'm not surprised. I think you've been disdainful of it all along. You only had to take one small step to reach no-man's-land."

She smiled. "You got it."

He took up his fork and scooped out a snail. "Oh, this is good."

There was a pause as they picked at their garlicky delicacies, and then he laughed to himself.

"What?"

"I was just thinking," he said. "There's such an incredible distance between you and Connie Falls. For you, sex is dispensable. For her, it's the most creative form of self-expression ever invented by the editors of *Cosmopolitan*." He wiped his buttery lips with his napkin.

"And where are you on the spectrum?" she asked, brushing a crumb from her sleeve. "Embracing the golden mean, I suppose. The sanest little fucker in god's universe."

"That's me!"

They laughed at their combined arrogance.

"With friends like me," Glenda began.

"Who needs enemies?" he completed.

"I wouldn't want to add you to the roster," she said, crestfallen.

They were silent as the waitress delivered the main course.

"What just happened there?" Eugene asked, after the waitress had gone.

"Please. I don't want to rain on your parade any more than I already have."

"Another cliché like that, and you're dead," he warned, brandishing his knife.

She smiled feebly. "The food looks delicious."

"Don't be evasive."

"My cousin's bugging me again," she said, slicing into the veal.

"About your stepfather."

"Yes. Only now she's making my relationship with her contingent on my going up there. I want to see her, and I don't know how to handle it."

He tasted the veal. "Simple. You go."

"That's easy for *you* to say."

"Easy for me to *do*," he amended. "I'll go with you, if you'd like some moral support."

"You'd do that for me?"

"Why not? I've always wanted to freeze my ass off. What's the temperature in Buffalo this time of year, about fifty below? This veal is very good."

"I don't think I've ever admitted I needed help like this in my life," she said.

"Then this is a landmark. Congratulations. Do you want to go this weekend?"

"Hey, wait, I haven't decided yet!"

"Oh, face it already."

"Face what?"

"It," he said. "Your demon. Whatever. When do we go?"

"This weekend we're registered at the Uris for the kids' program."

"I forget for what."

"The Horse in Art."

"I wouldn't miss it for the—" He remembered something. "I can't," he said. "Emily and I have one of our musical soirées to go to this

Saturday night. I'd better not cancel. Unless we can't wait another . . .
I mean, if your stepfather . . ." He moved the rice around with his fork.

"He's not on his deathbed," Glenda said, holding her glass of ice
water against her cheek.

"We'll go in two weeks," he proposed.

"I don't know," she wavered.

"You're not free? Myself, I'm looking forward to calling off racquetball with my friend Larry. He's been creaming me lately. He's also been
trying to force his sister on me."

"Doesn't he know about Emily?"

"Sure, but to Larry it's a non-factor."

"I'm free that weekend," Glenda admitted. "But I think it's a terrible
imposition on you."

"Cut the crap. I want to go."

She stared into his face, looking for the slightest hint of a con-
tradiction. She saw none. "I can leave Astrid with Irma Krauss," she
considered finally, putting down the glass of ice water. "Her daughter
Cheryl's stayed with us a couple of times. Irma's always reminding me
of it. Astrid would be thrilled. And I'm sure Irma would be delighted to
have Meredith stay with her, too. She loves being surrounded by kids.
She volunteers to chaperone every field trip."

"Emily will think we don't trust her," Eugene balked. "What if Meredith and Astrid both stay with Emily? She'd love to take them on her
musical missions. It will be an adventure for the girls."

"Emily might object," Glenda suggested.

"Emily's a very caring person."

"About your going with me, I mean."

"Didn't Emily go on tour with her composer friend Paul Scheinberg? And did I make a fuss? Of course, Scheinberg's not as pretty as
you are."

Glenda emitted a decorous laugh.

"Seriously, Emily trusts me," Eugene prodded. "She's very understanding. Anyway, she has to be understanding. She wouldn't want to
risk losing me." He grinned. "I'm such a great catch, you know."

"I know only from hearsay," Glenda said.

"Really? Whose?"

"Yours."

— 13 —

Glenda decided she and Eugene would take a cab from Buffalo International, but Janet countermanded that: her husband Rocco would pick them up. The deal was non-negotiable.

Rocco hailed them at the arrival gate. "It's a good thing Janet showed me a picture of you at our wedding," he said, bestowing Glenda with a hearty embrace.

"Glenda and I met once, and that was four years ago," he explained to Eugene as the two men shook hands. "I was a nervous wreck at the time. I remember nothing, except that I dropped the ring."

Glenda had recognized Rocco immediately as the great friendly bear who had made her delicate cousin look like a china doll. His heavy beard enhanced his broad features and drew attention to the quality of his smile and the direct focus of his eyes. From their first and only meeting, he had appeared to her as awkward in small things (like dropping rings) and graceful in matters of the heart—like kissing it after picking it up from the floor.

"I didn't want you to go to this trouble," she told Rocco, as he took her overnight bag from her. She glanced about.

"You're wondering where Janet is," Rocco guessed. "She didn't want to leave your stepfather. He was having a lot of stomach pain this morning." He steered them toward the airport exit. "Your stepfather has some money saved. He insists on spending it on home care. When Jan's at work she can't very well say no, but on weekends, forget it, she takes over."

"Why does she have to do this?" Glenda asked, the question rhetoric.

"Your mother was her aunt," Rocco nevertheless answered. "He's her step-uncle."

"She has no obligation to him."

Rocco smiled. "Obligation is not a factor. Patrick is a lost soul, and saving lost souls is Janet's calling."

"I hope he appreciates what she does for him," Glenda carped.

"Also beside the point."

Rocco tried to take Eugene's bag from him as they walked the corridor, but Eugene held fast. In the parking lot a gust of wind slapped Glenda's scarf against her face as they headed toward the car. Eugene reached out and anchored the scarf under her coat collar.

"When the wind roars over the Erie ice, it can sweep you off your feet, Eugene," Rocco said. "Welcome to Buffalo."

"We're lucky we haven't gotten much snow this year," he added as he fumbled in his pocket for the car keys. "Only about thirty inches so far. For early February, that's not bad." The keys dropped into a patch of snow the blowers had missed.

"'Not bad'?" Eugene repeated. "I guess everything's relative." He grinned and picked up the car keys, wiping them against his coat before handing them to Rocco.

Rocco stowed the bags in the trunk of the car and climbed in behind the wheel.

"You sit in front," Glenda suggested to Eugene, as he was about to slide into the back. "There's more leg room."

"I'm fine here. Get in the front and close the door. Gee, it's cold."

"You're sorry you came," she said.

"No, no!" Eugene laughed. "Do you want it in writing? Just get in the car."

"I want to thank you again."

"Get in!"

"You know," Rocco said, once they were out on the open highway, sashaying with the buffeting winds, "I better prepare you for what's ahead, Glenda. You haven't seen your stepfather since the wedding. He's, what, fifty-four years old?"

"Fifty-three."

"He looks twenty years older. He's changed a lot since you saw him. It caught up with him in the last couple of years. He's got cirrhosis of the liver, pretty advanced. Last month he was hospitalized with gastro-intestinal bleeding. He had to have a series of transfusions. Janet told you that."

"Yes. She did." Her words were clipped.

"He's also had what they call intercurrent infections, like peritonitis and pneumonia. He looks like hell. We're blasting him with Vitamin B and making him rest a lot, but the damage is irreversible. But, you know, people are still calling up with odd jobs for him, and he's telling them he'll do the work when he's feeling stronger. In about two weeks, he says to them."

"Janet told me that, too."

"I mainly want to warn you about his physical appearance."

"It's deteriorated," she said. "I get it."

"Glenda, whatever your feelings—"

"I know," she said. "I keep them to myself."

"That wasn't what I was going to say. I wanted to thank you for coming, in spite of how you feel."

She softened. "Rocco, I'm sorry. I really wanted to see you again, and Janet. I don't want to ruin things for us."

Eugene leaned forward and put his hand on her shoulder. "And I'm here to see she doesn't."

Glenda covered Eugene's hand with her own. "I don't deserve either of you," she said.

"If I didn't know you as well as I do," Eugene said, "I might have thought your remark was made for the effect." He squeezed her shoulder. "You're the most honest person I've ever met." He released her and leaned back in the seat. "Of course, that can at times be extremely trying."

"I couldn't agree with you more—the last part, I mean," she said, staring out at the bleak stretch ahead of them.

"I was just kidding," Eugene said.

She turned back to him and smiled. "No, you weren't."

"No, I wasn't," he reconsidered. "You'll make an honest man out of me yet."

A half hour later, as Rocco turned off the highway, Glenda felt a stitch of alarm as the encounter with her stepfather became imminent.

The snow was just beginning to fall.

Within a mile, a service road led them to the main street of Lintonville. Past the general store, the residential streets branched off in two directions. Rocco turned left, drove a short block, and then turned right.

The rows of houses that emerged as Rocco drove down the narrow streets of Lintonville reminded Eugene of his past. This is the kind of town you leave at childhood's end, he thought. A town with no distinctive character in itself, but one whose small houses—some shingle, some brick—are in friendly competition, their individuality highlighted through window treatment, landscaping, door color. A town you come back to during your college break, only to realize how small it is compared to Philosophy 101 and Professor Brockmann's grasp of Russian history. He felt as though he was returning home to the sparsely trafficked street where he had played dodgeball, afterwards cooling off on his screened-in porch.

Which was odd, considering he had spent his entire childhood living in an apartment in upper Manhattan and he had never played dodgeball in his life. What made him feel that the popular image of suburban America belonged to him, when it was no more a part of his past than the sight of his mother pruning a tomato plant (if that's what one did to a tomato plant)? Was it the cumulative and mystical power of all the movies he'd seen with shots of kids sitting on stoops, paper boys tossing *Daily Gazettes* onto front walks, and dogs barking at mailmen?

As Rocco pulled into a short asphalt driveway, Glenda turned around in her seat to look back at Eugene. Her lips were pressed together; her eyes were wide open. Eugene looked directly into them. Her history intoxicated and engulfed him, as if the essence of his own past had been hovering about like ectoplasm, first inhabiting the suburban form, now transmuting into Glenda's memory. He shuddered with the apprehension of seeing her stepfather, afraid of being hurt in some way.

"We're doing the right thing," he assured her. "You'll see."

The door of the modest white-shingled Colonial opened, and a woman appeared in its entrance bay. She stood there for a moment, hands clasped against her chest, then rushed to greet them. Glenda stepped from the car. She waited for Janet to reach her, and then she hugged her—or rather, fell into her arms.

"Janet—oh, Janet," she said.

"It's been so long!" Janet uttered finally, drawing out to arm's length. "Let me look at you." They held onto each other's hands—Glenda, Eugene noted, as though she might crumble to the ground without the connection.

"Don't get dramatic, you'll make us cry," Rocco intervened. "You want to break 'em up, Gene?"

"I don't have the heart," he said. "Pop the trunk."

Rocco did so and Eugene grabbed the bags as Janet laughed and introduced herself. For such a slight woman, Janet's embrace was surprisingly vigorous. Eugene felt instantly welcomed into the family, no questions asked.

"I'm overcome," he said. "Can I be your long lost cousin?"

"Any time," Janet agreed, patting him on his back.

With her delicate features, pale complexion, liquid blue eyes and long raven hair peppered with gray, Janet looked to Eugene like Snow White fifteen years into the happily ever after. Rocco, her swarthy prince, completed the picture.

The rosy image dissolved upon their entrance.

In the center of the living room stood an emaciated figure, his skin friable and yellow, like pages of an old paperback. He was wearing a neatly pressed but ill-fitting pair of dark blue serge trousers with a belt that gathered them in at the waist and marked the rise of a distended belly. A starched white shirt was buttoned up to the collar, which gaped miserably at the neck. Glenda barely recognized him.

"I thought you'd be standing out there all day," he said, taking a step toward them. He coughed, involuntarily releasing flatulence, and coughed again to distract from it.

"Sorry to keep you waiting, Mr. President," Janet said lightheartedly, clearly embarrassed for him. "This is Eugene Lerman, Glenda's friend. Eugene, Patrick Barnes."

"Glad to meet you," Eugene said, shaking Patrick's hand.

"Likewise." The exercise had caused Patrick's shirt to blouse out, and he tucked the excess back into his pants. His glance repeatedly strayed to Glenda, as if despite himself. "They told me I had a granddaughter," he directed to her general vicinity.

Eugene moved closer to Glenda and placed a hand on her waist, pressing her into a reply.

At the first sight of her stepfather Glenda had shrunk back, frightened not so much by his actual appearance as by its cause. She was struck by the irrational fear that she had caused his deterioration through some voodoo power over which she had no control, that she had created a disease to emaciate his body and stain his eyes the color of nicotine. She felt Eugene's hand on her waist, preventing her from escaping back, out of confrontation's reach.

"Why didn't you bring my granddaughter?" Patrick asked.

Glenda wanted to answer that it was a stretch, calling her his grand-daughter. Instead, she said, "I didn't want to," in the brittle voice she hadn't heard in twenty years.

"Maybe next time," he said, pulling at a shirt cuff. "I like the name Astrid." He turned to Janet. "Don't you like the name?"

"It's a lovely name," Janet agreed. "Why don't we sit down?" She took Patrick's arm to lead him to the sofa.

"Don't baby me," he said. "They'll think I'm feeble-minded."

"They'll think no such thing," Janet said.

He spun around to face the others in a habitual gesture Glenda remembered as having been more defiant. "Listen, I like to pull my weight around here, which I admit isn't a helluva lot right now, but I got what it takes. There's a list of customers a mile long that are waiting for me, and let me tell you, they wouldn't hear of anybody else laying a hand on their domiciles." He coughed. "Tell 'em, Rocco. How many loyal customers I got with carpentry jobs for me?"

Patrick attempted a proud stance, and Glenda found herself look-ing through him, at her recollection of what he once was. Without his swagger augmenting his presence, he was reduced to size, literally and figuratively.

"Pat, we know there's a bunch of folks waiting for you to work for them," Rocco reassured him. "I told Glenda that."

"How many?" Patrick whined. "Where's the list? My wife, Maggie used to keep my lists, and I always knew where they were!" He coughed again, more wretchedly. "Damn it. I feel so useless!"

"Don't get temperamental on us," Rocco scolded, with a conciliatory wink. "The list is in a safe place, and you'll get to it when you're feeling better."

"I'm going to lick this thing yet."

"You sure will," Janet encouraged.

"My staying here is a temporary arrangement," Patrick reminded his niece.

"You tell me that ten times a day."

"I'm grateful for everything you're doing, Janet." He shot an accusatory look at Glenda.

Glenda reached for Eugene. He took her hand and pressed it to his side.

"Just don't baby me," Patrick said. "I don't like to be babied."

Janet cocked her head. "Everyone needs to be babied one time or another."

"Not me. I don't need to be babied. What I need is a drink."

"Well, you're not getting one, Uncle."

"Christ, you hide the key to the liquor cabinet, but don't you think I've got something stashed away myself? You know I'll sneak one behind your back."

"That's your prerogative," Janet said. "I do what I can to encourage you from abusing yourself, but I'm not your warden."

"My stomach feels like someone is digging a hole in it," he announced abruptly.

"I was just going to serve lunch," Janet said. She started to head to the kitchen, Glenda following. "And I don't want any help. Sit here, all of you, and argue among yourselves for two minutes. You're not getting anything fancy. Turkey sandwiches and salad."

After the sandwiches were served, Patrick paused in a fit of coughing and sagged over the dining room table. "Why am I the only one who doesn't get the mayo? Never mind. I know. The turkey's dry. Give me a drink to wash it down."

"There's water right in front of you," Janet pointed out.

"Hell!" He started coughing again.

Glenda felt a pang of sympathy for the ailing man even as she felt impatience with her stepfather.

Rocco rose from the table. "Come on, Patty. You should be in bed now. Let me help you."

Patrick complied without resistance. "I think I may have to throw up," he rasped.

"You've had too much excitement," Rocco soothed. "You forget you're still recuperating."

Patrick closed his eyes and took a few deep breaths while Rocco supported him. "I think I'm okay," he said at last. "I'll take you up on the offer, though. Maybe I need to take a load off my feet. Isn't *that* a laugh!"

"Why don't you go up with them?" Eugene suggested to Glenda, his look embracing her qualms. "I'll help Janet with the dishes."

"All right," Glenda agreed. She felt protected from all harm by Eugene's understanding, as if by the mystical laying on of the hands.

"Rocco's terrific with your uncle," Eugene remarked to Janet as he was setting the plates in the sink.

Janet squirted detergent into the sink and turned on the hot water. "Rocco's had a lot of practice. He took care of his ailing mother in this house for many years. He was a very devoted son. We were married after she died." She took the cups from him and arranged them in the sudsy water. "That didn't sound right. He didn't wait until she died to get married. He just didn't have the time to court me." She grinned. "By the way, he's not a mama's boy. He's a natural at caring is all."

"Where were you so lucky to meet each other?"

"At work. He's a foreman at the steel plant, and I'm in payroll. In order to get him to notice me, I purposely made an error in his Social Security deduction—one too big for him to miss."

"How wicked of you."

"Yeah. You want to wash or dry? As you can see, we have a dish-washer, but I find this unwinds me."

"I'll wash," he said. "You know where the dishes go." They switched places.

"Glenda was really looking forward to seeing you," he said after a moment.

"Not her stepfather, though," she qualified.

"I know she blames him for her mother's death," Eugene said.

Janet sighed. "Patrick is maybe the only other person who blames himself. That's the irony of it."

"He didn't actually . . . *push* or anything?" Eugene ventured.

"Oh no!" Janet replied, adamant. "There was a scuffle. He was trying to keep her from going downstairs to get another bottle of whiskey. She broke away from him and fell."

"How can you be sure it happened that way?" he asked.

She stared at him in disbelief.

"Please don't think Glenda suggested the idea to me," Eugene added. "She blames him, but indirectly. I'm the one suggesting that maybe in the heat of the moment, he could have—"

"He would have taken the fall *for* her! He would have given his life for Maggie in a minute!"

"I thought he treated her badly," Eugene said, puzzled.

"What? Are you serious? The worst thing he ever did was to destroy a photograph album of hers, which he must have done in a rage of helplessness. He blamed that album for her depressions. During those last months she'd sit for hours, poring over all the old photographs."

"Why?"

Janet shrugged. "She was comparing herself to what she used to look like and what she aspired to. I'm not sure. But in his eyes that album must have become a curse. He finally burned it, not in a fit of jealousy as Glenda insists, but in a fit of frustration. It was an impulsive, desperate attempt to save Maggie from destruction."

"Prevent destruction by means of destruction," Eugene commented, handing Janet a clean plate. "Not what I'd call ideal therapy."

"Oh, of course they had their quarrels like everybody else," Janet went on, overriding Eugene's remark. "He'd make fun of what he called her fancy 'airs,' and she'd blame him for stifling her creative potential. That sort of thing. What did it amount to? It's true she was an artistic, sensitive person, but she really didn't have much drive or initiative. When it came down to it, she didn't want to be allowed to have a career of her own. As for Patrick, he adored her fineness and her delicacy—her 'airs' included."

"He never abused her when he was drunk?" Eugene interjected.

"He was loud, mainly. Rowdy. Maybe he even got nasty sometimes."

Eugene gave her a skeptical look.

"The answer is no," Janet declared. "He was sober on the afternoon of the accident, and he wouldn't have laid a hand on her, anyway. Look, Eugene, me and my family were living two houses away from them, in a town near Lintonville. Maybe you didn't know that? We'd see them all the time, and let me tell you, the most obvious thing about that couple was that they were absolutely crazy about each other. They had something between them that was stronger than anything else in their lives. No other attachment or interest came close to it."

Eugene stood very still. "If that's the case," he reflected, "Glenda must have felt like an intruder."

"Yes. But, you know, she handled it." Janet placed a dry plate in the cabinet above the sink. "She was more grown up than Maggie and Patrick ever were. Do you know how some kids go haywire when they aren't given some kind of structure to keep them in tow? Well, Glenda was her own taskmaster. You know what I mean?"

"Yes, I do." He realized Janet had been waiting for him to hand her something to dry. He ran a soapy glass under the water and handed it to her.

"That's my theory, anyway," she said. "After the accident, Glenda became more industrious than ever. It amazed me, how she could concentrate on her school work the way she did. She was only thirteen. I was sixteen, and not nearly as ambitious as she was. Then again, I ended up at an online secretarial school, and she went on to become a math genius."

"Don't put yourself down. You've got a lot on the ball."

"That's sweet. So listen—are you giving me the third degree, or am I just talking a blue streak?" She laughed, releasing tension. "What are you up to, anyway? I mean, nothing would surprise me about my cousin— heaven knows what kind of relationship she'd cultivate—but you seem like a normal kind of guy."

"Strictly an act." Turning serious, he said, "Glenda and I are good friends. Our kids go to the same school, and we do a lot of things together. With the kids, I mean."

"You're divorced?"

"About to be official. However, my relationship with Glenda is not . . . along those lines. As I said, we're friends. I came along hoping to provide moral support."

"I'm glad Glenda allowed that," Janet said. "I only hope she opens up to you more than she has been able to with me, or, I imagine, anyone else. She was never one to let it all hang out, and I don't think that's a good thing. I'm not saying she was all withdrawn and quiet; she could be outspoken and say the most outrageous things. But she was very careful about what she'd let on about her personal feelings. On the rare occasions when she revealed herself, there was always something she kept back, something important.

"How can I explain it? I remember one time we were walking home from school and we saw a couple of boys kneeling by the side of the road, laughing and playing with something blocked from our view. We were curious, so we went over to see what was happening. We discovered the object of their amusement was a flustered little bird with what I guess was a broken wing. The boys were prodding and teasing the poor thing, which they'd trapped within a wall of books. I thought what they were doing was terrible, but I have to admit it fascinated me. Still, I would have told them to stop, but I never got around to telling them anything because of the strange way Glenda behaved. At first she didn't seem to be able to catch her breath. Then she let out a high-pitched cry and burst into tears. It was so intense that even the boys were frightened. They grabbed their books and took off. You wouldn't have believed it."

Envisioning the sobbing girl by the side of the road, Eugene wanted to hold her in his arms and take away the pain. "You think maybe she associated the incident with her mother's death? Seeing her, like the bird, broken, helpless, a victim of—"

"No. This happened months before her mother's accident. I don't know why she reacted so violently. I tried to figure it out myself. I even blamed it on her entering puberty." Janet cracked a self-deprecating smile. "I asked her about it afterward. She said that I should have known she loved animals and hated to see them cruelly treated. She would say no more about it." Janet frowned. "The odd thing is, I knew she loved animals, but—"

"But?" Eugene urged, impatient.

"The odd thing is, she never once touched that lame little bird. She never even seemed to see it after the first shock. There was something else on her mind then. Maybe there still is."

There was nothing voyeuristic about Eugene's curiosity. He could not tear himself away from the scene because he could not part with the child. He stayed, not for his enlightenment, but to share her focus. "Glenda didn't say anything to you or to those boys that may have given you a hint? Something that may have seemed inappropriate for that particular situation?"

"Nothing."

They heard the irregular thud of footsteps on the stairway, and shortly Rocco was occupying the partition between the dining room and the kitchen. "I thought it would be a good idea to leave Glenda alone with Patrick," he said. "How's it coming down here? Doesn't look as though you've made much progress." He nudged Eugene aside. "Shove over. I haven't broken a dish in at least a week."

"I look like hell, don't I?" Patrick said, pulling the cover up over his pajamas. He leaned against the pile of pillows Rocco had jammed between his back and the headboard. "You know, I got this funny tingling in my fingers and toes now. I forget what it's called. The doctors, they do it purposely."

Glenda sat in a straight-backed chair some distance from the bed, her hands folded tightly in her lap. "The doctors give you the tingling?"

"No, they give things names you can't remember, so you always feel inferior to the bastards."

"I doubt that. Do you want me to turn on the television?"

"It's one helluva Sony. They took it out of their bedroom and put it in here for me."

"Do you want it on?" Glenda repeated.

"What do *you* think?"

"I don't know. I can't read your mind." She tugged at the hem of her skirt, which already covered her knees.

He raised his head then let it fall back into the pillows. "Do you think I'm an old fart who goes to sleep in the afternoon with the TV going?"

"I didn't say that."

After a pause, Patrick said, "You're staying in the room next door with your friend. He has a good handshake."

"Yes."

"You know why there's two beds in that room? It used to be Rocco's mother's room. Near the end, when she was very sick, he used to stay in the room with her in case she needed him." Patrick made a point of looking uncomfortable. "Could you fix these pillows for me?"

Glenda tried to avoid touching him as she adjusted the pillows, but he hesitated, then grasped her arm.

She pulled away.

"Why the hell did you come, anyway?" he snapped.

She backed away from the bed. "Why did you want me to?"

"To see you!" he cried. "To ask you to forgive me for not being able to save your mother!"

She held herself rigid, arms pressed against her body, as if she were trapped in a narrow passageway. "It's too late," she said.

"Too late to forgive?" he asked, peering into the blank television screen as if he had lost something there.

"Too late to save her," Glenda clipped, becoming sharp as he became remote. "She listened to you. You could have stopped her."

He sat up as if yanked by a leash. "I tried!"

"No, you wanted to bring her down to your level. She was too high-minded for you. You wanted to break her!"

He flailed his arms, beating off a swarm of recriminations. "You don't understand! We had such good times. She laughed at my stupid jokes. Nothing else mattered when we were like that. How did I know she wouldn't be able to control the drinking? How could I watch her like a baby?"

"Why didn't you quit drinking yourself? She would have followed you."

He sagged into the bedding as if his spine had been severed. "It wouldn't have done any good. Dear Jesus, I was weak!"

His body shook like a marionette's as he began to weep. She felt as if his tears were running down the back of her throat—burning, bitter. He continued to weep uncontrollably as she stood motionless at the foot of his bed.

"Can't you ever forgive me for being human?" he at last pleaded, sobbing still. Then, as if another question had been washed to the surface in the flood of tears—"Can't you ever forgive me for loving her more than I loved you?"

The utterance hovered over them before exploding. "That's why you really hate me, isn't it?" he gasped. "Why else are you making me beg for forgiveness like a dog?" His grief had turned fiery. "Do you think you're perfect? Do you think I have nothing to forgive *you* for?"

She was unable to move or speak.

"You say nothing. You know exactly what I'm talking about, don't you? *Don't* you?" he raved. "You also have sins to be forgiven for!"

She opened her mouth to speak, but instead a sharp cry like a bird's hooked the air. She fled from the room with her arms reaching out in front of her, as if she had been struck blind.

Eugene held her by the shoulders as she groped for the buttons of her coat.

"I want to go home," she insisted. "Please!"

"Glenda, it's not like it's just around the corner!" Eugene said.

Janet stood near. "You'd walk out on me?" she asked. "I don't know what happened up there, but you'd do that to me?"

"It has nothing to do with you," Glenda implored.

"Then don't leave me alone in the middle of it, cousin."

Rocco wrapped his arm around Janet's waist and drew her close. "Listen, Gene," he tossed out, "have you ever been to Niagara Falls?"

"No, I haven't," Eugene replied. He undid the buttons of Glenda's coat, which she'd fastened unevenly.

"It's a short drive," Rocco said. "You three go. I'll mind the store."

"That does sound good," Eugene agreed at once. "You wouldn't deprive me, would you?" he asked Glenda, who was fingering a button of his blazer.

Glenda looked up. "You make me feel so selfish."

Eugene smiled. "That's my intention." He detained her hands at his midsection. "We'll go?"

"Do you remember when we saw the Falls together for the first time, Glen?" Janet asked, on her guard.

Suddenly shy, Glenda directed her answer to Eugene, as if he had been the one to ask. "The day you got your driver's license."

Janet nodded. "It took me an hour to find a big enough parking spot."

"Parking was never her strong point," Glenda murmured.

Janet broke from Rocco and approached. "C'mon, Glen. We can talk on the way."

As they walked to the car, Eugene still held Glenda's hands pressed against his body, harboring them within his lapels.

When they reached the falls, Eugene stood at the railing between the two women, an arm around each of them. Before them crashed a vista of floods descending over glittering, molten emerald rock to the gulfs below, the mists created by the mighty turbulence rising halfway up the precipice.

"Bach-defying," Eugene exalted.

"I'm glad it stopped snowing so that nothing's marring your view," Janet said, stomping her feet to keep warm.

"The immensity of it," Eugene marveled. "The nobility—how immutable it all seems!"

"It is magnificent, isn't it," Janet agreed.

"Yet in another sense," Eugene continued, transported, "the form of the deluge is ever-changing. So it's like—like experiencing eternity and the fleeting instant, both at the same time."

"Is he *always* like this?" Janet asked her cousin.

Glenda returned a wistful smile. "I'd say he's usually more psychological than philosophical. By that I mean he's usually telling me what's on *my* mind, not his."

"What, am I stuck with two jaded women, here?" Eugene laughed, pulling them closer to him. "Look at this—how broken and fissured the rock is. I said immutable—but nothing stays the same." He turned to Glenda. "Everything evolves . . . gives . . . no matter how tough and hard you think you are."

Glenda leaned across him to address Janet. "See? Sooner or later he turns his wisdom on me."

"I see what you mean," Janet said. "Even though he's right."

"It's a conspiracy," Glenda sighed.

Eugene squeezed her shoulder. "Don't be negative. Change is good. This isn't a still life—that's why it's so beautiful. It changes, but it endures. Don't you feel part of it, Glenda? Doesn't it make you aware of your own enduring essence when you're—how can I say it—immersed in the sound of this vision?"

"Sorry to disappoint," Glenda replied, "but next to this I feel extremely temporary. I hope you weren't proposing to lecture us about our everlasting souls."

"If not your soul, then the fact of your existence. That, goddammit, will endure forever!"

"It's an interesting idea," Glenda conceded, "but it doesn't do much for me. I feel frail right now. Insignificant." Her voice drifted off. "Crumbling like parchment," she said quietly.

"Glen, what are you talking about?" Janet asked.

Glenda's silence rose above the roar of the falls. In the fullness of the moment, Eugene could have cried for anyone in the world.

In the evening, no mention was made of Glenda's earlier flight from her stepfather's room. She, Janet, Rocco, and Eugene were balanced in a delicate serenity, like a house of cards. No one cared to hazard the breath that might upset it.

Patrick himself chose to stay in his room. Rocco brought him his dinner and then joined the others in the dining room, where they were waiting for him before doling out the roast chicken and raising their glasses—Glenda's topped with sparkling water—in a medley of toasts. Afterward, the foursome gathered in the living room to continue a conversation that out of respect to Glenda, tacitly prohibited all reference to Patrick.

Sometime before retiring, Glenda and Eugene made calls to see how their children were getting on. Eugene spoke first to Emily, who sounded distressed.

"I'm trying, Eugene, really I am, but you must sit down and have a talk with Meredith yourself."

"What the hell happened, Emily?"

"We were invited to Paul's for dinner this evening, and—"

"Paul? Oh, yeah. Looney Tunes."

"Paul Scheinberg happens to be a marvelous composer, Eugene."

"I keep forgetting. What happened?"

"Meredith had a nasty little tiff with Paul's nephew, and the boy ended up hitting her. Meredith wasn't hurt, but Dwight was severely scolded. Maybe I shouldn't have, but I felt sorrier for him than her. She provoked him. I'm very fond of her, and I don't want to jeopardize my relationship with her by scolding her."

"I never heard you sound so agitated."

"I was embarrassed."

"Where is she now?"

"In the bedroom, doing her sewing homework. Hold on."

The next voice he heard was his daughter's. "Hi, Daddy."

"Hi, Mer. What happened today?"

"What?"

"I asked you what happened today. Emily seemed a little upset."

"*What?* Oh! Just a minute. I forgot to take the toilet paper out."

"Toilet paper?"

"It's okay now. I put toilet paper in my ears when we were at Paul's. They were practicing his music."

"Sometimes we have to sacrifice intelligence for tact," he mumbled.

"What?"

"Never mind. What kind of fight did you get into?"

"This kid Dwight hit me."

"What did you do to make him want to hit you?"

"All I did was tell him his uncle's music made me nauseous."

"Not nauseous; nauseated. And that was very impolite of you. I'm surprised at you. Did you apologize at least?"

"Sort of. When are you coming home?"

"Tomorrow night. I want you to behave yourself, Meredith, and listen to Emily."

"I will. Uncle Bob sent me this friendship card with a picture of the Care Bears on it."

"That's nice," Eugene said, trying to make his voice smile.

"No it isn't. Doesn't he know I'm too old for that kind of stuff?"

"Nobody's too old for friendship," Eugene managed.

"I mean I'm too old for the Care Bears!"

"Oh, I see."

What did he see? He was peering into the living room from the kitchen in order to catch a glimpse of Glenda, who was at that moment sitting on the couch explaining an aspect of her job to Janet and Rocco. Eugene was seeing Glenda's profile and imagining his forefinger tracing it from the bridge of her nose to the tip of her chin. Could remote tactility be an effective mnemonic device? he asked himself.

Without knowing it, Meredith was marooned on the isle of neglect.

When Eugene returned his attention to Meredith he took Glenda along, harboring her image next to his daughter's. "I guess you're too old for the Care Bears," he agreed. "But the card was a nice thought, anyway."

Glenda and Meredith were under the same aegis, sharing his attention like sisters.

A mere night table separated them. Although Eugene had come prepared for such an eventuality, the only pair of pajamas he owned (bought for him by his mother ten years ago and never worn) still lay folded in his suitcase. Changing into them, for all their conservatism, seemed too suggestive a statement for him to make. He was already feeling risqué from having brushed his teeth.

He slipped out of his loafers, rolled up his shirtsleeves, loosened his belt a notch, and stretched out on his back without turning down the bedclothes. Glenda must have felt the same way. Except for having discarded her shoes, she was dressed for a dentist's appointment as she slipped between the sheets.

They had both brought books to read. The books lay on the table between them. Neither reached for one.

"I feel like an old movie," he said after a while.

"You want to watch television at this hour?"

"I mean l feel like I'm *in* an old movie. You must know the routine—where through various plot convolutions the hero and heroine are obliged to share a hotel room, so they rig up something between them with a handy clothesline and a bedspread?"

"I'm not a movie buff," Glenda said.

"So they've got this bedspread draped over the clothesline, and all night long they hurl sparklingly nasty remarks at each other through the partition. You're not familiar with this formula?"

"No," she said. "What happens next?"

"The plot resolves. They find the lost relative or the stolen brooch, or whatever, and they realize they're in love, which is something the audience knows before they do. Every time."

Glenda offered a wry smile. "Sounds very believable."

"Got a clothesline?"

She laughed softly. "I thought we were more modern than that."

"You're right," he agreed. "We can be nasty *without* a curtain between us."

"You can say that again."

"We can be nasty without a cur—"

"Oh, shut up!" She buried her face in the pillow, stifling laughter that dangerously bordered on hysteria.

In old movies, such laughter dissolves immediately into tears. Glenda did not start crying for another two hours.

Eugene, who had been hearing—listening for—her every rustle, heard the muffled sobs and could not help but respond, even though he knew she might not welcome the intrusion.

"Do you want to talk, Glen?"

The sobbing continued.

"I'll leave the room if you like."

"No—please."

"I know you don't like anybody touching you when you're crying, but I wish I . . ." His voice trailed off.

In the scant light coming through the window curtains, he saw her hand reach into the divide. Amazed, he grabbed it before she had time to reconsider, lacing his fingers tightly through hers as if he were making a tourniquet to stop the flow of her tears.

"Talk to me," he said. "Let me help you."

Their arms formed a cable bridging the gap between them, and Glenda wished she could send her thoughts across the cable without speaking.

"I want to," she wept, turning her face toward Eugene. "I want to."

"Try, then," he coaxed. "Take your time. We have hours before day-break." Without letting go of her hand, he moved to her bedside and knelt there.

Her head sparked like an unattended switchboard. "It hurts," she said.

"Where?"

"My head."

"I'll get you something."

"No, don't."

"Not even a cup of tea? Let me feel like I'm being useful."

Her words came bunched between sobs: "You won't leave me—for long, will you? He's in the next room—I can't bear that he's so close!"

"Do you want to come down to the kitchen with me?" he asked. She could feel his lips brush inadvertently against a fold of her sleeve.

She coiled in on herself. "I don't want to go out into the hallway."

"Then I'll be right back." He rose from her side.

Not until Eugene was about to pour the hot water over the tea bag did the idea occur to him.

He transferred the tea bag from the cup to a hefty mug and poured a moderate amount of water over it. While the tea was steeping, he extricated the key to the liquor cabinet from under a dish in the back of the pantry, where he had seen Janet place it after dinner. From the cabinet—a section of the breakfront in the dining room—he removed a bottle of vodka and returned to the kitchen, there topping the mug with the tasteless fluid.

The guilt rising from the deception was mild as a poke from his mother's soup ladle, so confident was he of the honor of his mission. His intention was to loosen her tongue, nothing else; to get her to recognize the truth she stifled, that stifled her.

To your release from the demon, he silently toasted Glenda before taking a swig directly from the bottle.

Sitting in bed, the covers tucked beneath her legs, Glenda sipped the drink she had been given.

"Does your head feel any better?" Eugene asked.

"I don't know," she said. "You won't turn on the light, will you? I don't want you to see me properly. I'm a wreck."

"Love me, love my swollen eyelids is our motto." He sat on the edge of her bed. "Who cares if you're a wreck?"

She blew her nose into a tissue from a box on the night table. "What would I do without you? Didn't you want any tea?"

"No."

"Janet buys all the exotic teas. What's this one?"

"I'm not sure. Maybe SleepyTime."

She took a generous quaff.

"These pins don't help your headache," he said. "I'm taking them out." He began plucking out her hairpins.

"You mother me," she said. She could feel him smooth her hair back from her shoulders.

"You're easy to mother," he said.

When she was done, he took the mug from her and put it atop the books on the night table, "I hope you feel a little better." He tidied the collar of her blouse.

She pressed a hand to her temple. "I feel so woozy," she said.

"It's from all the emotion today," he said. "The remembering."

After a moment, her tears began to flow again. He rubbed her back. "Let it, let it, let it," he chanted.

"Why did I come here?" she wept. "Why did you make me come?"

"I didn't make you come," Eugene insisted. "I said I thought it was a good idea, and I still do."

She turned up to him, searching his face in supplication. "But I can't stop the . . . these pictures just won't go away!"

In the dim light her cheeks shone from her tears. He looked into her mystifying eyes and became acutely aware of the distinguishing features of his own physiognomy, his own private and decreed history.

And no sooner did their separateness appear to him as an absolute than their contact appeared as an exquisite possibility.

With great restraint, careful not to obstruct the flow of her purgation with too violent an embrace, he folded her in his arms, gently compelling her to rest her head against his shoulder. "Tell me," he crooned. "Tell me."

She rested against him, sobbing into his neck. "He looked so innocent," she said. "I went in to thank him—just to thank him for taking me."

Her stepfather on his stomach, facing the wall, one of his arms folded above his head, like a baby's, a bare knee jutting out from under the sheet.

Eugene stroked her head. "Where did he take you? Glen, I'm listening—I'm here."

"To the fair," she said. "He hardly took me anywhere, but that day he took me to the fair, and he rode the Ferris wheel just so he could be with me, even though he was the one afraid of heights. And I only wanted to thank him for being nice, and my mother was down the basement doing the laundry, and I only wanted to thank him."

"You went into his room, and he was sleeping—was he sleeping?"

"I didn't think he would be, but all that beer may have put him to sleep. He looked like a baby, and I remember his fixed grin on the Ferris wheel, he was so scared, and then I bent to kiss him on the cheek."

His whiskers, coarse. A flutter running along her ribs, tickling, like a feather brushing down her side.

She shuddered. Eugene held her more tightly. "I understand. I won't let you go. You're safe with me. Tell me."

"I don't know if he was awake or asleep," she said, her heart beating wildly, "but he turned over so quickly and grabbed me. It happened so fast, with his mouth, his hands—and I tried to say no, but my mouth was stopped. I tried to say no!"

His lips pressing, opening in on her. His tongue painting her mouth, nose, cutting off air. Choking on him, gasping for trapped beer breaths, her trachea in a spasm of protest—don't don't don't! His hand sweeping over her tender breasts, brutal under the gown to the place where she still blushed to explore, his man fingers parting, delving, where yesterday she had stroked a shallow depression, one slender finger delicately circling.

"His face shot back and I cried out, and he pushed away from me. And then he hit me—he *hit* me! He held one hand against my mouth, and he hit my face with the other. He said I tricked him into making him think I was my mother. He said it was my fault, coming in on him when he was sleeping like that. He blamed *me*!"

Her private smell on his hand, stifling her, degrading. Disgust contorting his face, more painful than the slaps. Afterward, in violent stealth, dragging her to her room, leaving her huddled on the floor, warning her to forget this forever, you slut, it would kill your mother!

"I wanted to run down the basement and tell my mother, but I couldn't. I was so afraid. Then later that night—I was still on the floor, I couldn't get up—I heard terrible noises coming from their room, and I thought maybe he was telling her after all, and she was angry with him, and he was hurting her. I was afraid, but I had to help my mother. Didn't I? But he wasn't hurting her, he was—I never saw her with such an expression on her face, like an animal! She yelled at me to get out— laughing!—and I couldn't move, but my stepfather turned and glared at me, and I ran from the doorway—even though it wouldn't have mattered, they never would have stopped what they were doing!"

Eugene tried to ease the trembling by caressing her head, her shoulders, her back.

"I never explained anything to her, and then it was too late. She was dead. A month later. Gone. I don't know if he ever told her—do you think he ever did?"

Eugene lifted her face from his shoulder so he could see her. The imploring look was that of a penitent, not of a child wronged.

"No," he said, "I don't think he told her, and if he did it wouldn't have changed the way things happened."

And he thought: *You were that trapped bird, weren't you—cornered by your stepfather and your own forbidden dreams. An only child who ought to have suffered from an overdose of love and attention, but who instead—instead! Love doled out sparingly, you grateful for every morsel, the guilt that is every child's compounded by one night's horror—and an accidental death that followed too closely behind it.*

He could hardly keep his thoughts from discharging like pellets, to prompt her to reflect. But he held back. "Oh, Glen, Glen," he said instead, rocking her in his arms, pressing back his own tears, wanting to rescue that elusive, incandescent being imprisoned just past his fingertips.

Impetuously, he kissed her. She responded.

Slowly, his protective embrace became an exploration. He reached into her garments, seeking beyond her flesh yet entranced by it. He lifted her skirt, drew off her underthings, spread her legs, while she, swimming deep in primordium, slid toward him, acquiescing.

Burying his face between her thighs, his nostrils, mouth, tongue penetrated her scent, texture, taste, in an act that for the first time in his life bore no reference to fantasy or morality. Directed energy, bending into another, was all. Her mouth, her ears, her breasts, the soft folds, the musky smooth interior, even his own desire were at the same time the means of access to her and the impediments to that access. When thought seeped into his actions, it was only to witness and condone. And when he mounted her, it was out of the same need to touch her directly, through and despite his own gratification.

Glenda was not truly with him. She was witnessing her mother's cru-cifixion beneath her stepfather as he hammered his passion against her delicate body, his bare ass rising and falling with heavy precision.

Her mother cries out in strange bursts of pain, and then a laugh, unearthly and wild. In that moment, she realizes it has not been a paroxysm of pain, but unholy pleasure that has twisted her mother's voice into alien shrieks. Her step-father sends a lightning look that strikes her down the center of her body, searing her insides and melting her into the spot where she stands in the doorway. She cannot move. She is transfixed. She watches until their bodies flex in a demonic seizure. Her expulsion from their dark paradise is absolute.

She reached orgasm, remembering this, and in her throes she saw her mother catapulted down a gigantic falls, her limbs flailing like an infant's, her eyes fixed in terror at a shrouded figure above.

She awoke in their disarray, the feel of Eugene's unshaven cheek against her breast and the smell of his dark matted hair insinuating itself into her brain. Her skirt was bunched about her waist, and his bare thigh rested heavily across her own. She thought it must be his ankle bone digging into her shin, but for reasons unknown she could not bring herself to move her leg out from under him. Her head throbbed dully, though her senses were sheared keen.

He stirred and opened his eyes, and immediately her higher faculties were alerted, causing her to draw back.

Eugene rose to a seated position and pulled the sheet over his nude lower half while she hastily rearranged her clothing to shield her own anatomy.

"Contrary to appearances," he said, "nothing happened last night."

She was silent.

"That was a joke. You were supposed to laugh."

"God, I must have really been disoriented," she said.

"Thanks."

"You know what I mean. I had no intention of . . . of . . ."

"Neither did I. Truly." A shadow of guilt passed over his face. "It was an unusual day all around."

"I have the worst taste in my mouth," she said.

"I'll check." He leaned toward her and kissed her lightly on the mouth. "Not bad."

"Please don't take what happened as an invitation," she said. "I mean, as an *indication*—"

"I will take this as a lapse in character, a quirk, as it were, in the normal flow of events."

She felt ridiculously shy. "How are we going to get dressed?"

"Very hastily."

"Eugene!"

"You close your eyes while I get myself together," he suggested. "Then I'll do the same for you."

She pulled the crumpled blanket up under her chin. "That seems very immature."

"Okay, okay. So you can go first."

Patrick appeared at the breakfast table carefully groomed and subdued. With deferential looks and excessive politeness, he tried to make up for what had passed between Glenda and himself the day before. Glenda was courteous, Eugene noted, treating Patrick like an ambassador of a warring nation, although this morning the threat of that nation seemed oddly reduced. Eugene was grateful for Glenda's unburdening—it was what he'd hoped for, although guilt for having spiked her tea still gnawed at him. He would have to tell her soon.

Janet, returning with the strawberry preserves, interrupted the cautious drama. "I don't know how you discovered where I hide the key, Uncle, but you're not kidding anyone but yourself."

"What are you talking about?" Patrick asked, his exaggerated confusion making him look guilty.

"You know very well what I'm talking about. The key to the liquor cabinet wasn't where I put it last. It was on another shelf. What kind of game are we playing?"

Eugene tried to catch Janet's eye with a quick hand-to-shoulder movement. Janet glanced at him but failed to register the message denoted by the subsequent twitch of his head.

But Glenda did notice. "What was that all about?" she murmured into Eugene's ear.

"Nothing," he whispered, his voice as faint as it could get.

"Why don't we talk about this later, Jan," Rocco urged, clearly uncomfortable about his wife having put Patrick on the spot. "Come sit down. Your toast's getting cold."

Janet softened. "Okay, but I've just had it up to here with his childish behavior." She took a seat.

Patrick slapped his hand against the table, causing the coffee cups to clatter against their saucers. "Wait a minute! You're accusing me of something, and I've got the right to respond!"

Eugene uttered a resigned sigh. "I'm the one who put the key on the wrong shelf," he confessed. "Sorry."

Janet reddened. "I didn't realize," she said. "Of course you're welcome to whatever we keep in the cabinet, Eugene. You should know that. What in heaven's name are *you* sorry about?" She turned to Patrick. "*I'm* the one who should apologize." She squeezed her uncle's hand.

Glenda peered at Eugene.

"Later," he mouthed.

Glenda was livid the instant Eugene told her. "You deceived me!"

"I thought it was a noble enterprise," Eugene replied, trying to lighten the mood.

"Cocktails?" the flight attendant inquired, pulling up alongside their two-seater row with her beverage cart.

Eugene shook his head. "I'm in enough trouble already."

"A ginger ale, thanks," Glenda relayed from her window seat. "No peanuts," she added as the attendant was reaching into the bin.

"I'll have her peanuts," Eugene said.

"Coming up," the attendant said, complying.

"Make that a Bloody Mary," Eugene edited.

"Instead of the peanuts, sir?"

"No. With the peanuts. Hers and mine."

"Give the man what he thinks he's *entitled* to," Glenda said, directing the jab at Eugene.

"Glenda, I've been trying to explain to you," he began, fumbling for his wallet. But before he could get it, Glenda handed the attendant payment for Eugene's drink.

"That wasn't necessary," he said when the attendant had rolled off. "You didn't have to pay for the devil's elixir." He took a swig of it. "But thanks, anyway."

She tore open one of the bags of peanuts and tossed it toward him. "I trusted you," she snapped. "How could you have deceived me like that?"

"I told you. I only meant to make it easier for you to talk."

"Was our conversation flagging?"

"I wanted to rescue you."

"Oh. The house was on fire. Why didn't you say so in the first place?"

He studied a peanut that had rolled onto his cocktail napkin. "You don't want to understand."

"I understand that you knew I had an aversion to alcohol."

"And to losing control of yourself," he added.

"If you knew I had an aversion to alcohol," she continued, "why did you intentionally disregard it?"

"Because I wanted to know you better."

"Hah! Tell me, since I wasn't quite cognizant of the situation. Was I *good?*"

"Oh, Glenda!" He started to move a hand toward hers, but he stopped himself.

She stared at the seat in front of her. "Don't think I didn't appreciate your coming with me this weekend, Eugene. I really did. But to extort such a payment from me!"

"Please don't say that. I lost control of myself, too."

"You were in full control when you poured that vodka into my tea, you bastard."

"Don't you care what my motive was?"

"Tell it to Emily."

The line stunned him. "I will," he answered, defiant.

"I can barely stand to look at you."

"Or at *yourself,*" he flung back.

Immediately, he winced from the sting of his retort. Glenda may have bared her soul to him, but this did not give him the authority to treat it as their joint possession.

"Look at me," he pleaded.

She turned toward him, hoping to find something in his expression to justify the level of her vexation, but finding only her distress mirrored there. "What do you want?"

"I want you to believe me."

"I'm not sure I want to," she said, hardly knowing what she meant.

— 14 —

Glenda had no choice but to regard Eugene's misconduct as an aberration. Somehow he had rooted his way into becoming her best friend. How, then, could she view him as her abuser? By putting her mind to it, she managed to have him acquitted of all charges, blaming the unfamiliar environment of Lintonville and her own unsettling behavior at her cousin's house.

Successful as she was in eliminating Eugene's wrongdoing from the picture, there remained an undercurrent of emotion that refused to be designated out of existence. It threatened to dominate reason and complicate her life, until she finally joined Sue at the Y in order to jog it out of her system.

Just as she believed she could work off an emotion like pent up energy, Glenda believed she could mend her cognitive ability, much like a splinted bone, if she didn't set eyes on the troubling emotion's cause for a prescribed number of weeks—say, eight to ten. Thus she avoided contact with Eugene, which added another level to her dialectic of despair: there was no one else, including Sue, with whom she wanted to share her problem.

From the way Glenda took on the indoor track like an Olympic contender or, as Sue put it to her, "like a dog trying to lose its tail," Sue deduced that Glenda was "working something out." She probed, but Glenda never confided in her, feeling—perversely, maddeningly—that she would have been breaking a sacred trust with Eugene.

One day while she was standing before the avocados in the produce aisle at Gristedes, a man with a small boy in tow emerged from the next aisle over, the boy whining loudly to his "Daaaddy!" about something denied him from the cookies section. Glenda watched the man turn and without warning smack the boy hard on his backside, causing the child's legs to buckle out from under him. The man scowled for a moment, and then, his hard visage struck forlorn, he went to scoop the boy up into the seat of the grocery cart, enduring a sharp blow to the head, possibly accidental, from a hard but tiny Oxford shoe. Glenda experienced a brief surge of feeling for the man, which surprisingly led to an admission that her stepfather really had felt remorse for his offenses against her mother and herself.

She tucked this acknowledgment, without fanfare, into the flow of memory and went to squeeze an avocado for ripeness.

Sunk into the velvet couch, his feet crossed atop the glass coffee table, the heels of his loafers scuffing its surface, Eugene analyzed the situation. *Fuck it*, he thought, punching the newspaper splayed across his legs. Why should he go on kidding himself, pretending it was best in the long run for Glenda to refuse to see him or that he owed Emily his balls like she was the goddamned Mafia? He was depressing Emily anyway, with all his strained affection. He'd noticed her getting all mopey lately, and how could he blame her? She was a sensitive woman. What was he doing, saving her a few tears by bleeding her to death internally?

He tossed the section of the *Times* resting on his legs to the floor. As he grabbed another section—Travel—from the couch, his eye chanced to fix on an ad for an air charter service, which pictured a "Wide Body aircraft configured to carry 100+ passengers." His thoughts latched on to Tillie Bernstein, not only because of the obvious reference to her hips, but because the flamenco skirt on the woman in the ad looked like one of the flowery skirts Tillie often wore.

As he threw the travel section to the floor, a peculiar idea came to him: if Tillie was, say, Spain, what countries were the other women in his life?

Francine was a familiar landmark: a vest-pocket park, a pleasant little spot like the one on Fifty-third Street, just off Fifth, only now she was becoming a Trump Tower. Connie was a country he had little desire to visit, like Malaysia, to which an irresistibly cheap charter flight had been arranged. Emily was a virgin isle, a place to which compassion and curiosity had drawn him, but from which he was looking to build a getaway raft. Glenda was a foreign country whose natives spoke to him in a language that resonated musically with his own, but whose dictator had cancelled all the goddamn flights to its shores.

He jumped from the couch. "This is insane!" he concluded aloud. "I've got to do something about this!"

"What did you say, Daddy?" Meredith called from her bedroom, where she was reviewing her spelling for Monday's quiz.

"I'm talking to myself," Eugene answered, striding toward her room.

"Will you test my spelling?" she asked him on his arrival.

"Sure. Listen, I'll be back in five minutes to test you. But first I've got to run down the hall to Emily's apartment and tell her something."

"Your shirt's coming out of your pants," Meredith pouted.

He tucked it in. "Okay? I'll be right back."

"Can we have McDonalds later? I don't feel like cooking tonight, Daddy."

"Mrs. Schmidt made us a casserole."

"I put it in the freezer. I was going to make salmon croquettes the way Grandma taught me."

"We'll go to McDonalds."

"You don't like my salmon croquettes?"

"I thought you wanted McDonalds."

"You don't like them?"

He sighed. "I love them."

"Good. Then we can go to McDonalds."

Ending his affair with Emily, he thought, should at least be easier than this.

Emily greeted him at the door in a flowing silk caftan, holding a cheese-cloth. "I was just polishing my instrument," she said.

"Ah," Eugene said, one side of his mouth curling upward.

"My cello," Emily said, sweeping her long hair back behind her shoulders and declining the invitation to smile. "Why don't you come in?"

"I'll only be a minute." He stepped inside the apartment and closed the door. His mouth had gone dry, and he licked his lips. "May I have a drink of water?" He shook his head. "Forget it."

"You seem so nervous."

"Do I? I don't like leaving Meredith alone." He scratched the back of his head and wondered if he looked as unkempt as he felt. "Would you mind going on with what you were doing? I feel uncomfortable standing here like this."

"Anything you say, Eugene. Come and sit next to me." Emily resumed the position she had been in before he had rung the bell: on the couch, her cello propped up between her legs. "Wait a minute. Would you like some green tea?"

He swatted away the green tea *déjà vu* and assumed a rigid position beside her on the couch. "No, please don't bother. Just go on with what you were doing."

"It's no bother." She began wiping the belly of the cello with her cloth.

"It doesn't matter if it's no bother. I don't want the tea. Look, I could have come here with the intention of starting an argument, which would probably have made this easier for me, but I figured, hell, we're adults. Why can't we say what's on our minds instead of contriving a situation that would produce the same outcome without us having to go through what I would consider the appropriate pain of honest speech?"

"You don't want to see me anymore."

"I—"

"I understand, Eugene. You don't have to explain." She went on polishing the cello without so much as raising her eyes.

"I didn't want to be brusque," he said, reaching out to touch her shoulder. "It's just that—"

"You don't feel we're suited for each other." She pivoted the cello on its support and began to work on its back.

"More of less that's what I've been thinking." Why the hell was she being so stoical? It was unhealthy. "I admire you tremendously, you understand."

"Thank you." She remained fixed on the job of rubbing something out of her cello.

Should he encourage Lady Macbeth to give him hell, or should he take advantage of the situation? "I guess I'll be going, then," he muttered, rising from the couch. "Please don't get up."

"I won't."

In a minute she would be crying hysterically, he decided, which should do her a world of good. "I feel very awkward," he confessed, nonetheless able to shuffle to the door before she had time to change her mind and speak up.

Later, in the deeply quiet insomniac hours of spiraling introspection, his departure became more callous with each replay. He finally stumbled out of bed, peed, threw on a robe, and pocketed the key to the apartment. He checked in on Meredith and told her briefly roused form that he was just going to look in on Emily. He confirmed the necessity of apologizing to Emily in person with the frazzled individual who reflected back at him from the vestibule mirror, and he secured the lock behind him.

There was no response when he rang Emily's bell. He tried the door, and to his surprise, it opened. Perhaps she had released the bolt when she had carried out the garbage and had forgotten about it.

He entered the apartment and reengaged the bolt. "Emily?" he called. "Don't be alarmed. It's only me."

There was no reply.

He walked down the unlit hall to her bedroom and rapped on the closed door. "Emily?"

No response.

He pushed open the door.

The room was brightly lit from the overhead fixture. Emily lay sprawled face down on the Indian print, her hair and her caftan spread about her as if she were floating. Her right hand rested on a sheet of paper. Eugene slipped it from under her hand, afraid all the while that she would awaken with a start and cry out in terror at the apparition before her.

The paper contained a handwritten poem. Eugene read it in guilty haste:

i've done with earthbound loyalties

born of inexperience

at last my soul unfurled

i fly to my renascence

in dawn's schein-ing light

city celestial in sight

my novitiate ends in a sigh

and to heaven go i

His pulse quickened. He stared at the prostrate figure, then fitfully scanned the room. When he saw the empty medicine bottle upturned on the night table, he dove to the bed, dropping the paper to the floor. "Emily, wake up!"

He tried to raise her to a sitting position, but she was a dead weight— oh god, no! "Emily, wake up, you have to walk! Walk, walk, damn it!" he yelled, trying to drag her to her feet, but succeeding only in toppling with her back onto the bed. He had to call 911.

Emily woke up, flailing. "Help, what are you doing!" she screamed, sending him to the floor. "Eugene! It's you!"

"Oh, thank goodness!" he cried, raising himself to his feet. "I thought you were dead!"

"Dead?"

He straightened his robe. "The empty pill bottle!"

"I ran out of aspirin. Don't you ever run out?"

"And the poem." He picked it up from the floor. "I thought it was a suicide note."

"A suicide note?"

Tapping the paper, he said, "You're finished with earthbound loyalties, and it's off to heaven you go? What was I to think?"

"How could you have misinterpreted the poem? Didn't you see the pun on the word 'schein-ing'?"

"I'm not in the habit of critiquing suicide notes," he said frantically. "I usually skim through them and miss the puns."

"Couldn't you see it was a love poem?" She took the paper from him. "I was referring to Paul Scheinberg."

He uttered a nervous laugh. "Really?"

"Let me explain. My 'novitiate' refers to my experience with you, of course. My 'renascence' . . ."

"Spare me," he interrupted.

"Oh, Eugene, Eugene, Eugene!"

"What, what, what, for chrissake?"

"It was good, but it's over," Emily said. "I was going to tell you, but after what you said this afternoon, I didn't think it was necessary. It just wasn't working out."

"I get it. You were expecting Madame Bovary. With me and Meredith you got Mother Goose."

She sighed. "That wasn't all of it. I'm sorry. I never thought it would ever happen with a colleague. It started innocently."

"Doesn't everything!"

"But Paul is not only creative musically. He is in other ways as well. I was innocent. I didn't understand these things. We experimented with a tuning fork, for instance. You would not believe the effect of vibrations on—"

"Thanks for sharing. So now you know what you were missing," he said, smiling, all at once gracious.

Emily rose from the bed and patted his head as if he were a stray cat. "Paul and I, we're kindred spirits. He's setting the poem to music. I'll be playing it. Do you see?"

"I do see. You make music together."

They laughed; she, lyrically.

"By the way," she reflected, "how did you get into my apartment—and why?"

"I wanted to apologize for my abruptness earlier. You left your door unlocked. Did you think I swiped a key?"

"Not at all." She made an upward-sweeping motion with her arms, the sleeves of her caftan unfolding, turning her into a gigantic butterfly. "It must have been when I brought out the trash. How stupid of me."

"Love makes us stupid."

She shrugged her shoulders. No gesture of hers could be described as petite. Even this negligible body phrase made him think of Isadora Duncan marking the end of a dance.

— 15 —

"Look, there's something radically wrong with my computer. You've got to come over to H and B and kick it or something."

"Eugene?" With her free hand Glenda fingered her mother's circle pin on the lapel of her suit jacket.

"Oh, yeah, sorry, it's me. Can you come right over? I've got to access something stat." He was clutching the receiver so tightly his fingers were turning white. "This might mean my job."

"Are you serious?"

"I am. Can you come?"

She had been refusing to see him, and the Term of Absence she had imposed on the relationship had not yet elapsed. "Are you sure the new assistant, Sara, can't—"

"She tried. No."

"Perhaps I can have Danny take a look—"

"You're the one who set up the system. You know it best. I'm begging you."

"I'll be right over."

Glenda was able to persuade Crowley to accompany her, ostensibly as a professional backup, but really to serve as a buffer between herself and Eugene.

"Old Henson's been trying to get me to lunch," Crowley submitted. "I guess it's as good a day as any to bring out the Zeta Tau jokes from the mothballs."

The receptionist led them to Eugene's new office, a larger room than the one he had occupied before his promotion to editorial director. Bookshelves lined all the walls but the one with the window, behind the desk, and the company's publications filled the shelves except for a few that contained medical and English usage books of reference.

Eugene, who had been reviewing the layout of an upcoming *Physician's Marketplace,* jumped out of his chair upon their entrance. "I didn't expect the *two* of you!" he exclaimed in a less than welcoming tone.

"Good to see you, too," Crowley replied, raising a brow.

"Didn't mean to be rude," Eugene amended, stumbling out from behind his desk. "It's just that I, well, I didn't expect it." He grabbed each of their hands in turn and shook them nervously, as if instinct would have him wringing his own.

Disturbed by her quickened heartbeat, Glenda thought perhaps she needed to extend the imposed hiatus of their relationship. After more than a month, her objectivity seemed hardly to have been secured. She gave her circle pin a forceful twist, as if it were her control dial. "Is Sara around?"

"No," Eugene said. "I sent her out to pick up some office supplies. Forget about Sara."

Crowley straightened his tie. "I'm off to see Jack. Let me know if you need me."

"I wish you'd stay with us," Glenda urged.

"Why?" Crowley questioned.

"Please stay."

"Reconciled, are we?" Eugene mumbled.

"Reconciled to what?" Glenda asked.

"The two of you."

"Who?" Glenda returned.

"You."

"Matt is only my boss!" Glenda whispered through gritted teeth, her back toward Crowley.

"What's your loss?" Crowley asked, mishearing.

"Boss, not loss. Boss," Eugene corrected.

"You piss me off, Lerman," Crowley said, "but you remind me of my kid, so I won't tell you to go fuck yourself. Excuse me." He left the office.

"What was *that* all about?" Glenda asked after he'd gone.

"Why haven't you allowed me to see you?" Eugene asked, disregarding her question. "The kids must be suffering some kind of culture withdrawal. We haven't taken them to a museum in over a month."

"I need a breather from all—"

"I mean, to hell with the kids," he interrupted. "I—"

"To *hell* with the kids?"

"I didn't mean that," he recanted. "I mean, shit, I want to see you."

"I just need a breather," she said after a moment.

"Who's stopping you from breathing?"

"Eugene, I came to look at your computer. I thought that was the emergency. Can I see to it now?"

As she approached his desk, Henson and Crowley entered the room.

"Hey," Henson bellowed, "what the hell's going on? I thought the new system was working just fine. What's the problem, Lerman?"

"Nothing Glenda can't handle, Jack! Just go back to what you were doing. As you were, gentlemen!" he ordered with false gaiety.

Henson's pudgy hand dove into his shirt pocket for his pack of cigarettes. "No, I'd like to stick around and see what's wrong with this thing." He dug for his lighter.

"I thought you quit smoking," Eugene detoured.

"I took it up again."

"You know it's bad for you."

"Get off my ass, Lerman."

Bill Blackman, on his way to the front desk with a parcel marked "Express Mail," loomed in the doorway. "What about your ass?"

"You know anything about the computer breakdown?" Henson inquired before drawing on his cigarette.

"Thought it was working just dandy," Blackman said, looking down at the smaller man.

Eugene mopped his brow with the back of his hand. "Don't make a big deal out of this."

Peering into the office on her way back to her desk from the restroom, Connie tittered. "It looks like you're having a party in here!"

"You having computer problems?" Henson asked her.

"Not that I know of," Connie replied, choosing to interpret this as an invitation. She sidled into the room. "Hi," she chirped, addressing Glenda.

Eugene began fidgeting with the lock mechanism of a file cabinet drawer.

"Turn the damn thing on," Henson said.

"Let's get this show on the road," Blackman joined in.

"I'm in deep suspense here," Crowley added.

"Oh, dear, did I leave your coffee coil on?" gasped a blonde sprite who appeared on the edge of the mob.

"Sara," groaned Eugene. "Back so soon?"

"I realized that half the things on the list you gave me we already have in stock!" She dropped her small bag of purchases onto a chair. "What's wrong?"

Glenda's lucid green eyes opened wide. "You mean *you* didn't know the computer was down?"

"The computer's down?" Sara asked with alarm, reaching toward the machine.

The group's anticipatory silence changed to one of surprise as the desktop image blipped into being.

"Okay!" Eugene fired. "If you must know, I have been trying to see Glenda for some time now, and she has been making it quite impossible. On the pretext of having an emergency computer problem, I finally got her over for what I thought would be a private discussion. I had envisioned a scene of civil rapprochement, not mass riot."

He peered directly at Glenda, who was sure she looked like she was suffering from a slipped disk. Actually, she was experiencing his embarrassment as her own.

In a moment more, he fled from the room and, as Glenda discovered after the group had released her from its inquisitive hold, from the premises altogether.

"Lerman behaved like a fool," Henson remarked at the tail end of lunch, surrounding himself in cigarette smoke and asphyxiating any inclinations he might have had to romanticize the incident.

"On the contrary," Blackman replied. "I found him rather endearing. How about you, Matt? What did *you* think of our boy?"

Crowley gestured to the waiter for more coffee, and instantly a young busboy hustled to the booth where the three men were tallying up their check. "Strikes me he's too far past puberty to cast himself as the star-crossed lover," he answered, putting up his hand at half a cup. "Although," he added, as his reflection in a hotel mirror with a pair of pantyhose draped around his neck came to mind, "I hear as an editor he's top-drawer."

— 16 —

If Glenda thought that by running out of the office Eugene was indicating he wanted nothing more to do with her, she was mistaken. He was saving his resources for the campaign. He would not be put off, as he had been in the past, by such obstacles as bodily attack by a doorman and passive resistance by the woman herself. His commitment, although seemingly akin to George Hayman's, was different in the profoundest sense. George's fixation had distracted the professor from reality, whereas Eugene's represented a mastery over his quirks and irresolution. It was a dedication to experience stripped of falsehood.

He had glimpsed beyond the forthrightness that Glenda had crystallized into a purity of design and purpose, her honesty that had become smooth and hard as bulletproof glass. Now he was determined to free the part of her nature incapable of such solidification. He would penetrate her wall of honest intentions and retrieve that disordered nescience, once violated and now denied relevance in the adult world.

In various ways, many of which he couldn't have guessed, he had already begun to do so. As far back as the P. T. A. meeting, when she had spilled coffee down the front of his parka, he had reacted with so blameless a look, beaming faith and blind trust, that it had lasered through her shield. When Diego had punched him to the floor in her lobby, he had conveyed not the slightest intimation of malice or accusation, even though she had been instrumental in causing the attack. The simplicity of his chagrin had touched her more deeply than any of her lovers' penetrations, for reasons she had long ago made inaccessible. Again and again he had communicated with her encysted child—sometimes unwittingly, sometimes not—and she had treated these contacts as signs of her weakness, gathering her forces to repel what she viewed as threats to maturity.

Ever since the night in Lintonville, though, her resistance had been showing signs of fatigue. Eugene, having sensed this, now planned to wear her defenses down. In order to accomplish this, however, he had to at least get her to see him. He approached the task with a fervency he hadn't known since the days of fighting for his life as his brother smothered him with pillows or sat on his face.

On the day of his computer ruse, he followed up with an afternoon call to her office to discuss an upcoming climate-change march. Glenda was surprised, but not unhappy to be hearing from him so soon.

"The march that Houghton's sending a contingent to? I don't think so," she said. "To believe a march will make a difference is naïve."

"Naïve?" Eugene repeated the word with the vehemence of a man who's just had a bad morning, only to have his ethics put down by a woman he admires. "Is it naïve to rage against a terminal disease? Is it naïve to seek a miracle cure? Shit, doesn't that in and of itself constitute a statement of life, huh? The *wish* to persist, even if it's futile? Would it be so terrible to make a gesture of sanity by marching in this march, even if sanity will never catch on? Can't you donate one lousy morning to a miracle?"

In the end she succumbed, not because she was convinced of the validity of his argument, but because she wanted to be with him on an occasion about which he felt so strongly.

Two days later, to mark the arrival of spring, Glenda found herself and her daughter, along with Eugene and Meredith, marching down Fifth Avenue behind a Houghton mother who carried a hand-lettered sign that read *This is it! There is no PLANet B!*.

She felt fearful at first, as if she and Astrid had been corralled against their will by the gawking crowd behind the police barricade. Beyond this, from what seemed like a world forbidden to her, the sunlight played on stylish men and women, bridled by cross-body bags, who scurried to venues more relevant to their lives.

Before long, however, she began to feel part of the demonstrating group of marchers, and more secure. The hecklers, with their unwarranted taunting, drew her closer to her companions. Rather than feel excluded by the non-participating crowd, she began to feel as if she had chosen to disassociate herself from it.

The temperature was in the forties, and tendrils of Glenda's hair, like the banners up the line, fluttered like telltales in the breeze. Eugene smiled and called her "comrade"—a jest, but vitalizing. She felt very young and hopeful. She wondered if perhaps the only way humanity could survive were if all its ministers became trusting as teenagers in love. In a wash of emotion, more compelling than any assessment of low carbon economy, her feeling of unity with the little group from Houghton extended to include all the demonstrators.

Glenda made no conscious analogy to her own situation when musing about humanity clearing itself of overthinking. But after the demonstration, when Eugene was trying to get her to agree to see him alone later that evening and she was demurring, she suddenly divulged not only the fact that she and Sue had begun jogging outdoors Saturday mornings, but also the hour they met and the duration and terminus of their route. Could she help it, she thought, if he chose to arrange a chance meeting some time?

He of course did so choose.

That Saturday, after his racquetball date with Larry, Eugene jogged over to the point where Central Park exits onto Central Park South, among the statues of the heroes on horseback who led the Bolivian revolution and across the street from the elegant Ritz-Carlton. Larry, with only a superficial knowledge of the setup, sensed the approach of new pheromones in his life and insisted on coming along.

For five minutes they jogged in place, studying the horses nearest them in the lineup of carriages at curbside and debating the pros and cons of preserving the practice.

"They look better on postcards," Larry remarked, as one of the horses lowered his head spiritlessly to his bucket of oats.

"So do we," Eugene suggested.

Offended even by small talk of this nature, Larry glanced down at the bare thighs bulging out from his brief white shorts in order to confirm his enviable lines. "Who is this Glenda, anyway?" he asked, establishing a pattern of jogging backward a few steps and then forward.

"I told you. A friend. We had a falling out. I'm trying to reestablish the relationship."

"Is this a détente or an affair?"

"I'd like it to be more than either," Eugene said. He switched his gym bag from his right to his left hand without breaking the rhythm of his gait.

"You can be one serious son-of-a-bitch, you know?"

"Yeah."

"I'd be insulted if my sister were still available—you've been so damned set against meeting her. But she's back in Duluth, reconciled with her periodontal ex."

Eugene hiked up his sweatpants. "How come?"

Larry shrugged. "What do I know? Her gums started to bleed. She took it as an omen."

"Is he involved with another woman?"

"Only if the name's GingerVitis. The man is devoted to his practice."

Eugene thought of Francine having a change of heart and returning home, repentant. Last summer he would have rushed back into the arms of status quo, which now appeared as the arms of Morpheus. Free of misgivings, he wished Francine continued happiness with Uncle Bob.

Tiring of his jogging pattern, Larry took an excursion around the statue of Simón Bolívar. "What's with this oblique approach of yours, anyway?" he inquired on his return. "Why don't you just drop in on the woman at her apartment?"

"I want to be forceful without appearing to be so."

"You don't want to scare her off."

"Right," Eugene admitted.

"Why don't we jog up her path at least?" Larry proposed. "Meet them en route?"

"I don't know if they come from the Pond or a more westerly direction. Listen, nobody's forcing you to hang around."

"That's okay," Larry insisted. "My pleasure." Determining that the bird excrement on the bench below José Martí was dry, he sat down on the clearest area and dumped his athletic bag at his feet.

Eugene circled the Bolívar statue once, then dropped down beside Larry. "They should be along any minute," he said.

From the Pond path, Glenda saw the cityscape glistening like Monet's Paris, colored in nature's muted tones and rising loftily as if through an innate sense of grace. From the same palette, the oaks and locusts, the stones by the Pond, the trodden path, all sparkled with colors found by the sun. On the water, a toy boat with a bright yellow sail was creating a small wake as a boy pulled it along on a string. Up ahead a man and a woman were jogging with a dog running alongside. Every now and then the dog scampered between the couple, wagging his tail furiously, and Glenda found herself feeling part of the merry turmoil. It was a young spring morning, basking in itself, admitting no hint of any other season or any other time of day.

"Isn't it beautiful here," Glenda declared, lengthening her stride.

"Can we sit for a while?" Sue rejoined. "I'm running on empty."

Glenda slowed her pace. "This is unusual. I thought you could go on forever."

"Not when I'm depressed. And I'm depressed." Walking now, Sue tore off her terry sweatband and stuffed it into the jacket pocket of her salmon-colored warm-ups. The curls sprang from her head in lovely disarray. "Let's claim it," she said, nodding at an unoccupied bench.

When they were sitting, Sue heaved a sigh and dug her hands into her pockets. "I didn't tell you because I thought maybe it wasn't final, but it is. Malcolm's left me."

"Hell." Glenda reached over and squeezed her friend's shoulder.

"He finally let it be known that, as he put it, our marriage is 'no longer extant.' It made me feel like a tyrannosaur."

"Maybe he's only gesturing."

Sue smiled wryly and shook her head. "He's moved in with his maternity ward. The one from the office."

"Oh, no."

"I allowed that pair to happen, and now it's taken on a life of its own. Literally."

"She's pregnant?"

Sue nodded.

"Could this be what you . . . wanted to happen?" Glenda proposed.

"Three weeks ago, I probably would have said yes. Now I realize I would have preferred to go on fighting over the issue indefinitely."

"I don't understand."

"Malcolm was my sounding board. I'd pick a fight to get things going. Descartes said 'I think therefore I am'? Well, with me it's 'I can *hear* myself think, therefore I must be.' Malcolm defined me as an entity to be reckoned with. By arguing with him I knew where I stood—or *that* I stood. What can I say?" She flapped her arms. "I'm weightless. My atoms are spinning off. There'll be nothing left for them to freeze."

"Freeze—you're talking about the cryogenics idea."

"Not an idea, Glen. A contract."

"This perception of yourself without Malcolm is a state of mind, not a state of being."

"Don't give me that crap, toots. A state of mind *is* a state of being."

Glenda gently punched her. "Don't be a hairsplitter. You're a beautiful and intelligent working woman. You've been perfectly independent, and—"

"I play off people, Glen. I either please or perturb. That's how I establish my whereabouts."

"You're feeling unsure of yourself. It's normal. But you'll get back your confidence," Glenda insisted, emphasizing the point by striking the back of the bench.

"You mean I'll cover up. Act tough."

"No. *Be* tough."

"Speak for yourself," Sue groused.

Glenda found the statement uncomfortably close, like a tiger brushing up against her side.

"My image used to bounce off Malcolm," Sue mused. "There's a strange aura of non-existence in the apartment now. I can see death. Malcolm used to block the view. I don't want to go out, but I don't want to be alone either. When I do go out, I talk a blue streak."

"It's a transition."

"To what?"

"To when you're comfortable with your new roommate."

"Who's that?"

"Yourself."

Sue shook her head. "I don't think I'll ever get used to it. You know, the quiet when you wait for someone to come home is like a rest in a musical composition. When he's gone for good, it's like the silence at the end of it. No notes about to happen. Nothing to listen for. I listen so hard for things. I discovered I make a funny sound in the back of my throat when I'm pulling up my jeans." She discouraged a pigeon strutting toward the bench by waving her foot at it. "The solution is to fill the gaps. Live it up. Being with one man atrophies whatever survival instincts you've got. You have the right idea, Glen. Don't tie the knot in the first place. It cuts off the circulation."

Glenda felt as if Sue had held up an unflattering mirror. The pigeon returned. She wished she had some morsel to offer it.

"Oh, well," Sue said at last. "Sitting around isn't going to help the circulation either." She rose from the bench. "Let's get on with it." She broke into a jog, Glenda following.

"Here they come," Eugene cheerfully pronounced, spotting the women as they approached on the path curving up from the Pond. He jumped to his feet.

"Stay cool," Larry directed, rising to strike a casual pose. "Which one's yours?"

"God, you're crude—the blonde."

"Fetching. Very fetching. Both of them."

"Well, hello!" Glenda exclaimed as she and Sue came to a halt before the men.

"Yeah, hey!" Eugene replied. "What took you so long?"

"I didn't know we had a date," Glenda replied.

Larry impetuously grasped her hand. "I think what he meant to say was, 'Bless my heart, what a fortuitous event!'"

Eugene laughed. "I knew that would sound far-fetched."

"I'm afraid I don't know what's going on," Sue said after the introductions were made.

"My friend was plotting a spontaneous meeting," Larry explained.

"And *my* friend has been acting a bit strange lately," Sue said. "The two things must be related. Have you been waiting long?"

Larry threw up his hands. "So long that this guy," he said, gesturing to the nearest hack perched on his carriage seat, "damn near hitched his wagon to *me!*"

The hack tipped his hat.

"I'm sorry I held you people up," Sue said.

"So why did you?" Eugene asked, elated by the reference to Glenda's strange behavior, which hopefully he had caused.

"Sue just wanted to sit for a while," Glenda said. "It's a rare occurrence."

"Actually, I wanted to whine about my husband's having left me," Sue supplied. "Although I can't blame him in the least. He wanted to establish a family, and I wanted to establish myself."

"I just went through a trying situation myself," Larry offered.

"Are you separated too?" Sue asked, perking up.

"I'm a happily married man," Larry said peevishly.

"Sorry," Sue said. "Don't go sporting the family photos to prove the point now."

Larry smiled. "I was talking about my sister. She had a bad time, but she just went back to her husband. I believe the financial situation frightened her. It was unfortunate because she's definitely the superior person."

"I support myself quite handsomely, yet I find myself going through a very unsettling identity crisis myself." Sue fluffed her hair with exaggerated grace, seeming to enjoy Larry's perusal. "Tell me, do you jog a lot?" she asked Larry, focusing on his calves with a look clearly calculated to arouse.

"Mostly indoors. You?"

"At the Y. Neoprene is a resilient surface, and knowing that twenty-eight laps equals a mile is reassuring, especially if you're prone to record-keeping."

"I'm with you," Larry agreed. "No pot holes or dog crap to contend with either. The hotel where I play racquetball with Eugene has an adequate track surrounded by exercise bikes. You never feel alone. Is the one at the Y pitched?"

"Yes," Sue said. "They suggest that you alternate directions daily."

"Sounds serious."

"Why don't you come take a look?" Sue suggested.

"Sure. Let's plan it over a hot chocolate at Benedict's Den, three blocks from here."

In shifting her weight, Sue subtly projected her breasts. "I can get strung out on hot chocolate."

"Not there. They've got an irascible soda jerk. He doesn't let his customers get carried away."

"I know the one," Sue said. "He's been there for years. I'm watching my weight, anyway."

"You're kidding," Larry predictably came back. "What's to watch?"

Sue's smile comprised the best of diffidence and witchcraft. "I'll have their fruit cocktail."

Eugene and Glenda, who had been silently re-tying their laces and pulling up their socks, were invited to join the twosome.

"I'd love to, but my sitter has a lunch date," Glenda declined.

"Me too—I mean, Mrs. Schmidt has to go home early," Eugene improvised.

As Larry and Sue started to cross the street, Sue abruptly turned back toward Glenda. "Call me?" she said, her eyes conveying the question *What am I doing here?*

"Tonight!" Glenda cried, as Sue, with Larry's hand at her elbow, was hurled into the momentary break in traffic.

"They'll never last," Eugene remarked with a smile.

The silence that followed shaped a thought: *Unlike us?*

"What do you want to do now?" he asked.

"I thought you had to get back to your housekeeper," Glenda said, watching Sue and Larry walking across the street.

"Actually, no. I don't have to get back until later," Eugene said.

"Oh. Is Meredith with Emily?" Jealousy tugged at her viscera. She was unaccustomed to the feeling.

"Meredith's with Mrs. Schmidt, only she doesn't have to leave early. I don't see Emily anymore, except in the elevator."

The words affected Glenda like a shaft of sunlight between her thighs. "Ah. I'm sorry it didn't work out."

"Don't be sorry. Emily's marching to the beat of a different drummer—well, percussionist, anyway. She's in love with a pianist."

"And you?"

"I'll let you guess. Come on, I'll run you home. Don't you have to get back?"

She hesitated. "Yes, but . . . "

"But what? Are you afraid of me? I only wanted to say hello to Astrid!"

She looked down at her sneakers. "Eugene, I need space."

"That expression's always made me want to puke."

"Just give me another week."

"Why? You taking karate lessons so you can fend me off?"

"Don't be ridiculous. I'm, well, rehabilitating."

"You've got me under your skin, haven't you?"

She looked up. "Talk about an expression that could make someone throw up."

"Yes, but mine was said with tongue in cheek. Never mind. I know what I'm going to do today. I'm going to Macy's to buy myself a bed."

Nonplussed, she asked, "Where have you been sleeping? In a shoe box?"

"On a waterbed. Rolling on the sea of inertia. Today I'm going to replace the thing with a bed of my choice."

"What brought this on so unexpectedly?"

"I don't know. I've been making decisions lately, and acting on them."

"You really are abstruse."

"You're cute, too." He kissed her lightly on the cheek.

They were jogging when they parted at Fifth Avenue and Central Park South. When they were on opposite curbs, he turned back toward her.

"Hey, Glenda!" he called, jogging in place.

She turned back toward the voice and, jogging in place herself, fired "What?" across the traffic and the dodging pedestrians before seeing him on the other side.

"Remember! One week!" he yelled across the busy thoroughfare.

"Yeah!" a young man among the passersby encouraged, giving Eugene a thumbs up.

"And on the eighth day God created the soccer ball," Eugene recited, as Glenda's apartment door opened. "And it was good." He tossed the ball to Astrid, who was waiting a few feet from her mother inside the doorway.

"Hey, this is regulation!" Astrid cried. "I thought you didn't have one!" She thumped the ball lovingly.

"I got it for you."

"Oh, thank you, Eugene!"

"*Eugene?*" Meredith repeated in disbelief, straightening rigid at her father's side.

"He gave me permission," Astrid sniffed.

"I did," Eugene confirmed, stepping into the apartment. "Let's not make an issue of it. Save the fights for the big game."

Meredith rolled her eyes. "I don't know why I have to play the stupid game, anyway," she muttered.

"We've got box lunches," Eugene said, disregarding his daughter's remark. "Meredith prepared her fantastic tuna salad. Put on your athletic gear, Fieldstons. We're going to the park."

"What's the weather like?" Glenda asked, pulling her robe together.

"Gorgeous," Eugene said.

Less than fifty minutes later Eugene and Astrid were defining the playing field.

"The goal area will be that tree over there," Eugene said.

"Where the black dog is peeing?" With one hand Astrid was shielding her eyes from the sun. With the other, she was clutching the ball to her chest.

"Yes, exactly. By the way, Astrid, have you been practicing heading the ball?"

"Mmhm! And I'm really good at trapping now, too!"

At a distance, Glenda and Meredith were standing on what the experts, their relatives, were about to designate as a sideline. Glenda touched the sleeve of Meredith's jacket. "I love your white warmups. They're lined, aren't they?"

Meredith nodded. "My father just bought them for me."

"They're so shiny."

"Thank you."

"So, you're prepared for our great soccer match?"

Meredith clasped her hands against her stomach. "No, I'm not. I don't want to get grass stains on the pants."

"But your father must have bought them for you to play in."

"They're DKNY Kids. They cost a lot of money."

"That's your father's problem."

"He spends too much money. Anyway, I don't like soccer."

"Did you ever try it?"

Meredith shrugged. "I don't want to."

"I'm not sure I want to either, but I'd feel silly standing here in my sweatsuit and sneakers like I'm waiting for a bus. Wouldn't you feel kind of silly?"

"No."

Having agreed on the conditions of play with Astrid, Eugene called to them. "C'mon, over here! We want to explain the rules and show you a couple of moves!"

"How about it?" Glenda said to Meredith. "Let's give it a try."

"You're not my mother. I don't have to listen to you."

"I want to be your friend, not your mother. Can't friends give advice to each other? Look, I didn't think I'd like jogging. I tried it. I liked it."

"I told you," Meredith griped, "white is an impractical color. The grass stains won't come out. Mrs. Schmidt will be mad."

"Is Mrs. *Schmidt* your mother?"

"Of course not."

"So?" Glenda probed.

"So what?"

"So your father got the warmups, and he'd rather see you getting them dirty trying to have fun than keeping them clean just standing around. I think that's what your mother would say. Am I right?"

"What if you are?" Meredith sulked.

"I don't know. Maybe you'll give me an award. You tell me."

"Yo! What's going on?" Eugene called. "You planning tactics already?"

Meredith turned to her father up the field. "My ankle hurts!"

"You didn't have a chance to twist it yet! How can it hurt?" He raised the ball over his head and playfully sent it toward them.

The ball dropped three feet away from Glenda and Meredith and continued rolling in their direction. Glenda took this as an opportunity to involve Meredith and kicked the ball to her.

"Stop that!" Meredith booted the ball back. "I told you I don't want to play!"

Glenda, refusing to obey, returned the ball to Meredith.

"Use the inside of your foot, Ma!" Astrid called, clapping her hands to her thighs like Mrs. Neilson always did when she fired instructions at her players.

The ball caught Meredith on her calf. "Hey!" She picked up the ball and threw it at Glenda, hitting her in the arm.

Unperturbed, Glenda recovered the ball and, heedless of her daughter's advice, toed it back to Meredith. "Get it out of your system, honey," she urged under her breath. "Hit me, c'mon. Let it out."

Meredith retrieved the ball and prepared to hurl it at Glenda as Glenda jumped from side to side, taunting her with come-and-get-me gestures.

"You can't throw the ball!" Astrid yelled. "You gotta kick it!"

"Let's keep out of it," Eugene quietly suggested. "They're warming up."

Glenda bounded away as Meredith, bent-elbowed and holding the soccer ball above her head in preparation for the throw, followed in angry pursuit. When her opponent feinted to the left, Meredith skidded in that direction and relaxed her grip, losing the ball over her shoulder. It fell at her heels. She spun around and trapped the ball between her feet. Glenda planted herself opposite her in an irresistibly challenging pose.

"Stop it!" Meredith screamed, kicking the ball at Glenda.

"Good kick," Glenda said, kicking it back. "Bet you can't get me." She took off again, Meredith booting the ball after her.

By this time the combatants were well out of bounds and well within the newly established territory of the black dog Astrid had noted earlier. The dog hurtled toward the ball before his master could stop him. Avoiding a collision, Glenda swerved, slipped on the grass, and fell.

Meredith, her face suddenly appearing furious, kicked the ball at her with all her force, catching her on the thigh. Glenda, sprawled on the ground, punched the ball back at her, daring Meredith with a merry yelp to persist in the assault. Meredith kicked the ball at Glenda again, bringing Eugene and Astrid on the run, but Glenda deflected the ball with her knee and waved off her rescuers with a commanding "No!"

The curious dog sniffed at the sole of Glenda's sneaker and then scampered off after a twig his master had sent into the air to divert him, and Eugene and Astrid watched as Meredith kicked the ball repeatedly at Glenda, crying "Go away! Leave me alone!" But Glenda managed to send the ball back every time until, sustaining a blow to her midsection, she let out a sharp moan and curled in on herself and the ball. Meredith froze in panic, and Eugene and Astrid again started toward Glenda. But surprising them all, Glenda leapt to her feet.

"What do you think I'm made of—jello?" She gave the ball a sharp kick in Meredith's direction. "Come on, come on, what are you gaping at?" Gesturing toward Eugene and Astrid, who had stopped dead in their tracks, she hooted at Meredith, "We've got them confused! Kick the ball to me and keep it away from them! What are you waiting for? You've got a fantastic kick! Hurry!"

Visibly tipsy with relief, Meredith giddily tapped the ball with her foot: beautiful, unharmed Glenda had just praised her for her athletic skill. And when Glenda started running off in a reckless pursuit of her team's yet-to-be-defined goal, bobbling with a ball that seemed determined to get away from her, there was no time for Meredith to tell herself that playing soccer was not something a girl in charge of a father and a tuna salad was supposed to be doing, only time to race to her teammate and prevent the others from gaining possession of the ball.

"Eugene! What do we do?" Glenda yelled, attempting to pass the ball to Meredith. "Where's our goal?"

Jabbing at the ball and intentionally missing, Eugene hooted, "That way! Go for it!"

What followed was more of a melee than a game, its only aim being to control the ball at all costs. Astrid objected to this lack of professionalism and voiced her disapproval with a blood-curdling howl each time the opposition succeeded in taking possession of the ball by means of an unorthodox maneuver, such as picking it up from the field and running away with it. Meredith forgot her concern with grass stains, falling on her knees repeatedly as she lunged after the ball.

In one particular play, Glenda freed the ball from Eugene's instep and sent it flying to Meredith with a sweeping kick. She then followed in the path of the ball to join forces with her partner. In her approach, however, she tripped on a stone and again went sprawling, colliding with Meredith and bringing her down with her. Despite the confusion, they managed to trap the ball between them, covering it with their bodies in a mutual attempt to keep it from the others. As Astrid and Eugene hovered over them, unsure of what their next tactic should be, Meredith and Glenda began to squeal out of excitement and ludicrous vulnerability. They rolled on the ground, laughing hysterically, clutching at the ball and each other, unable to rise and unwilling to surrender.

Eugene hadn't seen Meredith behave so giddily in a long time. He was remorseful about not having made this observation until now, but grateful that her capacity for enjoying the absurd was still intact. Moreover, he was overjoyed to hear Glenda's uncontrolled laughter in chorus with his daughter's. He nearly threw himself on top of them in an expression of affection and relief, but Astrid pounced on the pair in an attempt to wrest the ball from them first.

In a spasm of laughter Meredith ejected the ball from their midst with the slap of a palm and staggered to her feet to pursue it. Eugene deftly captured the ball and inched it away, alternately striking it lightly with his left and right insteps.

Play resumed.

"We didn't have any rules," Astrid complained later, when the reconciled parties were sitting under a tree unwrapping the sandwiches. "My coach would be so mad that there were no rules. I don't even know if we scored any goals. Did we score any goals?"

"Not any we could exactly call soccer goals," Eugene said, stealing a sidelong glance at Glenda. "But we had fun, didn't we?"

"Yeah," Astrid admitted, drawing her new regulation ball close to rest against her leg.

17

Rose Lerman stood on her tiptoes, but her son's dinner plates were out of reach. "Hand me the dishes, Eugene. Six—no, I'll need seven; one for the cake later." As he did her bidding, she remarked, sotto voce, "That Glenda is a nice-looking woman. Although with that delicate skin I only hope she doesn't age too quickly."

Eugene peered into the dining room, where Glenda and Meredith were arranging utensils on the table. He tried to nod cheerily, beginning to doubt that this dinner party would be as successful as last week's soccer match. "Come off it, Mom. Try to be nice."

"I'm an honest woman," Rose murmured. "It's always been a fault. I should learn to keep my mouth shut and be 'nice.' Where are your candles?" She began to rummage around in a kitchen drawer.

"We don't have to dress up the table with candles. The flowers you brought from the airport are beautiful." He stepped out of the kitchen to see what his father and Astrid were up to: they were sitting close to each other on the couch, and Abe was defending the Miami Dolphins. Eugene waved at them and returned to his mother.

"I want candles for the Friday night prayer, not to dress up the table,"

Rose informed her son, poking around in the cabinet below the sink. "Where are they? I could have sworn what's-her-name kept them in the kitchen somewhere."

"Francine."

"What about her?"

"It's still her name. Her lawyer twisted my arm and I agreed to let her keep it."

With a toss of her head, Rose returned her attention to the catchall drawer. "Ah, here they are!" She pulled two scarred white candles from out of the mess of string and discarded trivets. "The benediction must be made no less than eighteen minutes before sundown."

"I don't believe it. You haven't lit candles on Friday night since Grandma died ten years ago."

Rose was already on her way to the black lacquer étagère in the living room. "These will do," she said, removing two squat holders made of Austrian crystal from a shelf. She broadened the ends of the candles with aluminum foil so that they would stand in the holders, and she stepped in front of Glenda to place them on a corner of the dining room table. "Excuse me," she said, lighting the candles with one of the matches she'd found in the same drawer of sundries.

Directing all present to gather around her, Rose covered her eyes with her hands to aid her concentration and began to intone: "*Baruch atah Adonai, Eloheynu melech haolum . . .*"

Eugene bent toward Glenda. "I think my mother is marking her territory," he whispered.

"Shh!" Glenda scolded.

"With the odor of mendacity," he added.

"*Kidishanu b'mitz'votav . . . amein.*" Rose uncovered her eyes. "What odor?"

"I was quoting Big Daddy," Eugene said.

"I didn't hear your father say anything. Did you say anything, Abe?"

Abe shook his head.

"I was referring to Tennessee Williams' Big Daddy," Eugene said. "From *Cat on*—"

"*A Hot Tin Roof*," Rose finished. "You think I'm ignorant?"

"No, of course not. I'm sorry, Mom."

"Just because I like engaging in a little *tradition*"—she eyed Glenda—"you assume I'm an illiterate."

"I was making a joke. I said I was sorry."

A helpless smile graced Rose's countenance. "I don't know why I still love this boy." She pinched Eugene's cheek affectionately, twisting his flesh so that it would still be hurting ten minutes later, when they sat down to eat.

"Baked chicken. This was always *Francine's* favorite meal," Rose said, appearing to address her husband, who sat at the opposite end of the table. Whereas earlier her former daughter-in-law's name had been stricken from speech, for this occasion it had acquired a sublime resonance. "I taught Francine the recipe my mother passed on to me after she learned it from *her* mother."

Meredith, who, with Astrid, flanked Rose at the table, was miffed. "But *I* helped you cook the chicken this time. Didn't *I* do a good job?"

"Wonderful, darling," Rose answered her. "It will in all likelihood prove to be the best chicken ever." She stroked the child's head. "That's what I mean by tradition. Passing things on from one generation to the next." She gave Glenda a cryptic look. "Do you know what I mean?"

Glenda laughed good-naturedly. "At present I have no designs on your son, if that's what you mean."

Eugene rose. "Except for the tattoo she made me get. Wanna see?" He turned his back to the table and made the motions of starting to undo his pants.

"Eugene!" his mother warned shrilly. "What's gotten into you?"

"Sit down and behave yourself," Glenda admonished, smiling.

The remainder of the exchange at the dinner table ran smoothly. The soccer experience was described to the grandparents. Astrid enumerated the rules that had been broken, and Glenda extolled the girls' "natural ball sense." In an aside, Glenda asked Meredith if the grass stains had come out of her DKNY Kids, to which Meredith answered, "Well, not really," as a conspiratorial smile lit up her face.

Abe—who, with his scruffy gray beard and befitting paunch, seemed a kind of Semitic Santa, perhaps more approachable than the bellowing cherry-nosed stereotype—learned that Glenda worked with computers and promptly asked her for advice with his smartphone. "I can't seem to locate my iTunes files," he said. Glenda resolved his problem with a quick hands-on tutorial, and Abe apologized for picking her brains. "Just when you want to relax and feel like you're off duty, I bother you," he said. "You should have told me to give the thing two aspirins and call you in the morning." Glenda laughed and thought how much she liked this man.

After the main course was concluded, with Rose having exerted sufficient pressure for them all to have stuffed themselves, it was agreed they put off dessert to allow their digestive systems to recover. The children were granted permission to leave the table.

"You ever see a waterbed?" Meredith asked.

"No," Astrid said.

"We still have one, but my father says he's donating it to—who is it, again?"

"The Jacques Cousteau Society," Eugene said.

"Oh, yeah, that. You want to see it, Astrid? Macy's delivering a regular kind this week."

"Are we allowed to jump on it?" Astrid asked.

"Sure," Eugene said.

"We can watch TV," Meredith suggested, as she and Astrid made their exit.

Abe rocked back in his chair. "Too bad there aren't more educational programs on television," he contemplated.

Rose shook her head. "Violence, drugs and broken marriages." She sighed. "That's what's viewing material for these kids. If a Hollywood couple lasts more than five years they get applauded, and that includes the ones too modern to take the vows."

"How did we arrive at *this* subject?" Eugene asked, feigning ignorance.

"It's a wonder the children can maintain any sense of security," Rose continued, resolute, "what with all the unstable role models they are subjected to every day of their lives. Would you believe, there are actually lawyers who only handle palimony cases. Palimony. That says it all—Abe, are you my pal?"

"Well, I'm—"

"Of course not. You're my husband." She turned to Glenda. "Are you divorced?" she asked casually, as if the question had not been burning a hole in her brain.

"No, Mrs. Lerman."

"Call me 'Rose,' darling."

"I was never married, Rose. I had my daughter by means of artificial insemination."

Rose smiled blankly. "Oh, I see," she said, clutching at her midsection. "Uh, don't misunderstand me," she faltered. "I have nothing against a perfectly acceptable alternative. I was talking about commitments, previously established, that is to say—Abe, will you pour me a glass of wine, dear?" she piped in the range of Tinker Bell.

Abe got up from the table and walked to her end. "Here you go," he soothed, as he filled her glass with the Chablis. "How about you, Glenda?" he asked, returning to his seat. "Change your mind about not having a drink?" He brought the bottle toward her glass, but she covered it with her hand.

"Thanks, but I don't drink—ever."

"Oh?" escaped faintly from Rose.

"My mother became an immoderate drinker," Glenda was surprised to hear herself announce, "and I'm afraid of discovering that weakness in myself."

Rose emitted another feeble "Oh," a declarative one this time. "Then you're *not* actually an, an—"

"Glenda is a recovering non-alcoholic," Eugene said, beaming from Glenda's openness.

"That is an interesting concept," Abe remarked.

Glenda absently undid the top button of her blouse. "It is, isn't it," she mused.

Rose took a delicate sip of her wine, as if self-conscious about how this act would be perceived under the circumstances. Eugene reached for the bottle and refilled his glass.

"You know, Mom, how you were just talking more or less about the downside of sexual liberation—you know, looseness?"

"Yes," Rose replied, fearing the worst.

"It strikes me that it would be helpful to try for a minute and think of sex as art."

Rose looked to Abe for a supportive sign, but he was regarding his son with admiration, all ears.

"The traditional view of proper sex," Eugene continued, "would have it intrinsic to a marriage between one man and one woman. Now, that's like saying to paint is synonymous with to paint representationally—that any other way is disreputable, a desecration of the medium. Anything subjective, abstract—aberrant. But hey, when a couple of critics with rep—you know, the ubiquitous *They*—started to separate the paint, the stuff itself, from the style, the motive, then people started to see the method of applying paint as a choice made freely. The point is that once moral necessity or obligation is removed from art, the manner of expression is released. Aesthetics is stripped of guilt, and it's okay for a person to wallow in the paint or splatter his soul on canvas. Render the geometry of a steel factory or his own torment. And then, you see, once he is free to choose, he is also free to return, perhaps to representational painting—or in my case, to the monogamous life—out of a sense of self, not of necessity. To boot, he returns with a heightened awareness, an enhanced appreciation. Excitement. The desire to explore, to bring to play all his proclivities and talents within his chosen realm. The artist discovers what is inseparable from his being and what is simply presumed to be inseparable. In a sense, he re-forms—no, re-perceives—himself. Liberation did that, Ma. Now you can feel free to masturbate, meditate, change your gender, whatever—anything you like. With impunity."

Rose writhed ever so slightly. "Do you approve of this, Abe?" she inquired, affecting an attitude of urbane curiosity.

Abe gave a helpless shrug. "At this stage of my life I'm focusing on bladder retention. I find it refreshing to hear Eugene beating his brains out on the subject of sex."

"The point of view does not trouble you, then?" his wife asked.

"Forgive me, dear, but not one shit."

At that moment Astrid and Meredith, having decided they were ready for their portions of cake, were coming down the hall leading to the main expanse of the apartment. Upon hearing this last portion of conversation from the adults, they tacitly agreed to remain out of sight while it was still in progress.

Rose threw up her hands in surrender. "Okay, okay, Mister Big Shot. You win." She tapped her head. "I'm a little slow, Eugene. You just tell me if I understand you correctly. What you're saying is that all this open-mindedness on television and the Museum of Modern Art makes you feel free to sleep around and get yourself a good case of herpes. Did I get it right?"

Eugene laughed. "I was trying to explain the process of attitudinal change. Oh, I'm sure the general movement toward eliminating judgmental stigmata had a secondary influence on my thinking. But hell, it was Glenda who was the primary cause."

"Me?" Glenda blurted.

"Of course," Eugene replied.

Glenda leaned toward him. "What do you mean, of course?"

"I don't want to know," Rose said.

"By being with you," Eugene explained, focusing only on Glenda. "By listening to your ideas, even if I didn't agree with them. By touching you . . . in every way."

In the corridor, Astrid clapped her hand to her mouth to restrain the giggle.

"Oh, I don't want to hear this," Rose begged.

"You're getting your mother upset," Abe said, clearly hoping that this would not deter him.

"Glen, don't you see?" Eugene went on. "You spoke freely about sex. You thought of it casually, as a function. Even without agreeing with you, I became less rigid. And when I was with you that night in Lintonville, when we—"

"How *can* you?" Glenda interrupted. "How can you so cavalierly go and publicize that incident? Especially after making it sound like you met me at a seminar in a brothel! For god's sake, what will your mother think?"

"I'm trying not to think," Rose said without inflection. "Please. Don't make me think."

"Glenda, don't talk like that about yourself!" Eugene objected, becoming more impassioned. "If anything, it was I who took advantage of you!"

"Oh, wonderful. Look at your mother now!" Glenda reprimanded, as Rose appeared to be experiencing a spell of apnea. "I'm sorry about this, Mrs. Ler—Rose," Glenda crooned.

Rose caught her breath. "I thought I was going to go from complications of high blood pressure. Now I see asphyxiation is a definite possibility."

"Don't you understand how important this is?" Eugene pleaded with Glenda. "I'm talking about a major breakthrough!"

"Can I help it that you were such an uptight son-of-a-bitch?" Glenda mumbled.

"Vagina, vulva, pubis," Eugene chanted. "Do you understand the significance of this? This is the first time I am speaking these words in public, and in front of the matriarch, no less." He turned to his mother. "Don't be offended. This is a function of me, not you." He continued: "Labia, orgasm, clitoris—"

"Meredith!" Rose cried, seeing the figures of the girls at the foot of the hallway.

"—nipples, erection, semen—"

"We were just coming to get our cake, Grandma," Meredith said, as the girls approached.

"—fellatio, coitus—"

Rose covered Meredith's ears with her hands. "Your father has the flu, darling. Go back and watch television with your friend. I'll bring you the cake."

"I can't hear you, Grandma," Meredith said, tittering. "You're covering my ears."

"Uncover her ears, Mom," Eugene demanded.

Rose obeyed. Who knew? In his condition he might take it into his head to stick his own mother with a cake fork.

"—penis, testicles . . . um. Hmm."

"Ejaculation," Astrid suggested.

"Thank you," Eugene acknowledged. "Ejaculation, orgasm—"

"You said orgasm already," Astrid said.

"Yes. Well, I guess I made my point."

"You sure did," Glenda agreed. "You have a big mouth."

"Come on," Eugene cajoled. "The words are bullshit in themselves, as are the parts and functions they refer to. It's just that being able to say them means I can look at you and see you clearly, rather than through inhibiting taboos."

"Or through rose-colored glasses," Abe said, getting into the spirit of things. "Get it? *Rose*-colored glasses?"

Rose shook her head. "I think it is a general lack of sugar," she said. "I'll cut the cake." She pushed down on the edge of the table and brought herself slowly to her feet.

"What's that word you said before?" Meredith asked Astrid in a hushed voice, bringing her mouth right up to her ear. "Ejac-something."

"Ejaculation," Astrid said. "My mother gave me a book that has pictures—*real* pictures. It shows everything about sex. I'll let you see it when you come over. Okay?"

"Okay," Meredith said in her normal voice.

Glenda had been studying Eugene. "What do you mean, you can see me clearly?"

"Seeing is believing," Eugene said, flashing an enigmatic smile.

"You are impossible," Glenda sighed, rising from the table. "Excuse me, I'm going to help your mother fix the coffee."

On instinct she reached across the table and touched Eugene's cheek. He grabbed her hand, stood up, and before they knew who had initiated it, their faces were meeting under the chandelier.

"Will you marry me?" he asked, when their lips had finally parted.

"No," she said, with a giddy laugh.

"*Never?*"

"I can't say *never*. I don't like making promises I may not be able to keep."

"I'll drink to that," he said, raising his wine glass.

"What the hell, so will I," she said, reaching for the bottle.

They heard the sound of a utensil drop to the kitchen floor with a clunk.

18

On a bright afternoon in early May, the West Terrace of the Cloisters afforded a magnificent view of the Hudson River and the Palisades. Eugene and Glenda, standing near a corner of the low stone wall encompassing the lofty terrace, were virtually alone. Those visitors who did come out to the terrace through the heavy wooden door of the museum proper peered out at the panorama, posed for selfies against it—angled properly, a photo might include the graceful span of the George Washington Bridge—and then exited through the same door. Only a narrow bench of medieval character adorned the terrace, and it appeared to be in evidence more for display than use, so that a potential book-reader or box-luncher would have been discouraged from settling down there.

Astrid and Meredith were with a small group of children participating in a program about mythical beasts, given in the Hall of the Unicorn Tapestries. Eugene and Glenda had stayed for the informal talk but had excused themselves at the start of the creative hour, when the children were getting ready to invent monsters and legends of their own, lest they inhibit the free flow of imagination. The junior curator conducting the program was a shapely young woman with violet eyes and a knit dress that clung to her buttocks like an outgrown mitten. Eugene had admired her as he would an elegant verse, his sangfroid making him feel snugly virtuous.

The cord fabric of his pants melted against the denim of Glenda's jeans as he stood as close as possible to her without jamming her into the wall. She placed her hand flat on the stone ledge, and he covered it with his own. To his delight, she turned her hand under his so that their palms met and their fingers intertwined.

"I like being here with you," she said.

"Last week in Lintonville—I mean, it must have been terrible for you, Glen. Why didn't you let me go with you? I would have behaved. Haven't I been behaving?"

"I know," she said, tilting her head against his shoulder. "It was okay. I went with Astrid. Believe it or not, she gave me moral support."

"I believe it."

"I told her about Patrick's drinking and his health problems, and I told her about how I had been afraid to tell her before. I don't know if it helped her. It helped me. And Janet took care of all the—funeral arrangements. Janet. She's wonderful. You know?"

"Yes. But still, it must have been . . ."

"It wasn't like one of those touching reunions. No, he was gone by the time I got to the hospital. They said he had spontaneous hemorrhaging—'esophageal varices,' they called it—and they tried to save him. But he went very fast, and there were no parting words, and I don't know what I would have said if there had been. I felt empty and weak. Light-headed. I actually tried to work up some hostility, but all I ended up with was a stuffy nose from crying about I don't know what. It's strange. I thought of Sue, when she was telling me about how Malcolm gave her shape. Maybe that's what all that hate did for me. Do you think so?"

"Maybe it was more like your chaperone—something that protected you from getting involved with someone like me. That's an egocentric interpretation, but I don't care."

"Do you think I'm a mess?"

He smiled. "Why shouldn't you be? You know anybody who isn't?"

"I hope Astrid won't be."

"Don't count on it."

"Gee, thanks," she said, her smile wistful.

He brought their clasped hands to his lips and kissed hers. "Talking about Sue," he said. "Her torrid love affair with Larry is over. It lasted a week."

"I know. She told me. I'm glad. I had nothing to do with it, but I still feel like a sleazy matchmaker. Is his wife okay?"

"I hope so," Eugene said. "He does love her. It's his style, leading a double life. He's quite staid in it."

"Not like Sue," Glenda remarked. "Sue is confused. She wants to live forever, but she's not sure as what."

He let go of her hand to comb his fingers through her hair, which she recently had cut into a short, layered bob. "So when is *our* torrid whatever going to start? By the way, I love your hair."

"I was sick of the hairpins and everything. Do you really like it, or are you just being nice?"

"I like it, *and* I'm nice." He recalled the scene in the salon, watching Meredith's face in the mirror as she was getting her hair cut. It seemed so long ago. Funny. Meredith had tried to become the woman inside herself prematurely, and here was Glenda, allowing the carefree child to emerge, at last. "It's never too late," he murmured, close to her ear.

"For what?" she asked, gazing out at a small motor craft speedily approaching from the north.

"I don't know—to be seven years old."

She sensed accord without knowing exactly what he had in mind.

He felt a sudden nostalgia for his youth. For Richie, who wasn't all that bad (*I should give him a call*). For his mother's lovely smile, back when she had her real teeth. For his grandpa, who had bought him his blue tricycle. For his blue tricycle. He had an overwhelming sense of time lost forever and time that was becoming lost forever, like the wave of the motorboat passing them now—no, then—churning, subsiding, disappearing, marking the passage of some weekend sailor. (*Did he wave? Why didn't I wave back?*)

"Shit," he said at last.

"What is it, Eugene?"

"Meredith's going to leave me. She really is. I didn't want to wreck Francine's chance at happiness or use Meredith as a pawn, so I didn't put up a fight. And I've been kidding myself into believing Francine was going to say she couldn't hack it, that Uncle Bob really didn't want a child at this point in his life. But it's going to happen. I'm actually going to help Meredith pack her bags. We're going to cry. She's going to tell me to be grown-up about it. We're going to crack some jokes and cry some more. And then she's going to move out on me."

Glenda put her arm around him and stroked his back through the cotton shirt. "She'll come home to you summers and school vacations, and you can visit her any time, right? You'll never lose her."

He kissed her neck. "Glen?" he asked.

"Huh?"

"How do you feel?"

"The truth?"

"Yes. I can take it."

"I want you so much it's giving me cramps," she said.

"Oh." His grief and happiness sank into her shoulder. "My darling."

She felt control falling from her like a bridal gown, exposing her to the hazards, and other possibilities, of love.

Acknowledgments

Thanks to my father for steeping my childhood in Will Durant and Winnie the Pooh, and who, with his incisive intellect and earthy humor, showed me how to think freely and laugh uncontrollably. Thanks, too, to my mother, who bravely fought her prudish heart with liberated pronouncements and who unwittingly educated me on the conflicts of feminism.

I am forever grateful to Len Karlin of Hopkinson and Blake, whose candid critiques allowed me, early on, to sedate my inner censor in order to give my imagination free range of expression; and to Sol Stein of Stein and Day, who validated the effort by setting it to print.

As for present times, thanks to Marcia Rosen for her marketing skills and camaraderie; and to copy editor, Jeanne Thornton, who seamlessly tunes her sensibilities to the author's.

Most important, thanks to my husband, Bob, who even on the bleakest of his days can make me dance.

About the Author

Love and Other Hazards is Claudia's fourth novel. Her fifth, a sequel to her art suspense, *Stolen Light*, is in the works.

The author divides her time between the Hamptons and Manhattan with her husband, Bob.

For reviews of her books and to see what she's up to, visit her website, claudiariessbooks.com. To communicate directly, email claudiariess.w@gmail.com.